"Adam...than

The voice on the other ~~~~~~~~~~~
unmistakably to Adam's former mother in law.

"What's wrong? Is Jen all right?"

"Yes—yes, of course. I didn't mean to alarm you. And if it were just this David person, I wouldn't be so concerned. But there's a mystery man, too, and who knows what Jenna's getting herself into—"

"Slow down. What are you talking about? Who's David?"

"A very nice young fellow who seems enthralled with Jenna. But you're missing the point. I'm calling you so that you can do something about the mystery man in Jenna's life. Find out who he is, for one thing."

Adam stiffened. When he'd seen her last, he could've sworn Jen wasn't involved with anyone. Now, men were coming out of the woodwork. "Wait a moment. Jen doesn't need my interference. Look what happened the last time I—"

"What *did* happen?"

"Nothing." It was a lie, but Adam was damned if he'd tell his ex-mother-in-law that he'd gone to bed with her daughter.

Dear Reader,

What happens when "I do" turns into "I don't"? I've always been fascinated by the romance and drama of marriage—all those adventurous ups and downs between husband and wife. After eighteen years of marriage, I know a little about the adventure from firsthand experience! But not too long ago, the storyteller in me started to ask some intriguing questions: What happens when a husband and wife simply can't live together any longer? Can they divorce, yet fall in love with each other all over again? Can they solve the problems that pulled them apart in the first place—or will they keep repeating the same mistakes over and over, no matter how much they *do* love each other?

A Kiss Too Late is my answer to those questions. Telling the story of Jen and Adam has been a special experience for me. It's the first time I've written about two people who share a history. I found out just how much the past can intrude on the present, causing all sorts of trouble for my characters—and all sorts of fun for me. I hope you enjoy reading this story as much as I enjoyed writing it. I'm delighted that I have the chance to share it with you.

Sincerely,

Ellen James

Ellen James
A Kiss Too Late

Harlequin Books

TORONTO • NEW YORK • LONDON
AMSTERDAM • PARIS • SYDNEY • HAMBURG
STOCKHOLM • ATHENS • TOKYO • MILAN
MADRID • WARSAW • BUDAPEST • AUCKLAND

ISBN 0-373-70651-0

A KISS TOO LATE

A Kiss Too Late

CHAPTER ONE

JEN AWOKE to the smell of warm flesh and stale wine. As she opened her eyes, she tried to convince herself she was dreaming. It *had* to be a dream—the rumpled clothes strewn across the floor, the large hand draped over the curve of her hips, the singular gust of snoring next to her. Surely only one person in the world snored in that restless manner: Jen's ex-husband, Adam Prescott. That had to be it—she was having yet another dream about her ex-husband.

Jen closed her eyes and stretched. But when she opened them again, the hand remained firmly placed on her bare skin. And the snoring continued. With a sense of foreboding, Jen turned her head inch by inch on the pillow. A moment later she was gazing, appalled, into the sleeping face of her ex, stubborn features, luxuriant mustache and all. This was no dream! Adam Prescott was truly sprawled here in the flesh, his powerful, solid body tangled in her sheets. Oh, Lord. What had she done? What madness had she allowed?

Jen couldn't help a gasp escaping her lips. It didn't wake Adam, but his hand slipped lower, settling possessively on an intimate part of her thigh. Jen froze. Now the events of last evening came tumbling back into her mind in humiliating clarity. Adam's visit to New York— the first time she'd seen him since their divorce a year ago. His invitation to dinner at that posh restaurant, where they'd both had too much wine to drink. Far too much wine, for Jen had started to look at Adam through a hazy, romantic glow. And then the taxi ride back to her apartment, and the moment when Adam had taken her into his arms...

She stifled another gasp. How could she have been so stupid? She'd done the one thing she'd sworn she would never do—let Adam Prescott back into her bed!

She slipped away from him, leaving his warmth for the chill, early-morning air. Shivering, she glanced around. Her bedroom looked like a crime scene: discarded clothes, shoes tossed aside with abandon, even a dead-still body. Her dismay increasing by the second, Jen gazed once more at her ex-husband's face. Even in his sleep he seemed to be frowning a little. Then, without waking, he turned on the creaking mattress until his back was toward her. How wretchedly appropriate—Adam Prescott making love to her and then turning his back.

Jen scooped up what clothes she could find on the floor and made a beeline for the living room. Today she was actually grateful for her haphazard housekeeping skills. Her unfolded laundry was piled on the coffee table, and she rummaged through it. She found fresh underwear and a pair of jeans—but no shirts. Cursing herself, she shrugged into the blouse she'd worn last night. The silken material still seemed to harbor the expensive scent of Adam's cologne....

Jen rooted under the sofa, found a pair of sneakers and jammed them on her feet. She grabbed her purse, ran a comb through her hair with a shaky hand, and then tiptoed past the bedroom. One glance told her that Adam still slept.

Cursing herself some more, Jen let herself out of her apartment and fled the scene. Hadn't she learned anything during her year in New York?

WHEN ADAM PRESCOTT AWOKE, his head felt like it was stuffed with wads of cotton. He sat up slowly, grumbling to himself. What the hell had he done? What mess had he gotten himself into? Unfortunately it took him only a moment to remember where he was—the hovel that his ex-wife called home these days. He glanced around, noting the racked bureau, the threadbare carpet, the wallpaper grimy with age. Jen had left their spacious brownstone in Boston and their summer house in Newport for this seedy apartment in New York City. Was she crazy?

Admittedly last night Adam himself hadn't paid much attention to his surroundings. He'd been too busy holding Jen in his arms, relearning the curves of her body, the sexy tangle of her dark hair, the smoky depths of her eyes....

It had been damn good between them. That was the thing—sex had always been damn good between them. He'd missed it with Jen. He couldn't pretend otherwise.

Adam swung his feet down, waiting for the pounding in his skull to subside. He swore fluently. Maybe last evening he'd been a little drunk, but this morning he was stone-cold sober. And he knew it had been a mistake. No matter how good it had felt to hold Jenny, it had damn well been a mistake. Why hadn't he left well enough alone? He harbored no illusions: there'd be trouble because of the night he'd just spent with his ex-wife. Big trouble. Knowing Jen, he could count on it.

He made a circuit of her small apartment and found that she'd left. He wasn't surprised. She'd run away from him a year ago, and she still seemed to be running.

No longer able to ignore the sour taste in his mouth, Adam went into Jen's cramped bathroom and opened the medicine cabinet. Only one toothbrush poked out of a mug on the shelf. Adam smiled faintly. It was obvious that Jen didn't make a habit of sleep-over guests.

He closed the cabinet door, rinsed out his mouth with a glob of toothpaste and then went to get dressed—not an easy proposition, considering that his attire seemed to be strewn willy-nilly across the room. They had both been impatient last night—very impatient.

After what felt like a scavenger hunt, Adam finally managed to find all his clothes—suit jacket tossed over a chair back, pants strewn on the floor, shirt crumpled at the end of the bed. At last, fully dressed, he glanced around again. He still couldn't get over the sorry state of this place. The bedroom window was barred like a jail cell. Water stains pocked the low ceiling, and pipes rattled in the flimsy walls, as someone in the apartment next door used the plumbing. This place was a genuine dive. What did Jen think she was doing here? What was she trying to prove?

Okay, so she'd been making some cockeyed bid for independence ever since their divorce. She wouldn't accept any money from him. He'd had his lawyer contact her a dozen times, but to no avail. Yet Jen obviously couldn't even afford a decent place to live. Was this her idea of happiness and self-fulfillment? He just didn't get it.

Adam took his wallet from his back pocket and extracted several bills in the largest denominations he had. He tucked them under a bottle of lotion on the bureau.

At least now he wouldn't have to worry about his ex-wife's starving to death.

He left her apartment and stepped onto a musty elevator that shook all the way down to the lobby. Outside, the blare of car horns greeted him. This was what Jen came home to every day. What the hell was going on with her?

He flagged a taxi and settled in for the drive downtown. He had plenty of time to stare at the graffiti-scrawled walls, the abandoned scaffolding of once-ambitious construction projects, the trees barricaded behind iron fences. Adam disliked New York and always had. Boston was his city—big, rowdy, friendly. New York was just too damn tense.

At last the taxi burrowed its way among the skyscrapers of the financial district. A perpetual dimness lurked here, the old stone buildings rising like muted brown ghosts. Adam swung out of the cab and strode into one of the buildings. Now a perfectly noiseless elevator took him gliding smoothly upward. The atmosphere was hushed, as if the preoccupations of investment bankers demanded absolute quiet. That was something else Adam disliked—investment bankers. Yet today he had an appointment to meet with one. It had finally come to that.

The offices of Fowler, Meredith and Company on the forty-ninth floor were sleek and bland, all the walls and furniture in the reception area a subdued off-white. Even the sunlight filtering in through the blinds seemed off-white, a watered-down version of the real thing. An equally subdued secretary brought Adam a cup of hot coffee. He could use that, all right. He'd almost finished with it by the time he was ushered into the office of Jefferson Henshaw, a partner in the prestigious acquisitions-and-mergers department.

Henshaw looked too young for the exalted position he held, a shock of wispy blond hair falling over his forehead like a schoolboy's. Adam grimaced to himself. The last thing he needed was to deal with some hotshot fresh out of Harvard business school. He glanced at the framed diplomas on Henshaw's wall. Adam's list of dislikes was growing this morning. He didn't trust a guy who framed his diplomas in teak like they were works of art.

"Mr. Prescott," said Jefferson Henshaw. "Pleasure to meet you. Have a seat." He spoke a shade too heartily, his handshake a bit too firm, as if he'd been coached in some business-etiquette class to present a forceful image. With heavy misgivings, Adam sat down on the other side of his desk.

"I can tell you I already have Darnard Publishing very interested in your newspaper," Henshaw said, still in hearty mode. "You've picked a good time to sell."

More like sell out—that was how it felt to Adam. If he sacrificed the *Boston Standard,* he'd be betraying his family heritage. The problem was that family-owned newspapers didn't thrive in today's economy. It was a knowledge that Adam had been fighting for a long while. He'd put everything into the *Standard,* and the paper still wasn't breaking even.

"I'm looking at various possibilities," Adam said grimly. "Going public is an option."

"You start selling public stock, and you run the risk of losing any control of the paper at all. Let Darnard buy you out, and you can probably work a deal to stay on as editor." There was the slightest condescension in Henshaw's voice, as if he couldn't understand why anyone would want to be the editor of a middling New England paper like the *Standard.* Hell, was this what it had come to? Adam was being patronized by some snot-nosed kid who was supposed to be the newest financial wizard. Today Adam felt every one of his forty years, and then some.

"I don't enjoy the idea of editing a newspaper I don't own," Adam said.

"Darnard is the best way to go, believe me."

Adam shrugged. He knew that Darnard Publishing was a corporate conglomerate currently expanding into television, as well as gobbling up newspapers and magazines. If Adam agreed to the deal, the *Boston Standard* would become just another link in a nationwide media chain. It would no longer be the family paper that Adam's great-grandfather, Benjamin Prescott, had founded more than one hundred years ago.

Adam stood abruptly. "I'll think about it."

Henshaw frowned. "I'm ready right now to go over the details."

"I'm not."

"Mr. Prescott, I thought you were ready to seriously negotiate. You can't keep these people dangling—"

"Let them dangle."

Several minutes later, Adam was striding down the street, hands jammed into his pockets. It took him a while to realize where he was headed—Battery Park, to the pier where you caught the Statue of Liberty ferry. Although Adam disliked New York, he'd always had a fondness for the Lady, and there she was, with her great flowing robes and spiked crown. To the world she might represent freedom, but to Adam she held a much more personal appeal—she reflected belligerent determination, a determination to choose what was right despite all obstacles.

If only Adam could choose what was right for his newspaper. As for his ex-wife, hell, he'd never been able to figure out what was right where Jen was concerned. Last night had proved that all over again.

Adam turned and began striding in the opposite direction.

THE LUNCH RUSH at Gil's Deli in midtown Manhattan started to pick up speed at around eleven in the morning. Nearby office workers sought out the place, intent on beating the crowds for Gil's famed homemade sausage and potato salad. Jen, one of the deli's newer employees, still worked the sandwich bar, not yet trusted to mix the secret recipe for potato salad. She stood behind a long counter, lackadaisically slapping mustard and mayonnaise on slices of whole wheat bread.

"What's up?" asked her friend Suzanne, coming along to replenish Jen's supply of pickles, romaine lettuce and Swiss cheese. "You've been distracted all morning."

"Nothing," Jen muttered. "I'm fine. Just fine and dandy." She tossed a lettuce leaf and two slabs of ham on the thick, crusty bread. One decisive cut of her knife, and a number five, cheese-and-ham-on-wheat, lay waiting before her.

"Something's wrong," Suzanne said calmly, breaking out the pastrami. "I've never seen you like this."

"I can't talk about it."

"You'll talk," Suzanne said with an air of confidence. Jen tossed two slices of rye bread down on the counter and dug into the mustard jar. Then she glanced at her friend in exasperation. She'd quickly bonded with Suzanne, whose placid demeanor hid implacable drive. This morning, as usual, Suzanne's hair was swept back into a careless ponytail, and she wore her favorite uniform—corduroy pants and a madras blouse. In spite of Suzanne's casual appearance, however, she was a focused, single-minded person, intent on accomplishing the goals she'd set for herself. She juggled her job at the deli with a full load of class work, and she intended to be a lawyer someday. She was already tenacious in cross-examination.

"What happened?" she asked. "Come on, Jen. You stormed in here, hardly said good-morning and—"

"I've made a complete ass of myself!" Jen raised her voice more than she'd intended, and several interested faces swiveled toward her.

Suzanne's expression remained unconcerned. "Everyone makes an ass out of herself now and then. Why should you be different?"

"Damn," Jen said in despair, but she never once stopped wielding the mustard. Unbidden, memories of the night before came back to her. Adam kissing her in the foyer of her apartment building. Much later, Adam standing beside her bed, both of them fumbling with zippers and buttons...

Jen's face burned. She worked in silence a few moments, advancing from rye to pumpernickel and sourdough. "Lord...I slept with my ex-husband last night," she said miserably. "He shows up unannounced, informs me that my mother is getting married of all things, and I'm supposed to help with the wedding. And after that we...well, I can't believe I let it happen." There—it was out. The dreadful, mortifying truth. All Jen's bad judgment exposed. Suzanne, however, appeared unperturbed.

"What's so awful, Jen? The way you explained it before, your ex is gorgeous and rich. I still can't figure out why you left him."

Jen struggled with an all-too-familiar frustration. It seemed no one understood why she'd left Adam. Not her mother, not her friends . . . not even Adam himself. She pulled over a tray of sesame-seed buns and scowled at them.

"Outwardly Adam is a very...charismatic person. He sweeps up everyone around him. But inwardly, when it comes to emotions, Adam doesn't let anyone get too close. He never let *me* get too close, that's for damn sure."

Suzanne waved a piece of Swiss cheese. "I still don't understand. Your mother has money—tons of it. Your ex has money—tons of it. But you're here slogging it out, trying to land a job as an actress. Jen, your mother could probably build you your own theater. And if you'd let your ex pay alimony, you'd be rolling in dough, instead of slicing it."

Jen thought she heard a touch of envy in Suzanne's voice. Suzanne was very pragmatic, always counting dollars and cents. It must annoy her that Jen had walked away from so much family wealth. But Jen felt stifled by it—smothered. Two years ago, when she'd turned thirty, she'd begun to realize that never once had she proved anything on her own. The Hillard name—and then the Prescott name—had buffered her. Oh, she could have kept coasting along, safe and protected, never pursuing her secret yearnings. She could have done that—but courage had demanded otherwise.

She sighed deeply. "Speaking of acting jobs," she said, "I have an audition this afternoon. Will you cover for me?"

"Only if you relax about your night with the ex. It's no big deal."

Jen thought very much otherwise. She attacked a batch of caraway rye. "All I know is that Adam had better not be there when I get back. I left him in the apartment—asleep. I don't know how I'll ever face the man again!''

HOURS LATER, Jen hurried down the street, threading her way through the crowd. Even after a year in New York, the novelty of the place still hadn't worn off. She loved everything about it: the theater posters plastered one after the other on the walls, the fruit and candy stands with their cheerful umbrellas, the exotic shops and palm-reading rooms tucked into odd corners, the pots of flowers brightening the fire escapes, the high narrow buildings jutting up all around. She'd never known any other town like it. Boston didn't compare; it just didn't have the same excitement. As for Newport, well, she'd grown up in Newport. That was where she'd first fallen in love with Adam Prescott, reason enough to stay away from the place.

Jen glanced at the address she'd scribbled on a scrap of paper. The small theater where she'd be auditioning today didn't even qualify as off-off-Broadway, but no matter. Jen followed any prospect she could find. And now she had an agent—a serious young man named Bernie who actually returned her phone calls. That was worth something right there.

She pushed open the door and stepped into a dim foyer, then found her way to the theater proper, where rows of wooden seats sloped toward the stage. A cluster of people stood murmuring together several feet from Jen. The air was dank in here, the stage curtains sadly worn and drooping. Even so, the familiar reactions that any theater evoked for her kicked in: the tightening of anticipation in her stomach, the sense of magic. Ever since she was a kid, it'd been like this. When she was nine, her parents had taken her to see a play for the first time. She still remembered it—Shakespeare's *Twelfth Night*. All the lights shining on the stage, the glittering costumes, the vivid backdrops—every detail had imprinted itself on her young mind. She had vowed right then that someday she would be an actress. It had taken her two decades to finally put that vow to the test. . . .

Jen stirred from her reverie. Taking a deep breath, she walked toward the group of people. A bored-looking woman with dyed red hair turned to her.

"Not another one," she said wearily. "You're too old for the lead, you know."

Jen gritted her teeth, but managed a polite smile. It seemed she was always too old for the lead. "I'm just looking for work," Jen said. "Any work."

The red-haired woman gave her another bored look. "The aunt's part is a possibility. The spinster aunt. Here's the script—start at scene two. George will read with you."

Now Jen's anticipation turned to apprehension. She climbed the steps to the stage and sat down on a folding metal chair. George turned out to be a grizzled man who mumbled his lines so that Jen could hardly tell what he was saying. She stared at the script in front of her, trying to conjure up some idea of the proper emotions for a spinster aunt. But all that came to her were vague feelings of bitter resignation.

Then George mumbled her cue and Jen responded automatically. Her voice sounded tinny and unconvincing even to her own ears. She couldn't help wondering what Adam would say if he saw her here. He'd probably be incredulous—damn him. He'd probably laugh. His thirty-two-year-old ex-wife actually thinking she could break into a field brutal enough to girls ten years her junior. Adam would probably tell Jen to wake up and forget her dreams.

Somehow Jen got through the rest of the audition, knowing it was a miserable failure. Of course, the fake redhead had hardly seemed to be paying attention. She thanked Jen perfunctorily and went back to her conversation. Jen walked slowly from the theater and out to the bustling street.

She'd never botched an audition this badly before, not even during her first days in New York. Last night Adam Prescott had come back into her life. She'd allowed him to take her into his arms—and she'd allowed him to shake her confidence, as well.

She couldn't allow it to happen again.

CHAPTER TWO

JEN STARED out the window of the bus, already certain she was making a mistake. She didn't want to return to Newport. She wasn't ready yet. But here she was, traveling up from New York, regretting every mile that rumbled under the wheels of the bus, regretting every mile that brought her closer to home.

She knew she'd see Adam again, of course. He'd be here for her mother's wedding; he was practically an adopted son of the Hillard family. But it had been only a week since the tumultuous night Jen had spent with him. Her face heated just at the memory.

A book lay in her lap, open but unread. She slapped it shut and stuffed it into her carryall. The bus was now traveling through the narrow streets of Newport, Rhode Island, and she tried to resist the quaint beauty of the town: the old wooden houses standing cheek by jowl, the vines trailing from window boxes, the showy rhododendrons sprouting everywhere like colorful balloons.

When the bus pulled up at the station, Jen had to force herself to get off with the rest of the passengers. She felt tense as she made her way into the station with her carryall and one small suitcase. She tried to reassure herself that she wouldn't be staying long in Newport. A few days—would it really be so bad? Afterward she'd return to New York and to the life that truly mattered to her.

"Hello, Jen," said a voice behind her, the unmistakable voice of Adam Prescott. Jen drew in her breath. She'd expected to have a little more time to prepare herself. What was he doing here, anyway?

She couldn't turn to face him—she just couldn't! Not after that impetuous night they'd spent together. Jen remained frozen where she was, her back turned to Adam. Unfortunately, even though she wasn't looking at him, she felt his presence like an overwhelming force. Her nerves seemed to tingle uncomfortably, just because she knew he was there....

At last Adam came around in front of her, and she actually had to look at him. She struggled to present an aloof facade, but she didn't think she was very successful.

"Hello, Adam," she said stiffly. "It's . . . a surprise to see you. I thought you'd still be in Boston."

He gave a faint, skeptical smile. "You don't have to be polite with me, Jen."

She gazed at him. Adam had always been much too direct for her liking. And he was much too attractive and too self-assured. His dark brown hair with distinctive hints of gray waved back from his forehead. Prematurely gray hair was a Prescott family trait, and Adam had started to show the first silvery streaks when he was in his early twenties. He was forty now, and the Prescott trademark had worn well on him. Everything wore well on the man, including that dark luxuriant mustache of his. If possible, he looked even better than he had a week ago....

He was indulging in a perusal of his own. "I didn't get a chance to say goodbye the other day," he said quietly.

"Still, you managed to leave your message." She rummaged inside her carryall, found an envelope and thrust it at him. "There. I'm returning your money. I hardly expected payment for... services rendered." She was furious, but somehow she kept her voice cool.

Adam stared at the envelope. "I think you know that wasn't my intention. I was worried about you, Jen. After seeing how you live, it doesn't make sense..."

Jen sighed. "Let's drop it, all right? Everything. What happened in New York was a mistake for both of us."

He pocketed the envelope, regarding her with a dissatisfied expression. Jen gazed into his dark brown eyes a trifle too long. He was unsettling her all over again. Why did he affect her this way? Somehow she managed a shrug.

"I expected the chauffeur to come for me. I can't imagine you tearing yourself away from your newspaper. Did my mother bribe you?"

"I arranged to take a few days off. And I *volunteered* to pick you up. I thought we could finally clear the air about a few things."

"We've done enough damage already," she said tightly, but Adam had taken her suitcase and was leading the way out of the station as if he expected her to follow automatically. Hadn't it always been like that, Adam leading, Jen expected to follow?

She stood in the middle of the station, watching Adam's broad-shouldered back retreat. No matter that his shoulders looked wonderful in that dark, silk-woven jacket. Surely after all this time she knew how to resist his appeal.

She'd never been good at resisting him, that was the problem. Even during those painful times of their marriage, she'd longed for him, ached to have him near. With Adam, she'd always been like tinder waiting for the touch of flame. In the end, there'd been only one solution. Her one hope of making a life for herself had been to leave Adam.

Now he reached the door and turned to glance back at her, waiting. She was tempted to let him wait, but she couldn't ignore practicalities. She'd have to go with him, or walk—and if he had something he wanted to say to her, he'd stick around until he'd said it. She knew him well enough to know that. With another sigh, Jen went to the door and out to the parking lot with Adam.

He tossed her suitcase into the trunk of a tasteful sedan that managed to convey a hint of recklessness in its lines, as if at heart the vehicle was actually a race car. Adam himself was rather like that, his appearance subtly polished but suggesting reckless energy underneath.

Jen slid into the passenger seat, and a few seconds later Adam wheeled the car out of the lot. Pressing a button on his side, he lowered Jen's window. Feeling contrary, she found the button on her side and raised the glass. But soon the car became too hot, and with a grumble she lowered the window again.

"You used to do that a lot," Adam said. "Even before we were married, remember? We'd go out to dinner, and you'd insist on being the one to pay the tab. You'd argue with my opinion about a concert or a play or a book. You'd argue with me about anything."

Jen found herself tensing again. She'd been so young when she'd fallen in love with Adam. Young, in love and at the same time needing desperately to declare her independence. From the beginning, Adam's powerful personality had inspired both fascination and rebellion in her. It had made for a volatile combination.

"Oh, yes, I remember," she murmured. "But you never understood—"

"I knew what was going on. I'm not dense, Jenny."

Jenny. It had been his own private name for her, a name that no one else had ever used. It seemed to have slipped out just now almost against his will. He stared straight ahead, not saying anything more. Jen stared straight ahead, too. The silence was potent, filled with all the unspoken recriminations and misunderstandings between them.

Jen made an effort to concentrate on the scenery. After a short while they left the crowded downtown streets behind and began driving along the ocean. A few people were out with their fishing poles, and gulls sunned themselves on the rocks. Out on the water, sailboats skimmed easily along. Jen wished she could enjoy the relaxed view, but she was only growing more keyed up in Adam's company. And clearly he was determined to have his say. He pulled off the road and onto a point that overlooked the water. Waves surged against the rocks below, the ocean restless. Adam seemed restless, as well. He swung out of the car as if too impatient to sit still any longer.

Jen climbed out, too, and went to stand a short distance from him. Offshore, a tall ship rode the swells. It was a big, four-masted schooner at full sail, a ship that could have materialized straight from the nineteenth century—the past merging into the present on this lazy summer afternoon.

At last Jen glanced over at Adam. "If you're going to talk about the other night, please don't. We both had too much to drink, that's all. We got carried away."

The breeze ruffled Adam's hair until it was no longer so impeccably groomed. His voice was gruff when he spoke.

"I had a lot more I wanted to tell you that night. I didn't get a chance. The fact is, you've been trying to avoid me this past year, Jen. And you've also been avoiding your family. That isn't right. They need you, and you can't go on letting them down."

Jen stared at him. "That's what you wanted to tell me? You wanted to give me a lecture on my family? I suppose I should've known." She kicked a small stone. "And I'm not hiding out in New York, trying to avoid you. I'm simply leading my own life. A good, happy life, by the way." She stopped. Why did she feel so defensive around Adam? Why was she trying to justify herself to him?

His features were set in the hard, uncompromising lines so familiar to her. "A good life?" he echoed skeptically. "Don't forget, Jen, I've seen your apartment. I don't know what the hell you're doing in New York, but that's not the point. New York's only a couple of hours away. You've been acting like it's in another country, always making excuses why you can't come home. And that *is* hurting your family. All I'm trying to tell you is—don't do it on my account. You can start coming home again."

She made an attempt at laughter. "Now you're giving me permission to return. I guess you never really understood me or why I left you. And obviously you still don't understand."

"Explain it to me, then. Let's straighten this out once and for all."

Anger churned inside her. This was typical Adam Prescott—behaving as if she was someone he had to bring into line.

"I tried to explain it to you, Adam. A hundred times I tried. But you never listened."

They stood facing each other on the rocky outcropping, the waves splashing unheeded below. Adam jammed his hands into his pockets.

"This is about the newspaper," he said, "isn't it? You always resented how much time I put into it."

She made a gesture of futility. They'd been apart all this time, and still it seemed their arguments were destined to follow the same path.

"Adam, I knew from the beginning how important the *Standard* was to you. That wasn't the real problem." It dismayed her how fresh her memories were—how readily she recalled the pain and disappointment of trying to get through to Adam. During their marriage she'd been like someone pounding and pounding on a door, never to have it opened, never to know what was on the other side. How ironic. Living with Adam so many years, but never being allowed to know his private thoughts or emotions. She'd begun to wonder if she knew her own husband at all.

She still didn't really know him. Even now, his expression grew shuttered. "I gave you everything I could, Jen. Everything I had to give."

"It wasn't enough." She heard the edge of bitterness in her own voice. "Let's not start this all over," she said quickly. "I'm here for my mother's wedding, and that's the only thing that matters."

Adam studied her. "Don't let another year go by before you visit your family again."

"I don't know what's going to happen after this," she said, perhaps too sharply. "I'll just have to see how it goes with my great-uncles and with my mother. As for you and me, Adam . . . well, let's not have any more . . . unfortunate episodes."

"I call it lovemaking." His tone was final, yet he looked dissatisfied. He gazed at Jen a moment longer, frowning slightly. Her own gaze lingered involuntarily on the bold, expressive contours of his face. A week ago he had reawakened the passion between them, and now the familiar desire stirred in her again. She still wanted him. She still longed for his touch. Hadn't she learned anything—anything at all?

She turned away and was relieved when he went back to the car and pulled open the passenger door for her. She slid into her seat, and a moment later they were on the road.

"I'm surprised you haven't remarried," she said when the silence grew awkward. "You wanted children, after all." Jen paused for only a second. The issue of children had been one of the major sore spots in their marriage, and she felt it best to skim over the subject. "Anyway, these days it seems there's always a story about you in the society columns, and a picture of you with some new woman."

He drove the car smoothly along the winding ocean road. "I didn't know you read the social pages," he remarked.

"I don't read them. It's just that you can't help glancing at a picture of someone you know. Besides, you give the gossips a great deal to talk about."

"You believe the stories, Jen?"

"I believe the photographs." She stared out the windshield, refusing to mention the jealousy that twisted through her every time she saw a picture of Adam escorting yet another lovely socialite. "The women you choose, they're gorgeous," she said in an offhand manner. "Apparently you didn't waste any time after I was gone."

"You made it clear you wanted nothing more to do with me. You're still making that clear—even after I shared your bed."

Dammit, why couldn't they stop talking about that...incident? Jen feared her relationship with Adam was like a package she kept trying to wrap up and put away, only the paper kept tearing and the string kept coming untied. It certainly didn't help to be sitting beside him like this, his closeness almost taunting.

Adam turned off the road and stopped the car in front of the heavy iron gates that guarded Jen's childhood home. She frowned at them. She'd always detested these gates, convinced they'd been meant more to imprison the Hillard family than to keep intruders away.

Adam leaned out his window and punched a series of numbers on the security panel. A second later the gates buzzed and swung open ponderously. Adam drove through, the gates clanging shut behind the car.

"I don't even know the security code anymore," Jen said. "My family trusts you more than they do me."

Adam slowly took the car under the elms of the drive. "I know it bothers you, that I'm still on good terms with your family."

"I don't understand how you get along so well with them," Jen murmured. "I can never seem to agree with them about anything. I never seem to agree with my mother, that's for certain."

"Give your family a chance for once. You might be surprised."

"Surprised—I seriously doubt that. Some things *never* change."

He stopped the car in front of the house, although perhaps "house" wasn't precisely the right term for such an ambitious structure. The Hillard mansion had been built in the late 1800s, at a time when Jen's ancestors had harbored a fondness for Tudor architecture. The place resembled an English country estate, with its mullioned windows, stone walls, myriad chimneys and even a few conical towers. Architecturally the place was impressive, Jen supposed.

"Welcome home," she said wryly. "I never did trust this house. When I was a kid, I used to feel lost in there."

Adam sat with both hands resting on the steering wheel. "Jen . . . is it really so bad coming home?"

"It's uncomfortable at the very least."

"I could go in with you right now. It might help ease things."

Jen glanced at him. "It's better if I do this alone."

"Maybe some things do change, Jenny," he said in a quiet voice. "You seem different now. Stronger, I think. More independent, that's for damn sure."

Gazing into Adam's dark eyes, she felt trapped in the intimacy of his car. It seemed that long ago the touch of his lips and the caress of his hands had branded her in some irrevocable way. Perhaps she resented him for that, more than anything else. Adam had been her first lover. And, in spite of his emotional distance, he'd been a very good lover. Too good. She'd begun to fear she would find no other man who could compare with him that way.

She pressed the window button, raising the glass all the way up. "I appreciate your meeting me at the station," she said rather stiffly.

"There you go again, being polite."

Her eyebrows drew together. "Okay, forget polite. All I know is, I'm not looking forward to going in that house."

"I suspect you can handle your family. In a way, you handled all of us a year ago. This time just go a little easier."

She turned from him. How like Adam to align himself firmly on the side of her family. That was the way it had

felt back then: all of them, including Adam, lined up
against her.

She scrambled out of the car. Adam deposited her
suitcase and bag on the veranda, then jangled his keys in
his hand.

"Positive you don't want me to come in with you?" he
asked.

"Positive."

Adam gave her a fleeting smile and climbed back in his
car. Jen watched it disappear down the drive. And she
wished, quite suddenly, that she'd let Adam stay here
with her, after all.

ADAM DROVE BACK OUT the gates, only to slow the car to
a halt. He couldn't explain why he wasn't phoning the
newspaper. He usually checked in to see how things were
going; he rarely took this much time off. Hell, he
shouldn't be taking off time at all, not when he had Darnard Publishing looking to close a deal with him. They
were making a generous offer for the paper. Very generous. Yet Adam still couldn't force himself to sign on the
dotted line.

Now he thought about Jen. That his ex-wife was a distraction there could be no doubt. More than a distraction. These days she seemed to have gained a special
vibrancy, as if living in that run-down apartment of hers
in New York actually suited her. Of course, she still had
the patrician air that was her hallmark. That was the
joke: for as long as Adam had known Jen, she'd fought
against her aristocratic heritage, despising the fact that
her maternal ancestors boasted a distant connection to
Stuart royalty. And yet Jen moved with a naturally aristocratic bearing, something she couldn't disguise. It
showed in the confident way she walked, the way she

could make even faded jeans and a T-shirt seem like the
latest fashion. Meanwhile, her gray eyes betrayed the
passion she tried to keep hidden underneath. . . .

Damn. She was getting to him all over again. He'd
hoped he'd worked Jenny out of his system that night in
New York. He'd thought it would be safe, going to pick
her up today and setting her straight about her family.
He'd been wrong. Of course, he'd been wrong about
Jenny plenty of times before.

Adam started the car moving again, but he didn't call
the paper. Instead, he went down the road and turned in
at yet another pair of gates. A few minutes later he swung
the car around in front of a rambling, gabled villa built
of mellowed stone. It had been his parents' home, the
house where he'd grown up. He rarely came here anymore, and he couldn't explain the impulse that had
brought him today.

Adam climbed the porch steps and unlocked the front
door. He moved restlessly through the dim, musty rooms
with their shrouded furniture and drawn curtains. A
caretaker cleaned and dusted the rooms periodically, yet
still the place smelled of decay to Adam. All about him,
the air hung heavy and stale from disuse.

He knew he ought to have sold the house years ago.
After all, he wasn't a sentimental person. But it was one
more thing he couldn't explain—why he held on to a
house that felt more and more like a mausoleum with
each passing year.

Adam frowned as he paced the drawing room. He
didn't care for niggling emotions he couldn't explain.
Now he glanced at the portrait of his parents that still
hung in an alcove. It was a realistic portrayal, showing his
mother and father turned toward each other, focusing
solely on each other rather than gazing out at the rest of

the world. Adam paused and studied the portrait for some moments. That was a mistake, of course, for he felt remnants of the old sensations rise within him—sorrow and guilt and anger. But it had all happened such a long time ago. Surely with a little effort he could make himself forget.

Adam turned from the portrait and strode outside, gazing across the wide lawn. Off among the trees he could see the rooftop of the Hillard house. His family and Jen's had lived side by side for decades, and Adam couldn't help feeling protective toward Jen's two great-uncles and toward her mother. He didn't like the sadness he'd sensed in them, ever since his divorce from Jen and her refusal to visit Newport.

Adam gazed speculatively at the Hillards' rooftop. That was a problem he could tackle—convincing Jen her family needed more from her. He just had to make sure his involvement didn't go beyond that.

Where Jen was concerned, he wasn't about to make the same mistake twice.

CHAPTER THREE

JEN GLANCED once again at the elaborate clock that presided on the mantelpiece. She'd always disliked that clock, with its fussy, scrolled trim in gilded bronze. Nonetheless, the minute hand accurately indicated that Jen had been waiting in the living room for almost half an hour. This was so typical of her mother. Visiting her was like trying to see a head of state. The housekeeper had sternly ushered Jen into the living room, instructed her to remain there and stalked off to inform "madame" of this intrusion. Throughout the years, Jen's mother had employed a long line of equally stern housekeepers, who invariably considered it their duty to obliterate any homey detail in the Hillard mansion.

As Jen attempted to find a comfortable spot on the silk-brocade sofa, she felt more and more like someone waiting to petition the Queen. But she rejected the alternative of going upstairs to search for signs of life. Her great-uncles were never home at this time of day—not that Jen could have counted on them to ease the tension. At any rate, Jen would just wait here and let her mother make a grand entrance, if that was what she wanted.

At last the tap of heels sounded in the hall, and Beth Hillard appeared in the doorway. She smiled graciously, as if to an audience.

"Jenna, come here and give your poor old mother a kiss." Beth Hillard looked anything but poor and old. A slender woman of fifty-six, she could easily have passed for ten years younger. Her hair was still as dark as Jen's, her skin still fresh and barely lined. If on occasion Beth cultivated an air of frailty, it was simply to put others off guard. In reality, Beth Hillard was a shrewd, determined woman.

Now she held out her arms, and Jen went to give her a dutiful hug. As usual, a cloud of fragrance enveloped her, a floral perfume that Beth had been using forever. It reminded Jen of roses preserved under glass, and it always made her stomach tighten with some vague apprehension. Today was no different.

"We won't quarrel this time," Beth murmured against Jen's ear, like someone delivering a subliminal message. "Absolutely not."

Jen extricated herself from the embrace, battling a familiar annoyance. "If I recall, Mother, last time you were the one who quarreled with *me.*"

Beth surveyed her daughter. "Never look to place blame, dear. It's unladylike. Besides, today I'm willing to make allowances. I absolutely refuse to get upset."

Jen stifled a groan of frustration. During the past year, her mother had stirred up several arguments with her, usually via the telephone. On one awkward occasion, she'd insisted on meeting in New York. Lunch with Beth had not been a pleasant encounter, by any means.

Now Beth led Jen back to the sofa and urged her to sit. "Come, let's have a chat. You must be terribly surprised that I'm marrying Phillip—on the spur of the moment like this!"

Jen noted the sparkle in her mother's eyes. "Considering that you've been engaged to the man for years, Mother, 'surprised' isn't exactly the term. Let's just say I'm happy for you and Phillip. Really I am."

"You know, Jenna, I've been foolish to make Phillip wait so long," Beth said. "I'm glad I've finally made up my mind to go ahead. And that brings us to the subject of you and Adam..."

"I don't quite see the connection," Jen muttered.

Beth tucked up her feet and settled back in a corner of the sofa. In her bright turquoise blouse and flowered skirt, she made a splash of color against the pale cushions. Beth always dressed to stand out among subdued surroundings; it was part of her flair.

"I want to know how you've reacted to seeing Adam," she said. "Let's be frank, dear. Don't tell me the experience didn't affect you."

Jen struggled with another surge of annoyance. "Mother, how many times do I have to tell you it's over between Adam and me? It was an underhanded trick, sending him to New York to tell me about the wedding."

Beth shrugged. "I just think you ought to get your feelings out in the open. Let's be honest. You can't deny that Adam is someone special."

Jen hated it when her mother went into her honesty mode. Usually it meant Beth wanted *other* people to be honest, leaving Beth free to pass judgments and proffer advice. It was particularly irritating when the subject turned to Adam.

Jen stood abruptly and went to stare out the window. A lawn as perfect as green velvet sloped down toward the Hillards' own private beach. Nothing about the place had changed. The grounds were still exquisitely manicured, looking untouched, as if no one ever strolled across them. And Jen's mother still behaved as if Jen and Adam were meant to form an alliance. That was how the Hillard family had viewed it all those years ago: an alliance, not a romance. Jen suspected that even Adam had seen it in those terms.

She swiveled away from the window and faced Beth again. "Mother, you have to stop. You have to accept the truth about Adam and me. It's over."

Now Beth assumed a philosophical air. "You're just kicking up your heels a little, that's all. You never had a chance to be on your own before you got married, so you're doing it now. You just have to get it out of your system."

Jen clenched her hands into fists. "I'm not just getting something out of my system, as you put it. I'm building a life for myself."

"One you're quite mysterious about, if I do say so. What do you *do,* Jenna? I'm aware you haven't touched any of the funds in your accounts. How on earth do you support yourself?"

Jen wouldn't answer that question. No one in her family would understand her job at the deli, or how she lived. And her acting aspirations were too private, too special, to share right now.

"Mother, I'm doing just fine. You don't have to worry about me."

"Well, I do worry." Beth swung her feet down from the sofa and gazed at her daughter in consternation. "If only you'd had children with Adam. That would've anchored you."

"Anchored," Jen echoed. "Let's not get into this again, Mother."

Beth paused, apparently considering different tactics. "I'd always hoped that you and Adam would discover the joys of parenthood together. His poor dear parents dreamed of that, too, you know...."

It was Beth's guilt treatment, something she used with particular effectiveness. Jen refused to be swayed by it today, but she reflected on her mother's words. It was true that the Hillards and the Prescotts, long close in friendship, had always harbored the hope that eventually Jen and Adam would marry and produce children of their own. The marriage had taken place, indeed, on the eve of Jen's twenty-first birthday. She'd been wildly in love, and she'd imagined Adam felt the same way. She'd wanted to believe their union actually had nothing to do with family expectations. More than anything, she'd wanted to believe they were destined to be together for very personal and private reasons. Jen had been so damn naive back then.

Beth spoke again, still working on the guilt angle. "I don't understand you, Jenna, no matter how hard I try. If you can't make up with Adam, why don't you find yourself another husband? Someone suitable, of course, someone—"

"Someone appropriate," Jen finished. "Yes, I know. Someone with the proper family background who can live up to the Hillard standards."

"The right candidates *are* available. Look at me. I managed to find another man who can live up to the standards of our family. In fact, I'm sure your father would be very pleased that I've chosen Phillip."

Undeniably, Phillip Rhodes possessed flawless credentials. Master of his own considerable fortune in real estate, there was no danger that he wished to marry Beth Hillard for her money. Phillip and Jen's father had even been good friends. Jen could well imagine her father nodding his head in approval, endorsing the wise step his widow was about to take—the step of forming another proper alliance.

Jen pushed both hands through her hair. "Look, Mother, I really am happy for you and Phillip, so let's forget about me for the moment. This is your time. Let's talk about plans for the wedding. I'm ready to pitch in and get to work."

Beth smiled complacently. "I'm so glad to know that, dear. Because you're going to be a big part of the ceremony. You and Adam both, that is. You see, Adam is going to be the best man, and you're going to be the maid of honor!"

JEN WALKED QUICKLY through the grove of linden trees that marked the end of Hillard property. Prescott property began on the other side of the trees. For years, the Hillards and the Prescotts had been neighbors, the two families united in physical proximity, as well as in purpose and outlook. But Jen had always considered this grove between the two estates as a sort of no-man's land, belonging to neither of the families. It had often been her refuge, a place where she could simply be by herself, away from the combined demands of the Hillards and the Prescotts. It was only natural to come here now. She began to pace.

"Hello, Jenny," said Adam from the other side of the trees. Jen stopped abruptly. Just the sound of his voice seemed to transform her surroundings. Suddenly this grove seemed too outlying, too secluded.

Jen felt an odd mixture of defensiveness and anticipation. She turned and peered through the branches. "Adam, what are you doing out here?"

He walked toward her. He'd taken off his jacket, but his tie was still loosely knotted. "I have to admit I got curious. How'd it go with your mother?"

Jen frowned at him. "I suppose you already know she plans for me to be maid of honor—with you as best man, naturally."

"The best man has a lot of responsibilities," he remarked. "Taking charge of the ushers, being the toastmaster, supervising the rest of the wedding party."

Jen glanced at him sharply. "I never should've let my mother finagle me into this."

"You could always tell her you don't want to do it."

"She *is* my mother."

"So we're both in. I guess we'll be seeing a lot of each other the next few days."

Jen leaned against a tree trunk. "At least we can try not to get in each other's way."

"We can try," he agreed.

"What I mean to say is, I think it would be easier if you didn't come looking for me like this. Why *did* you come, Adam?"

For once he appeared at a loss. He didn't say anything for a moment. When at last he did speak, he surprised Jen.

"This place is where I first kissed you," he murmured. "Do you remember?"

"Of course I do," she said reluctantly. "But I never thought you remembered."

"You were, what, seventeen? I considered you much too young for me, but you seemed determined to show me otherwise."

Poignant memories drifted over her, but she resisted them as best she could. "What's the point, Adam? It was all so long ago."

Sunlight glimmered down through the leaves, and a breeze from the ocean stirred the branches. Adam crossed to Jen, a look of purpose in his eyes. She pressed back against the tree trunk, feeling the scratch of bark through the thin material of her blouse. Adam was standing very close to her now. He raised his hand and gently, experimentally, ran his thumb over the tender surface of her lips. Jen caught her breath at his touch. She felt herself trembling, and she couldn't move away from him.

"Do you remember when I first made love to you?" he asked, his voice husky.

Her eyelids drifted downward as he continued his light, seductive caress. But he was seducing her most of all with words and with those memories. Oh, she'd been crazy for him. Nineteen years old, and it had seemed to her she'd been saving herself all her life for Adam. She'd been so impatient to have him, and he'd taught her well the secrets of her own body. Too well....

"When I made love to you in New York, it was like the first time, wasn't it, Jen?"

It had been better than the first time, that was the worst of it. In New York, she'd brought to Adam all the experience he himself had given her. Their passion had been all the more intense for its familiarity. But she needed more from a man than physical passion. Far more.

She slipped away from him, furious at the tears pricking her eyelids. "Don't do this, Adam," she said, her voice shaking. She glanced away from him. They stood together among the trees, and Jen realized she would never find any neutral territory here. Her "no-man's land" was an illusion. In Newport she would always be haunted by all the poignant memories of her time with Adam—the man she had once loved so desperately.

"Leave it alone, Adam," she said tautly, wishing she could return to New York this very instant.

Instead, all she could do was retreat to the house where she'd never truly felt at home.

THERE WERE MANSIONS in Newport far grander even than the house where Jen had grown up. Tonight, for instance, she found herself wandering reluctantly about the spectacular edifice known as Hampton Court. Light from the chandeliers glittered on the marble fireplaces and gilded mirrors of the ballroom, and the ceiling frescoes and the carved wall panels only added to the atmosphere of exuberant Victorian excess. A hundred years ago, a wealthy society matron named Alda Hampton had thrown lavish parties here in her efforts to outdo other wealthy society matrons. This evening's gathering was an echo of those splendid affairs. The house now belonged to friends of Jen's mother, and they'd spared no expense in celebrating her impending marriage. At one end of the room, a chamber orchestra played on a dais. At the other end, tables had been laden with every variety of seafood: lobster, crab cakes, shrimp bisque, stuffed clams.

Jen continued to wander on the outskirts of the party, sipping a glass of champagne. She wasn't in the mood to socialize. She preferred smaller, more intimate gatherings, not large groups like this. But she knew that her uneasy mood couldn't entirely be blamed on the noise and chatter that surrounded her. The way Adam kept getting under her skin was what really vexed her.

At this very moment Adam was nearby, sharing a conversation with a group of people. As if sensing her gaze, he turned and glanced at her. It seemed to her that even from this distance, she could see a hint of mockery in his dark eyes. She couldn't look away. One glance, and he had captured her. Her fingers tightened around the glass of champagne. But the fizz of warmth through her body had nothing to do with alcohol.

"Having a good time, dear?" Beth Hillard appeared at Jen's elbow, her gaze assessing.

Jen finally dragged her eyes away from Adam's. "You don't need to worry about me, Mother. This is your celebration. Have fun."

"Yes, it's so pleasant to have an unexpected party like this." Beth was her usual immaculate self, hair perfectly waved, makeup expertly applied. Now she glanced about the crowded room with an air of contentment. "Ah, there's Adam," she said in a too-innocent voice. "He looks particularly dashing tonight."

Unfortunately Jen found that she agreed. Adam's masculine, broad-shouldered frame looked especially attractive in the slate gray jacket he wore. And no matter how restrained his outward demeanor, he conveyed a sense of energy coiled underneath. His vitality seemed to draw Jen even from here. She turned so that she couldn't see him anymore.

"Mother, I wish you and I could talk about something besides Adam."

Beth gave her daughter a disapproving glare. "You're not giving him a chance. I'm quite certain he wishes a reconciliation with you—whether or not *he* realizes it."

Trust Beth to disregard reality completely. Still, Jen couldn't help glancing at Adam again. By now a few couples were dancing, and Adam was among them. He was executing a waltz with a striking blonde Jenna didn't know. She tried to ignore her immediate, instinctive discomfort at the sight. Let Adam Prescott dance with all the blondes he liked!

Jen's mother became distracted by the approach of several friends, and Jen was able to slip out onto the terrace. Leaning against the balustrade, she gazed at the ocean. The evening had deepened into night, and the line between water and sky was barely perceptible. The noise of the party was subdued out here, and Jen tried to lose herself in the sweet, humid fragrance of the air.

"You have a habit of running away, Jenny."

She stiffened at the sound of Adam's voice and went on staring at the ocean. The stone balustrade was cool against her hand, and she tried to focus on that sensation rather than Adam's nearness. "I'm not running away. I just don't like this type of party. So many people..."

"So many of the wrong people, you mean," he said, coming to lean next to her.

In some ways, Adam knew her very well. Too well. "I've never really belonged in this world," she said, gesturing to include the ornate mansion and the expansive grounds that swept down to the bluff. "Everything's on such a grandiose scale. I prefer things small and manageable. I'd rather look at one single wild rose than acres of garden flowers. But *you* belong in this world, Adam. You're very comfortable in it."

"And that gives you one more reason to despise me," he said. The light spilling from the ballroom revealed the hard lines of his face.

"I don't despise you," she answered. "Believe it or not, I've gone on with my life. I haven't spent every minute thinking about you." That wasn't entirely the truth. Jen had spent a lot of time over the past year thinking about Adam.

He studied her intently. "Tell me about this life of yours in New York City."

She stiffened again. She'd never told Adam about her secret dreams, knowing instinctively he would dismiss

them as absurd and farfetched. She knew how farfetched they were. She didn't need a dose of Adam's
cynical realism.

"I'm happy," she said. "That's all you need to know."

"From what I can tell, you've carved out a lonely place
for yourself. Is that how you want it? No family around,
no kids..."

She set her glass down on the balustrade, the champagne no longer enticing her. "I can see where this is
headed. But I had good reasons for not wanting children
while we were married. Dammit, Adam, you were never
around. You didn't have any time for me, let alone a
baby."

"We could have worked it out. I would have made
adjustments—"

"No. You wouldn't have. You refused to change for
me. Would a child really have made the difference?" She
took a deep breath, struggling to calm herself. It dismayed her that Adam could still provoke her emotions so
easily.

"Be straight, Jen," he muttered. "It wasn't just about
my working too much. You always behaved as if you'd
be jealous of any child we'd have—as if you'd resent my
giving attention to someone else."

Turmoil churned inside Jen as she gazed at him.
"Maybe if you'd really been in love with me, maybe then
I wouldn't have been afraid children would come be-
tween us."

"Your idea of love is completely unrealistic." Adam
sounded impatient. "You expected us to be enthralled
with each other twenty-four hours a day. But marriage
should be a partnership, not a ticket on an emotional
merry-go-round."

"Well put," she said caustically. "Except that I'm no longer asking you to be enthralled. You're off the merry-go-round. You're free."

"It's not as simple as that." Adam stepped closer and drew her into his arms. Startled, she placed her hands against his chest and frowned at him in the glimmering light from the ballroom.

"Don't do this..."

"We've proved that at least one thing is right between us. Very right, Jenny."

His touch was dangerous, sparking memories of all their secret, impassioned hours together throughout the years. "It's not enough," she said, her voice unsteady.

Adam didn't answer. He and Jen stood clasped together in the shadows. As the music drifted out from the ballroom, he moved her into a dance. They swayed together, and she found her cheek nestled against his chest, certainly a deterrent to rational thought. They had always danced well together, moving so naturally in each other's arms, and tonight was no different. She trailed her hands up over his shoulders, raising her face toward his as if she possessed no will of her own.

She trembled in his arms, alive to his touch, and knew she had to do anything she could to break the spell between them. "Adam...there's something you should realize," she said. "My mother wants to get us back together. Let's not make her think she's succeeding."

He drew Jen even closer. "Your mother has nothing to do with this," he said.

"She's up to something, I tell you."

Adam wouldn't listen, and against her own will, Jen relaxed deeper into his arms. The pounding of the ocean against the shore seemed to grow louder, until she could almost feel the rhythmic throbbing of the waves—or was that simply Adam's heartbeat next to hers? It was difficult to tell where one sound began and the other left off. And then she realized that the music had ceased entirely. In fact, an expectant sort of silence seemed to weight the air. From the direction of the ballroom, someone gave a discreet cough.

Jen pulled away from Adam, only to find her mother peering out at them. Even from this distance, Jen could see the satisfied glint in her mother's eyes. Behind Beth Hillard, several other faces peered out with interest, too. It was impossible to tell how long Jen and Adam's embrace had provided a source of entertainment for the other guests, but Jen's mother fairly beamed. She gave Adam and Jen a perky little wave from the doors of the ballroom.

"Damn," Adam said. And Jen had to agree.

CHAPTER FOUR

OUT OF SORTS. That was the only way Adam could describe how he felt this morning. Out of sorts, as if everything in his life had subtly shifted and become just a little displaced. Could he blame this sensation on his problems with the newspaper? Or could it be the fact that his ex-wife was back in town? Back in Newport.

Adam didn't know the answer. Apparently he didn't know a whole hell of a lot about his life anymore, and that bothered him as much as anything. He was accustomed to being in control. Not that long ago he'd known exactly where he was headed, but these days it seemed that all the familiar signposts were gone.

For the moment, Adam stood in front of the Newport offices of Hillard Enterprises, the shipping firm that had provided his ex-wife's family with a substantial fortune over the past few centuries. The firm was a venerable one, originally founded by Jen's shipbuilding ancestors in the early 1700s. Not that Jen's forebears had been all that respectable; the family history included tales of smuggling and privateering—more than a few skeletons in the closet. These days, however, Hillard Enterprises occupied itself with the mundane details of supervising its fleets, calculating tonnages and monitoring worldwide freight rates.

Even with branches in New York, San Francisco and London, the firm still maintained its original small building in Newport—almost a museum, really. Adam studied the place: its bricks mellowed with age to an ocher red, the ancient window sashes painted a fresh white as if to belie their years, the hipped roof giving the structure a rather ponderous, top-heavy air. Heritage. The place was all about heritage. It stirred something in Adam, some restlessness he couldn't quite define. More vague dissatisfaction, it seemed. He didn't like it, but once again he didn't seem able to do anything about it. He also didn't seem able to do anything about the way his ex-wife kept coming to mind. Jen, with her gray eyes and her dark hair tumbling to her shoulders....

Adam pushed open the front door of Hillard Enterprises and passed through a room where relics of the business were carefully preserved: yellowed maps, old-fashioned typewriters and adding machines, framed photographs of Hillard ships through the generations, even a crusty old anchor dating back some two hundred years. Adam climbed a simple, graceful staircase of polished pine, walked down the second-story hallway and knocked on a closed door.

"Come in," called a voice that quavered just a little, like a scratchy phonograph recording. Adam pushed open the door and walked inside an office where the walls were paneled in more glossy pine. All of this honey-colored wood gave the room an impression of airiness, as if Adam had just stepped into a forest clearing. Jen's great-uncle William was seated by the window in a slatted chair, taking full advantage of the early-morning sunlight. Recently old William had been complaining that Newport weather had become too brisk even in the summer. William liked to theorize about changes in the earth's atmosphere, refusing to admit that his own advancing years might account for stiff joints and cold toes.

"Adam—right on time," William said with obvious approval. Adam shook William's hand with the requisite formality. He'd known William Hillard all his life, and he also knew how much William appreciated the small grace notes of respect.

Now Adam took a seat across from the elderly gentleman. "You made things sound pretty urgent on the phone, William. I came right over."

William nodded. "Yes, it's a matter of some importance. But where is Thomas? He knows we can't start without him. He does this sort of thing on purpose—"

"Contain yourself, Will," Thomas Hillard said from the doorway. Thomas, William's older brother, had turned eighty this year. He walked slowly and stiffly into the room. As stubborn as his sibling, he refused to make concessions to his age and wouldn't use so much as a cane to help himself get about. The Hillard brothers had other similarities. They were both tall and thin, and they both had snowy white hair. In some ways, however, the two old men were a study in contrasts. William wore outmoded flannel trousers and an equally outmoded cardigan; Thomas wore an elegant, hand-tailored suit. William favored drab, unobtrusive colors; Thomas sported a jaunty red handkerchief in his jacket pocket. The two old guys reminded Adam of a set of mismatched bookends.

William watched with a frown as his brother lowered himself inch by inch into a chair. "You're almost late, Thomas."

"Check your watch, Will. I still have fifteen seconds to spare." Thomas finally settled all the way into his chair and gave Adam a roguish smile. "You're in for it today, my boy. Will's on a tear about Jenna."

Somehow this didn't come as a surprise to Adam. William was always on a tear about his great-niece.

"I'll explain, given the chance." William stared at his older brother, looking peeved, but that was nothing new, either. William always looked peeved with Thomas. "Adam, we're worried about Jenna. Very worried, I might add—"

"Speak for yourself, Will," Thomas interrupted. "I'm not worried about Jenna at all. It's the best thing she could do for herself, kicking up her heels in New York. Let her have at it, that's what I say."

William looked more annoyed than ever. Now he pointedly ignored his brother, addressing Adam once again. "We called you here so you could do something about Jenna before it's too late. This escapade of hers has gone on long enough. Keep her in Newport, Adam. That's what we're asking."

Thomas interrupted once more, lifting a hand that shook slightly. "Calm yourself, Will. I think it's fine that Jenna wants to be an actress in New York. Just fine."

Now it was Adam who glanced at Thomas. "Jen? An actress? What are you talking about?"

Thomas's expression seemed purposely bland. "You haven't suspected? But it's true, you know. That's why Jenna ran away to New York—to become an actress."

Adam stood and began pacing. This office, for all its sunlight and airiness, felt too confining. Perhaps it was the age of the place, or the age of its inhabitants, but Adam felt restless. Besides, he was having a difficult time accepting this claim Thomas had just made. Jen, an actress. He'd been married to her all those years, and she'd never once mentioned anything about wanting to act.

"It can't be true," sputtered William. "It can't possibly... But, Tom, if you knew something about Jenna, why didn't you tell *me?*" William sounded hurt, like a kid asking why he hadn't been allowed to join the sand-lot baseball game. Occasionally that happened—William seeming to echo the long-ago child he'd once been, longing to be let in on his older brother's secrets.

Thomas appeared pleased to have stirred up a reaction. He was always trying to stir up his younger brother. "I'm telling you about Jen now, Will. Not that it's a very sporting thing to do—she's made it clear she doesn't want anyone to know what she's up to."

William looked offended. "*You* seem to know all about her. Are you implying that she's confided in you?"

Thomas looked complacent. "Let us say she almost confided. I was speaking with her yesterday, and she started to tell me about her acting class. She tried to catch herself, but it was too late. After that, I made a few phone calls. I still have friends in the theater, you might remember, and I've learned that Jenna's been making the audition rounds in New York." Old Thomas leaned back with all the satisfaction of someone who'd just displayed his trump card.

"You investigated... and you didn't tell *me,*" William muttered.

Adam thought about Jen. She'd always loved to attend the theater, but she'd never confessed to having any serious acting aspirations. It bothered the hell out of him that his own wife hadn't confided in him....

"Adam, it's more imperative than ever that you do something about Jenna," William continued. "It's absurd for her to be alone in New York chasing some wild fancy. What are the chances she'll succeed? The odds are against even the most talented..." For just a moment, William sounded forlorn, and Adam could guess why. Almost fifty years ago, William, too, had chased a wild fancy, causing his own brief scandal. He'd announced to his parents that he wished to be a novelist, instead of joining the family shipping concern. Against all their admonishments, he'd moved into a small apartment in Boston and proceeded to write. He'd actually completed a novel and sent it off to one editor after another. Unfortunately even the Hillard name hadn't helped him sell the book. He'd given up in discouragement and returned quietly to the family fold.

Adam rubbed the back of his neck. He didn't know if his ex-wife had any acting ability or if this really *was* just some crazy dream of hers. No matter what, though, her great-uncle William was right. The odds were against Jen. She'd chosen a very difficult career, one notorious for its harsh disappointments.

Adam wasn't prepared for the sudden protectiveness he felt at this moment. Protectiveness for his Jen—

Except that she wasn't his Jen anymore. Why couldn't he seem to remember that?

"Adam, you look perturbed," Thomas commented, a gleam in his eye as if he hoped for a ruckus of some type. "I'll bet you don't like the thought of Jenna's being an actress, either. Maybe you and Will should join forces—lock the poor girl up and prevent her from going back to New York. Between the two of you, I'm sure you could manage it."

"I'm talking about a realistic plan to dissuade Jenna!" William snapped. "For once in your life, take something seriously, would you?"

"If I took life seriously, I'd be long dead by now. In fact, I'm amazed *you're* still ticking away..."

Adam watched the great-uncles go at each other— Thomas trying to stir up a reaction, William obliging him by getting peeved. For decades these brothers had been doing the same thing, locked in familiar, time-worn patterns. Over the years Adam had developed affection for the two difficult old men, but today it was being tested.

He went to the door of the office, glancing back for a moment. "Forget it, William," he said. "I'm not going to interfere in Jen's life. Whatever she wants to do, she can do it. I already asked her to come to Newport more often for visits. I can't ask anything else of her."

William looked disappointed. Thomas looked disappointed, too, but no doubt for different reasons. He'd probably been hoping to cause more trouble.

"Forget it," Adam said again, and then he left the offices of Hillard Enterprises, feeling more dissatisfied and out of sorts than ever.

JEN DISLIKED being here in the rambling garden behind St. Matthew's Church on Seabell Lane. This place stirred too many conflicting emotions in her, no matter how lovely the surroundings—wisteria vines growing over the arched gate in competition with the yellow trumpet flowers, a forsythia hedge adorning the brick wall, drifts of David's harp and lady's mantle spreading a froth of greenery along the walk. This was the same church garden where generations of Hillards and Prescotts had taken tea with a succession of pastors and pastors' wives. This was also the very same garden where Jen had married Adam twelve years ago. She didn't want to be here. She didn't want to remember the promises she'd made that dazzling summer day.

Now it was another dazzling summer day, the sun shining down through a sky as clear and deep and translucent as blue glass. The beauty was lost on Jen. She felt tension radiating along her neck and through her shoulders. She just wanted her mother's wedding rehearsal to

be over and done with, but it hadn't even started yet.
Reverend Kiley was deep in consultation with the under-
pastor in regard to some minute detail of protocol, the
musicians couldn't decide where to set up, and the groom
had abruptly disappeared ten minutes ago. For that
matter, the best man hadn't yet arrived.

As if she'd compelled his appearance with her
thoughts, Adam came walking through the gate. He
looked good—he always looked good. Those hints of
silver in his hair only made him seem all the more virile,
and she knew from experience that his mustache had an
unexpected, enticing softness....

Jen curled her fingers into her palms. Adam made her
feel as if she were sitting in a darkened theater, watching
a movie projected boldly on the screen—a movie in which
the leading man overshadowed every other player by the
sheer force of his presence.

When would it stop being like this? One glance at
Adam, and her tension had turned to something different—a disquieting awareness of him. She watched as he
came purposefully toward her. Adam always moved with
purpose.

He stopped beside her, his silk tie casually loosened, his
shirtsleeves rolled up over strong forearms.

"Hello, Jen," he said, his gaze intent on her.

"Hello, Adam."

For a moment it seemed that would be the extent of
their conversation. Adam, however, didn't excuse himself and go off to speak to someone else; that would have
been too easy. Instead, he remained beside Jen, allowing
the silence between them to grow heavy and potent.

Just when she thought she'd have to blurt out something—anything—to break it, Adam nodded toward the
opposite side of the garden.

"Your mother seems upset," he remarked.

Jen followed the direction of his gaze to where Beth Hillard was deep in consultation with the Reverend Kiley's wife. Jen, too, had already noticed the subtle lines of strain on her mother's face. Usually Beth appeared so on top of things, an optimistic manager of people and events. But at this moment Beth wasn't managing anything, not even her own wedding rehearsal. She just stood there, listening to the pastor's wife and looking almost...anxious. Jen couldn't help being worried about her mother; Beth simply wasn't the type to succumb to prewedding jitters.

"You're very observant," Jen said to Adam. "Most people wouldn't realize anything's wrong with Mother. They'd just think she was being a little restrained."

"We both know that your mother being restrained is enough of an oddity," Adam said dryly. Jen couldn't help smiling at that, and for a moment she and Adam seemed to share something—a sort of insider's knowledge, born of their long history together. But then Adam spoke again, and this tenuous sense of intimacy vanished.

"Maybe I'm not so observant," he said. "One thing escaped me entirely—the fact that you want to be an actress, Jen."

She glanced at him. "How on earth...? Uncle Thomas, I suppose."

Jen should have expected something like this, particularly where Uncle Thomas was concerned. He was the most sympathetic of her relatives, and she had a habit of letting her guard down around him. Of course, sooner or later someone in her meddlesome family had been bound to find out. She'd just hoped that she'd have a bit more time to establish herself in New York before it hap-

pened. She hadn't wanted anyone judging or dissecting
or analyzing her plans until they were a little more substantial, a little more shaped.

Now Jen glanced over to where her two great-uncles sat
together on a wooden bench among the delphiniums.
They looked so...old. They were both officially retired,
although they still spent long hours at the offices of Hillard Enterprises, keeping an eye on things. It had to be
difficult for them, knowing that the family business must
pass into younger hands. Worst of all, there were no
Hillard heirs to take over. William had never married;
Thomas had gone through two marriages and a few volatile love affairs without producing any progeny. Jen had
never been able to envision a career in shipping, and she'd
supplied no children who could eventually do the job.

The familiar guilt swirled over Jen, the stifling sense
that the whole burden of the Hillard name rested on *her,*
and that she had failed to carry it. She'd refused to have
kids with Adam, she'd divorced him, she'd gone off to
New York to pursue her own idea of happiness... By
Hillard standards, she'd been amazingly selfish. Yet her
own choice had seemed clear. She could either continue
being selfish, or suffocate—

"Don't look so disgusted with your great-uncles,"
Adam murmured at her elbow. "If Thomas pokes his
nose into your life, he's just hoping for some excitement. Not to mention the fact that he genuinely cares
about you, Jen. And William...William is very concerned that someone in New York might hurt your feelings. You know how sensitive he is about artistic
rejection."

Oh, yes, poor Uncle William and the novel no one
would publish. It was a famous family story, although
William himself refused to talk about it anymore. Jen

suspected, however, that William still guarded that manuscript somewhere, the pages moldering away in a desk drawer or ancient filing cabinet, a constant symbol of his failure. William hated rejection of any kind, and somehow he'd seemed the most hurt of anyone when Jen had left for New York.

Damn. Jen had been afraid it would be like this coming back to Newport, all the old guilt and the old tenderness taking her over. Because no matter what, she truly *did* love her great-uncles and her mother. She cared about them and worried about them and wanted desperately for all three to be happy and well. She just couldn't live with them.

"You don't need to appeal to my better sentiments," she told Adam in a low voice. "I'm not completely unfeeling, you know. It's just that— Don't you realize, Adam? For the first time in my life, for the very first time, I'm doing something on my own, without help from my family, from you, from anyone." She wondered at this sudden impulse to explain things to him. How would he possibly understand? Adam stood here now, stroking his mustache in a judicious manner as he observed her. It was a disconcerting gesture on his part— first of all, because it gave her the unaccountable desire to reach out her fingers and stroke his luxuriant mustache herself. That was distracting enough. But Adam really did seem to be contemplating her in judgmental fashion, like a professor wondering how to bring a recalcitrant student into line. It put Jen immediately on the defensive, giving her even more knots of tension in her shoulders.

"I can't figure it out," Adam said after a moment. "All those years of ours together and I never once suspected that you wanted to be an actress. How could something like that slip by me? Just tell me that."

Jen folded her arms. "It annoys you, doesn't it? Finding out that something about me was outside your control. But it's not that simple, Adam. It's not like I went around all the time wishing I could be an actress and hiding the wish from you. For such a long while I pushed the whole idea away. I mean, it seemed so foolish, so impossible. I'd never acted in my life. I had no reason to believe it was something I could do..." Her voice trailed off. Once again, she was explaining too much to Adam. It made her feel more foolish than ever, but somehow she had to finish.

"It wasn't until...until our marriage got into serious trouble that I started thinking about what I really wanted to do with my life. And that was when I knew I had to give it a shot. I had to see if I could be an actress. I had to know I'd tried at least. So that's what I'm doing now. I'm trying." She didn't mention the immense insecurities about the endeavor that assaulted her every day—every minute, really, if she was honest. But she was going ahead. She could be proud of that much.

Adam continued to study her. "You've been away from me a year," he murmured. "An entire year, all that time attending acting classes and going to auditions. But your life is still a mystery to me. I don't know what you're doing to support yourself. I don't even know if there's a new man in your life."

Jen flushed. She could feel the heat rising through her body, reaching her face, staining her cheeks. More confusion churned inside her. She simply could not admit the truth about *that* to Adam. In the year she'd been in New York, she hadn't been with any other man. Oh, she'd gone on a few dates, that sort of thing, but nothing serious. And that was part of the problem. No doubt she needed to be with another man, someone who could erase the memory of Adam's kisses, the memory of Adam's caresses....

Jen felt her flush deepen, and she had to glance away from Adam. She was thirty-two years old, and yet she had known only one lover in her life, one love. No wonder Adam still had such power over her senses. But she hadn't met anyone in New York who attracted her the way Adam did. It was a hopeless circle. Jen almost laughed thinking about it, even though it wasn't a particularly humorous situation.

"So I'm being nosy," Adam admitted, when she didn't answer him. "So I'll stop. You don't have to tell me anything."

This was a surprise—Adam's backing off before he obtained what he wanted. Jen glanced at him suspiciously, but it seemed at last the rehearsal was starting. The groom had reappeared, the violinists and cellist had finally set up, Jen's mother looked comparatively more composed, and Reverend Kiley had opened his prayer book with a flourish.

As best man and maid of honor, Adam and Jen were obliged to walk down the aisle together, the aisle in this case being the flagstone walk that traversed the length of the garden. Twelve years ago, Jen had walked down this exact same path in her beaded silk wedding gown, a great-uncle ready on either side to give her away.

"Steady," Adam said, as if reading her thoughts. He placed his hand under her elbow. "Remember, you're not the one getting married in two days. You don't have any reason to be nervous this time around."

"I'm not nervous," she muttered back. "Not in the least." Jen stared straight ahead and saw the pastor smiling nostalgically at her and Adam. Reverend Kiley, after all, had been the one to perform their wedding ceremony all those years ago. How many other memories would assault Jen before this rehearsal was over?

Just then she heard a beeping noise, as if her own agitated pulse had suddenly acquired sound. The noise, however, was coming from Adam. He had one of those obnoxious little beepers, it seemed, heralding some important phone call.

Adam frowned, but he excused himself to use the telephone inside the church. The rehearsal came to an awkward halt, and Jen reflected wryly that she'd just been abandoned while walking down the aisle.

Adam returned a few moments later. He glanced at Jen and then at the rest of the wedding party. ''I'm very sorry, but there's something of an emergency at the newspaper. I'll have to drive into Boston. Please go on without me. I'll have Jen fill me in on what I miss.''

All Jen could do was stare at him. She saw the expression on his face, the focused intensity that always came to him whenever he spoke about his newspaper. So things hadn't changed over this past year—not at all, it seemed. Adam couldn't take even a day or two off without the *Boston Standard* intruding.

He gazed at Jen for another minute or so, his expression growing enigmatic. But then he turned, striding away, going out through the garden gate—and vanishing from her sight.

CHAPTER FIVE

ADAM COULD TELL that something was wrong with Russ Billington. He could tell that, not by looking at Russ, but rather by examining the story in front of him. For years, Russ had been one of Adam's best reporters, dependable for his accuracy but also for his ability to bring unusual insight to just about any story. However, this one was neither accurate nor insightful. Adam glanced up.

"Okay, Russ," he said quietly. "Mind telling me what's going on?"

Russ Billington sat on the other side of Adam's desk, looking harried. Russ had been with the *Boston Standard* ever since graduating from college. He'd started out as a reporter, and he'd remained a reporter. He'd never wanted to move up, never wanted even to be an associate editor when the opportunity arose. As far as Adam could tell, Russ had liked his job, was good at it and hadn't asked for much more from life. He'd seemed one of those rare people content with what he was doing. But now, well, the quality of Russ's work had been steadily slipping for the past few months, and this was the worst so far.

Russ leaned forward, elbows propped on his knees as if he suddenly felt tired. "I know it's bad," he said. "It shouldn't have happened, I realize that—"

"It didn't just happen. You wrote the thing. Lord, if Sandra hadn't caught this, you could've caused us one hell of a mess. Think about it."

"That's all I've been doing—thinking about it," Russ said with an edge of anger to his voice. Maybe he was mad at Adam, maybe at himself. Adam pulled the copy in front of him again. Russ had put together what should have been an in-depth story regarding recent problems with parole violators.

"Hell, Russ. This just isn't like you. Usually you're so thorough. But this reads like you just tossed it off. Obviously you didn't try to interview one person who actually had any facts in the case."

Russ stood up abruptly. To all appearances, he seemed the same as usual—a bit flabby around the middle because he kept making plans to get to the gym but somehow never managed it, his thinning hair cut just a little too short in back because he never made the effort to find a good barber. Yes, Russ looked just the same—but something had to be way out of kilter for him to write like this.

"Trouble with your personal life?" Adam hazarded. Not that Russ had much of a personal life. He was a long-term bachelor.

"Everything's fine," Russ muttered. "Just fine."

"Health? Finances? Just spit it out, whatever it is," Adam said.

"It's nothing. Let it go. This won't happen again, I'm telling you—"

"It's already happened too many times. That's why Sandra's been checking your work so carefully. Russ, take some time off—two weeks to straighten things out. Because if you can't straighten things out, I'll have to let you go—permanently." Adam spoke gruffly. He'd always been able to fire an employee when necessary, but Russ Billington was someone special. He didn't want to fire the guy, but Russ needed to help him out with this.

Russ just stood there, face gone stony. "I don't want any time off. All you have to do is give me one more chance. That's all I'm asking."

"You don't have a choice in the matter, Russ. Two weeks—that's what I'm giving you. Make the best of it."

Russ turned and strode out of Adam's office, banging the door behind him. Adam leaned back in his chair, feeling more than discontented. It seemed to him that Russ might very well represent the problems with the *Boston Standard* right now. Russ was an excellent reporter who for some reason or other seemed to be burning out. And the *Standard* was an excellent paper also in danger of burning out.

Adam glanced around his office. It was large, messy and comfortable. The shelves along the walls were wide and deep, able to hold any number of books, magazines and newspapers. Adam's desk was the bulky, green-metal type, big and solid, with enough space for all the pieces of computer equipment that sprouted from it like so many electronic mushrooms. The desk even had a few corners free for piles of research reports, as well as scatterings of layout designs, print tests and ad broadsheets. It was a capacious office, the sort of place where you could settle down to work and not be overwhelmed by your clutter. Adam liked it, liked spending hours surrounded by his own friendly chaos. At least, he'd liked spending hours in here before that odd restlessness had taken him over of late.

Adam stood and moved toward the blinds at the glassed-in portion of his office. They were the old-fashioned wooden kind that made a rattling noise and were always getting snarled in their own cords. Adam supposed he should replace them, but they'd been installed way back when his grandfather was editor in chief of the *Standard*.

Adam had lowered them earlier so he'd have some privacy for his talk with Russ. Now he raised them and stared out at the newsroom. It was late, and the day's commotion had died down. Some of the reporters still worked at their desks, but tomorrow's early-morning edition was already humming on the presses downstairs and most of Adam's staff had gone home to eat a meal with their families. It occurred to Adam that he'd been eating dinner alone more often than not the past few weeks. It was usually a mediocre dinner, too. Either he'd grab some potato chips and a stale sandwich at the vending machines down the hall, or he'd go across the street to the café that overgrilled its burgers. His appetite for good food seemed dampened.

A knock came at his door and Sandra Koster, the managing editor, poked her head inside. "Got a minute, Adam?"

"Sure. But I thought you'd left already."

Sandra plunked herself down in the chair across from his desk and gave a heartfelt sigh. "I was just on my way out, but I had to come in first and tell you how sorry I am I interrupted your vacation in Newport. It was just that we were in such an uproar, and I felt you should know what was going on. Then again, maybe I ought to have handled everything myself..." Sandra was a fine manager, but occasionally she had the unfortunate habit of second-guessing her own decisions. Adam wasn't concerned, though. He'd promoted Sandra only recently to this position, and he figured all she needed was a little more experience at taking charge.

"You had to call me," he said. "This damn system is still too touchy. We don't have all the glitches worked out yet. Wonder if we ever will." The newspaper's mainframe computer had crashed today, setting off a chain reaction that had shut down the entire photocomposition system. It made Adam long for the old days, the less sophisticated days of typewriters and Linotype machines. But finally they'd gotten things up and running again.

"Then on top of everything, to have Russ botch a story the way he did..." Sandra muttered. "It's been the most awful day. The worst." Suddenly, unexpectedly, her eyes filled with tears, and she looked like she was going to start sobbing any minute. Adam felt his gut tighten. A woman's tears—he'd known far too many of those while growing up. Even now seeing a female cry always produced the same reaction in him—impatience, distrust, but almost a weariness at the same time. Jen, though, she'd never been much for weeping. Adam had always been grateful for that.

Sandra's tears had begun trickling down her cheeks. What was happening? Was his entire staff going to fall apart at the seams while he watched? First Russ, and now Sandra.

She didn't actually begin sobbing, though. She just let the tears run down her face while she searched through her pockets. "Damn," she said. "Damn! I'm sorry, Adam. I feel really stupid. You can't imagine how stupid I feel right now."

Adam figured it was time to lower the blinds again. They stuck a little, but he finally managed to bring them rattling down. Then he sat behind his desk and waited.

He was good at waiting out another person when the occasion demanded. Jen had often accused him of trying to unnerve people with his silence, but he knew when words weren't necessary.

Sandra was silent for a long moment, too, and she avoided looking at him. She'd found a crumpled tissue in one of her pockets and used it to blot the tears trickling down her cheeks. It didn't seem to do much good; more tears just came leaking out. Adam continued to wait. He'd never had this much uninterrupted time to observe his managing editor. Of course, she'd never sat and cried in his office before. Sandra was undeniably attractive, with clear blue eyes—when they weren't reddened by tears—curling brown hair and a pleasant hint of roundness to her body. Attractive, yes, but even so, she didn't possess Jen's grace, Jen's innate air of confidence....

Adam couldn't believe he was doing it again. In the year he and Jen had been apart, he'd developed an irritating habit of comparing every woman he met with his ex-wife. And somehow, in one way or another, they always came up lacking. He'd have to get over the habit—it was a damned nuisance.

Finally Sandra blotted the last few tears from her face. "I think I'm under control now," she said, although her voice was a bit shaky. "I thought I was handling things so well—the divorce, you know..."

Adam nodded carefully. He knew that Sandra had recently been divorced. He also knew she had something more to say; he could sense it coming. He just wasn't sure he wanted to hear anything about Sandra's private life.

"My ex-husband is seeing someone," she said. "Some girl who's barely twenty, for heaven's sake. I could deal with that much, I really think I could, but last night I found out she's going to move in with him. You know who told me? My own son. My own child. My eight-year-old informed me that his father is soon going to be living with some juvenile twit . . . Oh, I know it's crazy, Adam, but I'm so jealous and furious about it. I'm a basket case, I really am."

Adam had the uneasy feeling that those tears were going to start again. But he felt a reluctant empathy with Sandra. The thought of his own ex going to bed with someone else—yeah, he understood the jealous part. It was driving him a little crazy, not knowing if Jen had some other guy in her life. He hadn't seen any signs of a man in her apartment that time, but still . . .

"Divorce is tough," he said. He knew it wasn't a particularly helpful statement, but it seemed to get Sandra's interest. At least she wasn't crying anymore.

"How long has it been for you now?" she asked.

"A little over a year." He stopped there. He didn't like talking about his divorce. He didn't like admitting he hadn't been able to hold on to his wife.

"Please tell me that things get better," Sandra said, sounding rueful. "If I could just believe they *will* get better . . ."

"They will—trust me," Adam said, perhaps a shade too heartily. His own experience with Jen was more complex than he'd like it to be. After his initial sense of loss, he'd managed to adjust to single life. He'd immersed himself in the newspaper more than ever, and in his few off hours he had started seeing other women. No matter that he kept comparing those other women with Jen, things had actually started to go along pretty well. But then Beth Hillard had announced she was getting married and had asked Adam to deliver the message personally to Jen. He'd obliged, seen Jen—made love to her—and his new life had been out of kilter ever since. So who was he to offer advice to fellow sufferers?

"I think I feel better now," Sandra said with obvious resolve. "I'm sorry I dumped all this on you, Adam, but it helped to talk about it." She stood and went to the door. "Thanks for lending an ear. Good night."

"How about dinner?" he asked, surprising himself. It wasn't an invitation he'd planned to offer, but he went with it. "I'm starved, and I imagine you are, too."

Sandra hesitated, staring down at the tissue wadded in her hand. "I don't know..."

"I suppose you have your son waiting for you."

She grimaced a little. "Actually, no. He's sleeping over at his father's tonight, and I guess that's just one more thing that's been getting me down. All day I've dreaded going home to an empty house."

"It's settled, then." Feeling a welcome energy, Adam grabbed his jacket from a chair back and shrugged into it. After another moment, Sandra gave a nod, capitulating.

"Why not? It so happens I am starving. Blubbering and making a fool of myself really worked up an appetite."

Adam liked her ability to poke fun at herself without being too self-deprecating. She was a nice woman. She was also a woman who stirred none of the turmoil that his ex-wife could provoke in him. He'd always felt relaxed around Sandra, and he could do with a little relaxation tonight.

He escorted her out to his car, and soon they were traveling through downtown Boston as the last of dusk gave way to night. Driving here was something of a free-for-all, cars and trucks and buses squeezing haphazardly in and out of lanes, pressing around each other frenetically but with little malice. It always made Adam feel like he was in a car rally, and it got his adrenaline going. He and Jen had often joked that you could tell where you were in this city just by people's driving habits. Downtown, drivers were inventive, but in the suburbs, they stayed in their own lanes.

Jen again. He tightened his grip on the steering wheel and made an effort to concentrate on the woman beside him, not the woman in his head.

"How's your son handling everything, Sandra? Brian, isn't that his name?" Adam thought back to the last company picnic and seemed to remember a little boy with curly hair just like his mom's. He tried to keep tabs on his employees' families without being too intrusive. After all, he subscribed to the belief that a boss should be cordial while maintaining an appropriate distance. That, of course, brought up another question—what was he doing taking his managing editor out to dinner?

He didn't have an answer, so he merely listened while Sandra talked about her son.

"Brian seems to be okay, he really does. But how do I know for sure? I mean, maybe the divorce has caused some horrible, irrevocable scars that won't surface for years and years. Maybe he'll turn out to be a neurotic, or a psychopath. I lie awake at night and worry about it."

Adam downshifted and wheeled around a corner. "Do you always imagine such disasters?"

"I'm a worrywart," she confessed. "But it's parenthood that's made me that way. I have this philosophy. I believe that if I worry and stew enough, somehow I'll prevent anything really bad from ever happening to Brian. It doesn't make any sense, I know, but there it is. Don't all parents get silly ideas like that? Of course, you'll find out someday," she added hastily, as if remembering too late that Adam didn't have any children of his own. She seemed embarrassed and lapsed into silence.

The way Adam looked at it, there were two types of parents. The first type behaved as if having children was the most stunning, all-encompassing activity in the world and felt sorry for anyone who didn't share the happiness. Such enthusiasts generally equated the term "nonparent" with "nonperson." The other type of parent took you aside and warned you with bitter, graphic descriptions never, ever to let yourself in for the grief, disillusionment and pain of spawning children. Adam suspected that Sandra belonged to the first category, the kind of parent who treated you as if your lack of children was some pathetic, unmentionable disease. Of course, he'd wanted kids himself. Maybe that was why he was so aware of the whole thing.

He parked in front of the Hamilton Tower, gave his key to the parking attendant and ushered Sandra inside to the elevator. A few moments later they emerged on the fiftieth floor. The restaurant here was one of Adam's favorites, good food combined with understated comfort, and the windowed walls provided a glittering view of the city lights below. Carl, the maître d', greeted Adam with his usual affability.

"Mr. Prescott, haven't seen you in a while. I know exactly what table you'll like . . ."

Once they were seated and perusing the menus, Sandra glanced around. "Imposing," she commented. "When you suggested dinner, I was hoping maybe you meant that taco takeout place everyone in the newsroom is raving about—not that this isn't just fine," she amended quickly. "Of course it's fine. It's just that— I'm really making a fool out of myself tonight, aren't I?" She set down her menu, looking chagrined.

"Take it easy," he told her. "You're not up for employee review right now."

Sandra stared at the menu again with great concentration, as if determined not to make any more social gaffes. She was an odd sort of person—very earnest, raw around the edges, unexpectedly humorous, intelligent, but at times unsure of her own abilities. When he'd first hired her some four years ago, she'd brought excellent recommendations with her—high marks from the journalism school she'd attended at a small state college in Vermont, praise from the editors she'd worked for at two dailies in Pennsylvania. Adam had promoted her first to city editor, then to managing editor. She seemed well liked by other staff members, but in fact, she was too afraid not to be liked. Take the problem with Russ Billington. Sandra hadn't wanted to be the one who would come down hard on Russ. It was fully within her authority to do so, but she had backed off from being the bad guy and had deferred to Adam.

Adam knew he had to find a way for Sandra to become more resolute in her job. She was denying her own talents, her own chances for greater success. He considered the matter, but then caught himself. It seemed, he *was* subjecting Sandra to an employee review tonight. Maybe he should just try to enjoy a decent meal and some congenial companionship.

Sandra, however, deferred to him again when it came time to order the wine. "Whatever you'd like," she said. "Anything's fine with me."

How different it would be if Jen were sitting across from him. Jen would have argued with him about the merits of different wines. And when at last a vintage could be decided upon between the two of them, she would have required to taste the wine herself, never accepting that it was Adam's prerogative to do so. He smiled a little.

"You're thinking about your ex-wife, aren't you?" Sandra asked abruptly.

He gave a reluctant nod. "Yes...I was thinking about Jen. I seem to be doing more and more of that lately. I'm sorry to be so distracted...."

"Don't be," Sandra said with obvious relief. "I mean, I think about my ex-husband far too much myself. Isn't it crazy? I brood about Don a lot more now than I did when I was actually married to him. I brood about him and that twenty-year-old he's taken up with..."

Sandra seemed glad to have established the parameters for this encounter: she and Adam were simply two embattled survivors of divorce, commiserating together. Maybe for a while there she'd feared Adam was extending more than an invitation to dinner. This kind of thing got so damn complicated. It seemed you could never just share a few casual moments with a woman; the undercurrents were already in place.

They ordered, and the food soon arrived—steamed clams for an appetizer, and then plates of salmon fettuccine. Sandra commented a few too many times about how delicious everything was, but the conversation gravitated naturally toward the newspaper.

"Something will have to change pretty soon," Adam said grimly. "Either I sell out to Darnard, or I come up with a damn good way to plug the leaks in our advertising revenues—not to mention our circulation base. I'm investigating some options, but nothing I'm happy with yet."

Sandra leaned toward him, propping her elbows on the table. "You shouldn't sell," she said emphatically. "Believe me, I'm not being altruistic—I'd just like to protect my own position. If a bunch of corporate bigwigs take over, all they'll want to do is hire MBAs to run things. It'd be awful.'' She made being an MBA sound like evil incarnate, but Adam was inclined to agree with her general assessment. And he liked Sandra best when she was riled up, expressing her opinion blatantly, not worrying if she'd said or done the right thing.

The next hour or so passed quickly. He and Sandra went on discussing the newspaper over dessert and several cups of coffee. Sandra shared his enthusiasm for the unvarnished, day-to-day details of the editing business—ferreting out a good story, knowing who would be best to cover it, knowing which unexpected leads should be followed, secretly itching to write the story yourself. And then putting the different stories together, discarding bits and pieces, adding other ones, as if you were assembling some intricate mosaic or puzzle—and all the while the clock ticking toward deadline. Then at last, the newspaper taking shape, all the pieces adding up somehow and shooting through the presses, while already you started to think about doing the whole process over again tomorrow.

It had been a long time since Adam had just sat back, talking to someone about the business he loved. It was turning out to be an enjoyable evening, but it could only go on so long. Finally, most of the other patrons having already left, Adam paid the check and escorted Sandra back down to his car.

As they drove toward the newspaper building so that Sandra could pick up her own car, they suddenly seemed to run out of things to say. Adam blamed those pervasive male-female undercurrents again. He hadn't intended for this to be anything like a date—just a friendly dinner. Except that he and Sandra weren't friends. They were boss and employee—and maybe it hadn't been such a great idea to take that relationship outside the office. Hell, he'd probably known all along that it wasn't a good idea, but he'd gone ahead with it, anyway.

When he pulled into the parking lot, Sandra immediately started talking.

"It was kind of you to do this, Adam. Really, I do feel a lot better. So I appreciate the effort you made to cheer me up. You're still supposed to be on vacation, and all—"

"Sandra, I had a good time. It's not like I was doing you a favor."

She gave an explosive sigh. "I'm babbling again, aren't I? It's one of my worst failings. I just get nervous, and— Not that you make me nervous. Well, actually, that's not true. I think you make everybody nervous, me included. You *are* just a little overpowering, although I'm sure you don't intend it . . ." Her voice trailed off. "Look, do me a favor, will you?" she muttered after a few seconds. "Ignore everything I just said. Hit the erase button."

"Sandra, take it easy. You're not on probation."

"That's reassuring," she said, her tone dry. "Well, good night, Adam. Go back to Newport for your mother-in-law's wedding. Your ex-mother-in-law, I mean. And enjoy yourself. I'll handle everything from here. No more emergencies—I promise." She seemed very eager to get out of the car and away from him. So people like Sandra saw him as overpowering. Jen was a little less diplomatic about it. Jen liked to call him domineering and controlling and just plain arrogant.

Adam waited until Sandra was safely in her own vehicle—a clunky, somewhat battered station wagon that probably got about two miles to the gallon—and watched as she drove away. There was something oddly valiant about her, sailing off in that behemoth of a car. He hoped she got over her ex-husband sometime soon. She was a nice woman who deserved to be happy.

Adam sat for a while longer in the parking lot, wondering why he couldn't seem to resolve his murky feelings about his own ex. Ever since making love to Jen a week ago and then leaving her to the new life she'd chosen, he'd felt an emptiness, almost as if a hole had been eaten away inside him. He'd tried to fill that emptiness a little tonight, and it had worked for a while. He'd had dinner with a woman he liked, and talked to her, and started to feel at ease.

But the effect had only been temporary. The damn emptiness was still there inside him, and Jen still haunted his thoughts. Adam drummed his fingers on the steering wheel for a long moment. Then he cranked the engine again, swung out of the parking lot and pointed the nose of his car toward Newport.

CHAPTER SIX

"THE WEDDING IS OFF!"

Beth Hillard spoke these words forcefully and dramatically. Jen, however, could scarcely believe she'd heard correctly. She stared at her mother.

"You can't mean it."

"I'm very serious, Jenna. I have broken my engagement to Phillip. There will be no wedding tomorrow." That said, Beth sank onto the reclining chaise lounge in front of the drawing room window. Instead of her usual bright colors, this evening she wore a sober brown dress that made Jen think distressingly of dead leaves. Beth acted as if she'd gone into mourning. But it had to be more than her flair for drama. In the fading sunlight, her face seemed very white and drawn—too startling a contrast to her black hair—and her mouth had a pinched look. She appeared genuinely miserable.

Jen wanted to help. She just wasn't sure how to go about it. All day her mother had seemed on edge. Finally Beth had gone out to dinner with her prospective groom—only to return home and announce that she never intended to eat another meal with the man. Jen's mother was clearly full steam into a crisis. Always before, she'd been the one who orchestrated *other* people's crises. It wasn't like her to have one of her own.

Jen tried perching on the edge of the chaise lounge, not an easy proposition because the thing was rather narrow. She patted Beth's shoulder.

"Whatever the trouble, surely you and Phillip can work it out. You always told me it's natural for a couple to have a few spats before the wedding."

Beth glared at her. "I never thought the day would arrive when my own daughter would patronize me. This is not a mere 'spat,' Jenna. Phillip and I have a serious difference of opinion that cannot be resolved."

"Mother, I wasn't patronizing you. I just want you to be happy—"

"If you wanted me to be happy, you wouldn't be off in New York doing who knows what. You'd be here with your family, where you belong."

As far as Jen was concerned, they were getting off the subject, but trust Beth never to lose an opportunity to apply a little guilt. Jen decided to ignore it. "I'm here now," she suggested gently. "Talk to me. Tell me what's wrong between you and Phillip."

"There isn't any point. It's over."

Jen patted her mother's shoulder again, but it felt an awkward, futile gesture. Beth sounded so... bleak. Jen could only wonder what had happened to cause such a rift with Phillip. The two of them had always seemed to have such a steady, affectionate regard for each other. They hadn't appeared passionately in love, perhaps, but for years now Phillip Rhodes had been a fixture in the Hillard family. Jen was fond of him.

"You know, Mother, Phillip is a reasonable man. I'm sure if there's a problem, you can talk to him about it and work it out. I'm absolutely convinced of it, in fact."

Beth straightened and frowned at Jen. "You're one to talk. I seem to remember saying exactly the same thing to you. I seem to remember telling you, before your divorce, that Adam was a reasonable man and perfectly willing to discuss any problems the two of you might have.''

Jen fought down a swell of frustration. ''It's not the same thing at all. The problems between Adam and me just . . . couldn't be resolved.''

''How do you know my own situation is any different?'' Beth asked, pursuing an infuriating logic all her own. ''Since I haven't told you what the problem is, you're hardly qualified to judge. And I've always felt that you were too harsh on Adam, in any case. You should have accommodated yourself a little more to him. You should have been willing to listen to his side of things.''

It was all Jen could do to stifle her rising anger. Her mother had just broken off her engagement, but instead of discussing that, she wanted to pursue an in-depth analysis of Jen's divorce.

Jen, however, tried again. ''Mother, let's have some coffee. Then maybe we can figure out what to do about Phillip—''

''Oh, Adam, thank goodness you're here,'' Beth exclaimed, gazing toward the door. Jen twisted around and watched her ex-husband come into the drawing room. She hadn't seen him since he'd left the wedding rehearsal yesterday and had no idea how he'd been spending his time. It was annoying to realize how much she'd been wondering about him.

Now, with Adam's presence, the atmosphere in the room seemed to change subtly, to grow more rarified and intense at the same time. More exciting, to be honest. It made Jen feel as if she'd suddenly found herself high on an alpine slope breathing in the bracing mountain air. Why did he always disorient her this way?

Even at this hour he looked ready for any contingency. He was wearing a tie again, striped silk, so that his khaki pants and oxford-cloth shirt lost any chance of appearing casual or relaxed. He could just as well be on his way to an executive meeting somewhere. Not to mention the fact that he had that beeper attached to his belt again, making him available for any phone call from the newspaper. Jen wondered uncharitably why he didn't just live at the *Boston Standard*.

Adam's dark gaze held hers for a moment, and he seemed to be appraising her. She wished, suddenly, for a little more dignity. Her arms and legs were bare, for she wore a sleeveless cotton blouse and denim shorts, her plain leather sandals doing nothing to dress up the outfit. When she'd started over in New York, she'd opted for comfortable, utilitarian clothes, leaving her sophisticated designer wardrobe behind, shedding it like an old skin. But at this moment she would have been happy to wear anything with a little style or verve. She needed a dose of verve right now. All she seemed able to do was perch here on the arm of this ridiculous chair, clad in her bargain-basement clothes, staring back at Adam.

He was the one who broke the unspoken contact between them, addressing Beth. "You sounded pretty upset on the phone. What's this about you and Phillip?"

With alacrity, Beth moved to the sofa and gestured for Adam to sit beside her. "I'll tell you exactly what happened, and I know you'll see my point of view. I'm sure of it."

Jen was left balancing precariously on the chaise lounge. Not happy with this arrangement, she crossed to the sofa and sat down on her mother's other side. She reflected that to an outside observer, it might have appeared cozy: Jen and Adam settled on the sofa, Jen's mother ensconced between them. But then Beth angled herself slightly away from Jen, turning toward Adam. This gave Jen a back view of her mother's well-coiffed head. Even in the worst disaster, Beth Hillard would no doubt comb her hair, apply her lipstick and clip on her best earrings. No one could fault Beth's grooming habits under any circumstance—just as no one could deny her attentiveness toward her former son-in-law and her determination to ignore her own daughter.

"Adam," Beth said now, "I'll be as concise as possible. Out of the blue—out of nowhere—Phillip has announced that he won't live in this house with me after our wedding. He absolutely *refuses* to live here."

Adam seemed to consider this. "What reasons does Phillip give?"

Beth waved her hand dismissively. "He says he can't live in the same place I once shared with another man. But Phillip and Jen's father were good friends! Why all of a sudden is my poor dead Jonathan seen as a rival? And that's not all. Phillip refuses, categorically refuses, to live in the same house as the uncles. As if either one of those dear old men could cause any trouble at all...."

Jen gave this her own consideration. She knew that right now her great-uncles were upstairs, arguing over a game of chess. The two elderly Hillard gentlemen were capable of causing any amount of trouble. William could get the entire house into a swivet if his meals weren't prepared properly, and Thomas on occasion would stay out until all hours, making everyone think something terrible had happened to him—only to find that he'd been playing cards with some of his cronies.

"Mother," Jen said to Beth's back, "I hate to say this, but Phillip has a point. Any marriage should start on fresh ground—someplace that belongs not to the bride, not to the groom, but to both of them. Otherwise, one person is always going to feel at a disadvantage—left out somehow. That's just not right.''

As Jen spoke, she became aware of Adam studying her over the top of Beth's head. He had to know what she was talking about, for Jen had always lived in *his* territory during their marriage. The beach house in Newport, the brownstone in Boston—Adam had chosen those residences for himself well before he'd even started dating Jen. She hadn't questioned moving in with him as a bride, but gradually she'd come to realize that she lived in two luxurious homes not truly her own. She would gladly have traded both of them for one small house that she and Adam could inhabit on equal terms. Adam, of course, had dismissed any such suggestion—it would be inefficient, unnecessary. And for too long, Jen had given in.

Now Jen stirred, glancing away from Adam. Their problems with living arrangements were all in the past. At issue here were her mother and Phillip. Unfortunately Beth's shoulders had gone rigid at Jen's advice.

"Adam, what do *you* think?" Beth asked, continuing to ignore her daughter. "Surely you see my side of it. I can't possibly move out and leave the uncles here alone. They need me. With Jenna away in New York—" Beth paused significantly "—I'm the only family William and Thomas have. And there's certainly room enough in this place for all of us, Phillip included."

Adam leaned back against the Italian brocade of the sofa. "I have to agree with Jen," he said. "Phillip will always feel like an outsider in a house that belonged to you and Jonathan—no matter that they were good friends. As for the uncles, I believe they'll get along just fine here on their own. They're both in remarkably good health, and you already have a live-in housekeeper who can watch out for them. Jen has the right idea. Start fresh with Phillip.''

For the second time this evening, Jen wondered if she'd heard correctly. Was Adam actually agreeing with her about something?

Beth didn't look pleased. She stood up and moved away from the sofa. "Adam, I can't possibly leave this house." Her voice was pained. "A housekeeper won't care for the uncles the way I do. But it's not just that. My first marriage was a happy one. I'd feel disloyal to Jonathan if I left all my memories behind. Why, this is the Hillard ancestral home and it's my duty to preserve it. Can't Phillip understand that? Can't *you* understand it?" Finally Beth looked at Jen, almost with pleading. "And you, Jenna, don't you understand that this is the house where I loved you from the time you were born, where I watched over you and nurtured you every possible moment? So many happy memories… This home holds my entire life.''

Jen couldn't help feeling sympathy for her mother. Beth Hillard could be impossibly manipulative, and maybe even at this moment she was playing the scene for best effect, but Jen knew her mother was sincere about having loved Jonathan Hillard. She'd been devastated when Jonathan had died of a heart attack. Even though Jen had been only twelve at the time, she still vividly remembered her mother's grief. However, Beth *was* exaggerating when it came to the part about nurturing Jen every possible moment. Beth had liked the idea of raising a child more in theory than in practice, and over the years had relied heavily on a succession of nannies.

"Oh, Mother," Jen said at last, "no one's asking you to give up your memories. There has to be a solution to this."

Beth looked strained. "I'll tell you the solution. I won't marry Phillip. I won't marry a man who can't understand how I feel." With that, she turned and walked quickly from the room.

Jen began rising from the sofa to follow, but Adam placed a hand on her arm.

"Let her have some time to herself," he said quietly. "She needs to think it over."

Jen sank back again. By now the emphatic sound of her mother's heels had clicked down the hallway and up the stairs, and Jen and Adam were left on this too-plump, too-formal sofa. Jen felt the fussy brocade scratch against the bare skin of her legs. What an absurd situation to be in, she and Adam confronting not only each other but the remains of Beth's broken engagement.

"Well," Jen said at last, feeling grouchy, "no one can ever change her mind once she's decided on something. All she wanted from either one of us was confirmation, and we wouldn't give it to her. The big surprise, though, is that you actually agreed with me, Adam. What gives?"

He leaned back a little more against the overstuffed cushions. Trust Adam to be able to make himself comfortable in spite of the most pompous of furniture. "I don't see what the surprise is. I was always willing to admit the validity of your ideas."

"Validity... right."

"Don't be so skeptical, Jen," he murmured. "Give me a little credit."

She made the mistake of gazing at him again. It seemed to her that Adam's eyes always held some mystery she couldn't quite fathom. But for a moment she stared into them, anyway, as if the mystery would somehow reveal itself to her this time around.

She stood and went to one of the windows. The sky had turned the deep thick blue of dusk, the last sunlight shimmering against the clouds. Those untouched Hillard lawns sloped downward, a green so improbably rich in color they looked as if they'd been painted by the expert brush of an artist. That was how everything about this place felt to Jen: beautiful, artistically arranged, but lacking in spontaneity and spirit. Much of the decor in the house dated to previous generations of Hillards. Beth herself had changed only a few details here and there, content to let her husband's family set the tone. How could this house be so important to her when she hadn't truly created it?

Adam came to stand at the other side of the window. Against her will, Jen glanced at him.

"I suppose it doesn't matter anymore that you missed the wedding rehearsal, not if my mother's really going to call the thing off. How did your emergency at the paper go?"

"I find it hard to believe you're actually interested. You lost patience with my newspaper a long time ago."

"Adam . . . can't we just make a little polite conversation?"

He looked reflective. "Okay, let's give it a try. Everything went as well as can be expected—when you're dealing with the eccentricities of a mainframe computer. Anyway, I got the system back on line. I also put one of my best reporters on probation for mangling a story. And then I took my managing editor to dinner. I believe you met her once or twice—Sandra Koster."

Something in Adam's tone made Jen uneasy. She seemed to remember meeting a Sandra Something-or-other at a few of the newspaper functions she'd attended with Adam before their divorce. Sandra—a pretty, down-to-earth sort of woman, pleasant to talk with.

"I hope you had a good time," Jen said with no sincerity.

Adam looked out the window, frowning slightly. "It was a fine evening. Just fine."

"I'm happy for you." Jen was still on automatic, saying words she didn't mean in the least. But Adam knew her.

"Come off it, Jen. I can guess how I'd feel if you told me you'd gone to dinner with some other man—and you'd had a good time. I wouldn't like it."

Adam always had been direct. More confusing emotions swirled through Jen. She felt a brief satisfaction, knowing that he could still be jealous, still be possessive. But Adam had always been possessive of her. That didn't mean he'd ever really loved her.

"We're not married anymore," she reminded him. "We both have to move on...."

"So why hasn't either one of us become seriously involved with someone else?"

She stared at him in exasperation. "What makes you so certain I'm *not* involved with anyone?"

"I've been thinking about it. And I've decided that if you were seeing someone, you wouldn't have gone to bed with me last week."

She felt her face begin to flame. Why did he have to keep bringing up that humiliating episode? "Listen, you can speculate all you like, but it's none of your damn business."

"You're not seeing anyone," he stated with conviction. "And for the past year, I've made sure not to become serious about any of the women I've met. Why do you think that is?''

So much for polite conversation. Jen found Adam's train of thought to be fascinating and perplexing all at once. "It *has* only been a year," she pointed out rather acidly. "Give yourself more time. You're bound to meet up with the right woman—someone who can give you a home and children, someone who doesn't mind putting your needs first."

Adam stepped closer to Jen, still frowning. She could feel the rhythm of her pulse, a relentless beat to remind her how readily her body could respond to him. What she felt for him seemed the most elemental attraction, a pull of the senses that obeyed no logic or reason.

"You and I, Adam, in so many ways, we weren't good together," she said, her voice low. "Even more, we weren't good *for* each other. But somehow, in spite of that, we always had one thing going for us. We were . . . very good in bed."

"It seems we still are," he said, his voice rough.

She pressed a hand to the cool glass of the window, as if that would quell the warmth gathering in her. "Very well, we still are," she admitted reluctantly. "But we have to . . . forget about it and get on with our lives."

"That's your solution? We pretend nothing happened a week ago?"

"I don't have any other answer!" she burst out. "All I know is that I have to go back to New York and not see you anymore."

Adam looked dissatisfied, pacing across the room to the piano that hardly anyone played anymore. He plunked two fingers down on the keys, hitting a jarring note. "Avoiding each other—not good enough," he muttered. "There has to be a better way. Believe me, Jen,

I want to get you out of my system. I'd like to go on to something else . . . someone else."

"Someone like Sandra Koster," she suggested.

Adam's fingers made another discordant sound on the piano. "I'd be a damn fool to take up with Sandra. She works for me, and she's just getting over her own divorce. But someone like her . . . hell, yes, she's probably the kind of person I should be looking for."

Jen found herself impelled by a perverse curiosity. "You make her sound different than the women you've dated so far. Those women who end up with you in the society pages . . ."

Adam shrugged. "At one of the dailies where she worked before, she was in charge of the society page herself." He smiled faintly. "Yet she's the type who likes taco carryout and spending time with her eight-year-old."

Jen gritted her teeth. "Congratulations. Sounds like a match made in heaven."

"You're laying it on a little thick, Jen. All I did was take the woman to dinner."

"And you made sure to tell me about it," Jen muttered.

Adam looked disgruntled. He stroked his mustache. "Maybe I thought telling you would serve some obscure purpose."

"Maybe you just wanted me to be jealous. Or maybe you just wanted to make some official announcement that you're looking for another woman. A woman who can win your approval the way I never could. A woman who loves your newspaper as much as you do. A woman whose whole life is built around *your* dreams." At last Jen managed to clamp her mouth shut. She knew she'd said too much, revealed too much. She knew it by the way Adam came over to her and took both her hands in his.

"Jen...I never wanted you to spend your life trying to please me. All I wanted was for us to build a life together."

She moved her fingers in his warm grasp. "No, Adam," she said, "you didn't want to build our life. You wanted to build *your* life, and I was supposed to meekly help you. You already had the specifications all laid out. I was just supposed to follow."

He frowned, even as he kept her hands clasped in his. "I've never wanted someone meek. Part of the reason I married you was because you had so much fight in you. All the trouble you gave me—I actually liked it, Jenny." He pulled her gently, inexorably toward him. She stared at his chest, at its rise and fall with his breaths. Her own breath seemed to quicken in answer. He was working his magic on her all over again, capturing her under his masculine spell. She raised her gaze slowly to his.

"Adam...maybe you wanted trouble at first," she murmured. "Maybe it attracted you. But then you just got impatient. You just wanted me to fall into line."

His own gaze held turbulence. "I wanted a partner. A partner, and a lover. You were one, but never the other, Jen. Always you eluded me." He bent his head toward hers. She knew he would kiss her in another second or two. She ached for his kiss, even as his words stirred all the old arguments inside her. But they could argue later. Right now she craved the touch of his lips. She craved that—and more.

CHAPTER SEVEN

ADAM DENIED JEN her kiss. He moved his cheek over hers, nothing more. She knew the brief, tantalizing whisper of his mustache against her skin, but then nothing more. He raised his head and stepped back, leaving her feeling strangely bereft. She was still breathing unsteadily, wondering how he had the power to resist when once again *she* had succumbed.

He observed her with that disconcerting intensity of his—disconcerting because she never quite knew what lay behind it.

"Come with me tonight, Jen."

She held her arms against her body, dismayed to find herself trembling. He hadn't even kissed her, and she was trembling. "I don't know what you're talking about...."

"Just come with me." He took her hand and began pulling her toward the door. This was Adam at his annoying best—forceful, imbued with purpose, expecting her to comply without question. Jen knew she ought to refuse him. She ought to just let him go and do whatever he wished on his own. But there was something else about Adam—he'd always made her feel as if important things were happening around him. He'd always made her feel that if she refused to go along, she might miss something exciting, something significant.

And so, against all her better judgment, she allowed him to sweep her along tonight. She went out to his car.

Soon they drove through the gates and were headed out onto the winding ocean road.

"I wonder what adventure you have in mind," she said sardonically.

He took a curve of the road with practiced ease, then glanced at her. "What makes you so sure I'm taking you on an adventure?"

"Sometimes I think everything you do turns into an adventure." As she spoke, Jen realized what she was really saying: that her ex-husband, Adam Prescott, could turn even the most ordinary of endeavors into something special and memorable. Living away from him was like celebrating the Fourth of July without fireworks. The job got done, but the sparks were missing.

"Why do you look so perturbed, Jenny?"

"It's nothing. And I really wish you'd stop calling me that. I'm not 'Jenny' anymore. Maybe I never was."

He had no comment on this and just kept driving as dusk deepened into night. Suddenly Jen suspected where he was taking her. She sat with her hands held tightly in her lap, her body tense. And then, several minutes later, Adam made a turnoff, and she knew for sure. The car jounced along a narrow rutted path among the bayberries, beach grass flattening under the tires. After another few moments, Adam came to a halt.

"Why did you bring me here?" Jen asked, her voice barely above a whisper. "Anywhere but here, Adam..."

She sat beside him in his car, gazing out the windshield. All she could do was stare at the beach house where so much of her life with Adam had taken place—some of it joyful, a lot of it painful. This was the house where she had first made love to him. This was also the house where she'd told him she wanted a divorce.

It was a wild sort of place, built of weathered, silvery wood, all rough angles like a pile of driftwood rising above the rocky cliff. Primitive steps hewn into the cliff led downward to a stretch of tawny sand. Nature prevailed in this spot, waves spuming against the shore, the ocean stretching beyond in a dark limitless expanse. These surroundings had always suited Adam, reflecting his own vitality and power.

"Why?" Jen asked him again. "Why did you bring me here?"

He moved his hands restlessly over the steering wheel. "It's not something I planned. It was just..." He frowned a little, as if he regretted bringing her here. But then he pulled the key from the ignition and swung open his door. "We might as well go inside," he said.

"No—"

He didn't listen to her. Already he had come around to her side of the car, holding the door open. She stayed where she was.

"Come with me, Jenny," he said again.

She didn't know how to answer. All manner of emotions churned inside her, as confusing and unpredictable as the sea. But she did know one thing. It was not her past with Adam she feared. It was that they were here together now, very much in the present. She closed her eyes briefly, and then climbed out to stand beside him. The air was humid, clinging to her skin, and the breeze from the Atlantic whipped tendrils of hair against her cheeks. The breeze riffled through Adam's hair, too, making him look subtly reckless. He gazed at her while the salty perfume of the ocean surrounded them and the waves crashed against the rocks below.

Every bit of common sense told Jen not to go into the house with Adam. But he turned, climbing the porch steps to unlock the door. After a second or two, Jen followed, listening to none of the warnings that clamored inside her.

They entered the house together. Adam switched on the lights, and Jen went to stand at the threshold of the living room. She glanced around. She saw the rustic pine settle she'd purchased years ago at an antique shop— she'd made the cushions for it herself in a pattern of lavender and jade. She saw the captain's table and the button-back sofa she'd discovered at an estate sale, the corner cupboard she'd refinished and stacked with her favorite books, the rag rug she'd chosen for the polished wood floor.

"You haven't changed anything," she said in surprise. "Not a single thing."

"Did you think I would?" he asked, standing beside her. "You always made this place seem...lived-in. I liked that feeling—I still do."

Jen didn't answer. When she'd first married Adam, this beach house of his had been indifferently furnished, a place he used merely as a weekend getaway. She'd envisioned it as more of a home—and she'd also naively imagined Adam and herself strolling together hand in hand through antique and furniture stores, choosing items that would reflect both their tastes. Adam, however, had simply never had the time for such activities. Jen had ended up redoing the beach house herself. It had been an engrossing, enjoyable pursuit, but when she'd finished with the job she'd experienced a letdown. In spite of the imprint she'd made on the place, it hadn't seemed a shared home. Perhaps that was because Adam had never placed his own favorite books next to hers, had never added to her collection of music or her stock of board games. Neither had he included any Prescott fam-

ily photos or mementos on the shelves. Right now that
struck Jen as odd and a little sad. Adam believed so
strongly in family heritage, family tradition, yet he kept
no signs of that here.

By now the sky was completely dark beyond the windows. Adam went to the liquor cabinet and took out a
bottle of brandy. He poured two snifters, then handed
one to Jen. She frowned at it.

"Relax," he said. "I'm not trying to seduce you.
That's not why I brought you."

"Why *did* you, then?"

He looked reflective. "As I told you, I don't know.
Unless I just wanted to see if you still fit here."

Jen gave a mirthless laugh. "You make me sound like
something of yours that's escaped from its box."

Reaching out, he tilted her chin with one finger and
studied her thoughtfully. Warming his brandy in one
hand, commanding Jen with the other... because, even
with this light touch of his finger on her skin, desire and
longing plaited through her, weaving a dangerous pattern.

"You did escape me, Jen," he murmured.

"I had to." She heard the shakiness in her voice.
"Adam, if only you knew how hard it *was* to leave. Don't
do this to me now..."

But he kept on doing it. He kept on touching her, and
looking at her. And this time Jen knew he was going to
kiss her. She knew it with all the yearning and misgiving
in her heart.

Adam bent his head and brushed his lips over hers.
Once, and then again, he tantalized her with just the
briefest touch of his mouth, his silky mustache tickling
her skin. She closed her eyes and felt as if she were float-
ing, skimming the surface of desire.

But then Adam deepened his kiss. His mouth possessing hers fully now, he somehow still managed to set down his glass of brandy. Eyes closed, Jen set down her own glass. But occupied as she was with Adam's kiss, she missed the table and the glass went tumbling onto the rug.

"Damn . . ." she whispered against Adam's mouth.

"Forget about it." He brought his arms around her, pressing her close to him. All the warning bells inside her clamored once again. She and Adam had to stop now. Only a little damage had been done so far. Only a kiss, and a brandy stain. If they stopped now, it wouldn't be too late. . . .

With a soft moan, Jen brought her arms around him. She needed to feel him pressed to her, needed to relearn the way her body curved into his. But it wasn't enough. As quickly as this, it wasn't enough. She molded herself even closer to him, reckless and provocative in her haste. His answer betrayed his own need.

"Ah, Jenny . . ."

Still kissing, still holding each other, they began to move toward the bedroom one step at a time. They both knew the way, yet they bumped against the wall as they went. One last warning echoed faintly in Jen's head. *Stop. Stop! It's still not too late. . . .*

She didn't listen. She was beyond listening, all her senses drenched in a liquid heat. She and Adam made it through the door of the bedroom, and he lowered her onto the bed. And still they kissed. He tangled his hands in her hair, and she arched her neck, her head thrown back. His lips pressed to her throat, finding the pulse that beat so tumultuously there.

"Adam . . . Adam, please . . ." She tugged at his shirt, impatient with the fabric that kept his skin from touching hers. Fingers trembling, she started to undo his buttons, first one, then another, then another. He lifted himself up a little so he could work on his tie at the same time. Jen took care of just enough buttons so she could reach inside Adam's shirt. She allowed herself a few delicious seconds to run her hands through the dark swirl of hair on his chest. But still she needed more.

Adam started on her buttons. She helped him, and at last her blouse was peeled away. But even that wasn't enough. Aching with the heat that bloomed inside her, Jen wondered almost frantically why anyone had invented such contraptions as pants and underwear and socks. Adam reached behind her, working at the fastening of her bra, but they were both in too much of a hurry to let him complete the job. Jen yanked the bra straps down over her shoulders, freeing her breasts for Adam to caress. His skin was hot, as hot as her own.

He unzipped her shorts; she unzipped his pants. But shoes and sandals were in the way, too—laces to be undone, buckles to be unbuckled. Alive and flaming to Adam's touch, Jen needed every square inch of his flesh next to hers. And at last there were no more barriers between them, no more clothes to unbutton or unsnap. Jen wrapped her body around his.

"Adam...Adam, please," she said again, her voice taut. But now he refused to hurry.

"I want to look at you," he murmured. He reached over to turn on the bedside lamp, and light cascaded over them. His gaze lingered intimately upon her. And then he went on kissing her, stroking her; he used his hands, his mouth, taking his time with her until she could submit no more, the pleasure he gave her so keen it bordered on pain. And so she caressed him in turn, knowing how to give the pleasure back to him. She was rewarded by the sharp intake of his breath and by the way he crushed her still closer to him.

"Adam..." This time she spoke his name almost on a sob, clutching at his shoulders. And at last there was only an exquisite union, Adam entering Jen, Jen welcoming him. She closed her eyes, lost in sweet desire.

But Adam wouldn't let her hide, wouldn't let her lose herself completely. "Look at me, Jenny," he said, his voice husky and strained.

Reluctantly she opened her eyes. His own eyes were very dark. She wanted to glance away, but somehow she couldn't. His gaze possessed hers even as they moved together more urgently, even as Jen cried out her intense fulfillment, even as Adam gave a shuddering groan a moment later.

Afterward they lay tangled together on the bed, their bodies moist with lovemaking. Gradually Jen's breathing slackened to a normal rhythm, and she realized that her bra was twisted down around her waist—she and Adam had never managed to get the fastenings undone properly. She felt ludicrous.

But it was not her own disarray that made Jen feel a growing sense of humiliation. It was the way it had happened all over again: making love to Adam, giving herself to him, and then sensing the subtle, irrevocable shift as he shut himself off from her once their passion was sated.

He didn't actually turn away, nothing so simple as that. Even now, he lay here beside her, one arm draped across her body. But she could sense him closing himself off nonetheless. She knew it by the slight tensing of his arm and by his having no words of tenderness to offer her at this moment—no words of any kind. She could also see it in the way he seemed to look past her, not directly into her eyes. That was the amazing thing. In the most intimate moments of lovemaking, Adam often gazed at her, *into* her, it seemed. But afterward... afterward, he always gazed past her, exactly as he was doing now. It made her feel as if she'd just gone to bed with a stranger. How many times had she felt like that when she was married to him? Too many times.

Jen slid off the bed. She pulled up her bra, yanked the straps back over her shoulders, grabbed her shorts and shirt and sandals. But even when she was dressed again, the humiliation remained. Her ex-husband, Adam Prescott, still gazed right past her.

THE MUSTY SMELL of the theater rose around Jen. She imagined it as the odor of a thousand shabby dreams. Well, today she'd brought her own slightly shabby dream into this small, decrepit theater. This was the same theater, in fact, where she'd performed such a rotten audition two weeks ago, reading the part of a spinster aunt. Yesterday, however, Bernie informed her that the role of the aunt was still open. He'd somehow managed to wrangle a copy of the script for Jen, and she'd studied it thoroughly. She could tell from the script that this was destined to be a rather rambling and pretentious play, but the role of the aunt did have possibilities. And who was she kidding, anyway? She wanted to act. She wanted to desperately. She didn't care how good or bad the play was, if only she could be in it. So much for her pride. A solid year of rejections had taken care of *that*.

Jen walked briskly down the narrow aisle of the theater, behaving like someone who felt confident of her abilities. That required an acting job right there. Three or four people were clustered in front of the stage, among them the same bored-looking redhead from last time. The woman's hair looked more fake than ever, hanging in limp strands as if it had lost all ambition.

"Have a seat," the woman told Jen with little apparent interest. "I'll get to you in a minute."

Jen hated the thought of a delay; she was geared up right now to audition. However, she had no choice but to sit down on one of the ratty velvet chairs. She settled back and took a few deep breaths as she'd learned to do in acting class. She opened the script and flipped through a few of the pages, rereading lines. But she couldn't seem to relax. Too many thoughts kept intruding—thoughts of failure, of success . . . of Newport.

She'd left Newport four days ago, and she'd been worried about her mother ever since. It didn't help that every time she called her mother and tried to begin a sensible discussion, Beth lost her temper and hung up on her. Beth had branded Jen a traitor for siding with Phillip. It seemed that Beth had broken off all negotiations with her ex-fiancé—and was ready to break off all negotiations with anyone who so much as even mentioned Phillip's name. From the sound of things, she wasn't spending very much time with her friends. She was just holed up in the Hillard mansion, clinging to memories of her long-ago first marriage.

And then there was Adam. Here in the dimness of the theater, Jen's face burned at the memory of going to bed with her ex-husband again. The first time she'd had a bit of an excuse. She'd had too much wine to drink. The second time she'd had no excuse at all. She hadn't taken a single sip of her brandy. It had all ended up on the damn rug.

Jen fanned herself with the script. One mistake she could forgive herself. Two mistakes she couldn't forgive. She despised her own weakness—

"...of course, you could just sit there," the tired-looking redhead said to Jen. "Fine with me."

Jen gave a start, and scrambled to her feet. She couldn't believe she'd been so distracted she hadn't heard the summons to the stage. Firmly she reminded herself that thoughts of Adam had ruined her first audition. She couldn't allow him to ruin this one, as well. She walked briskly down the aisle and up the steps.

"Act two, scene five," said the redhead. "I suppose you might as well read with David."

A man of about twenty-five climbed onto the stage beside Jen, carrying another copy of the script. Her stomach had tightened nervously, but she managed to give him a brief, professional nod. Quickly she thought about the character she was supposed to play—a woman slipping off the far edge of middle age, seeking any way she could to make herself young again....

Jen clenched her script and took another deep breath. The first line was hers, and as she began speaking the words she knew she was rushing them. Emotion—where was the emotion she ought to feel? Dammit, she wasn't supposed to be Jen Hillard anymore. She was supposed to be a woman named Eileen, speaking to a young man half her age, a man she desired....

Except that Jen didn't feel desire, or any other emotion appropriate to this character. She just felt awkward and ridiculous, and she was reading too fast.

"Start again," interrupted the red-haired woman, sounding impatient. Jen couldn't believe she'd already bungled things. Her throat had gone dry, her chest felt constricted, her palms were sweating—

"You'll do fine," murmured the man beside her. "Remember, it's just a part."

Jen glanced at him. He was pleasant-looking, with fair coloring and hazel eyes. And somehow he'd managed to say just the right thing. He made Jen realize she was taking this part too seriously. She had to play around with it a little. She had to think of it as trying on a new dress—not as wearing a straitjacket.

She waited a minute or two, and then she spoke her lines again, more easily this time.

"'Lisa isn't here, Mark. I don't know when she'll be back.'"

"'I don't mind waiting. It's nothing new, waiting for Lisa.'"

Jen kept trying to relax. It was a short scene, but it was also one of the best in the play—where the aunt comes to suspect she has feelings for her niece's boyfriend.

"'Suit yourself,'" Jen went on, as she took a turn around a small crate littered with shredded newspaper. The stage directions read, "Eileen walks to the mantel shelf, keeping her back to Mark." Jen tried to improvise. "'Lisa says you're considering leaving school. I thought you wanted to study medicine.'"

"'My parents wanted it, perhaps. But never me.'"

"'Oh . . . what *do* you want, Mark?'"

"Okay, okay," the bored redhead interrupted. "No need to drag it out. Thank you, Ms. . . . Whatever."

Jen lowered her script. It took her a second or two to let go of Eileen, the spinster aunt. It seemed that the audition was already over. Usually that made Jen feel relieved. Today she just felt a peculiar sense of loss.

The red-haired woman, however, was already speaking to someone else. Jen turned to the man who'd read with her.

"Thanks," she said.

"Hey, no sweat. You did great."

Jen wasn't sure at all how she'd done. Obviously the redhead wasn't impressed. But, anyway, the session was over. Jen went down the stage steps and walked back up the aisle. She moved automatically, a sharp disappointment going through her. One more audition, one less part to play. It didn't make for the most balanced equation.

"Be here at seven tomorrow," the redhead called after Jen, still sounding bored.

Jen twisted around. "You want me to read again?"

"I want you to know the damn lines."

For a long minute Jen didn't understand. "Do you mean—"

"You want Eileen or not?"

Still not daring to believe, Jen wished the woman could just come out and say it. Well, if she wouldn't, Jen would say it for her.

"I got the part!"

The redhead looked resigned. "You got the part. Seven o'clock tomorrow night."

Jen didn't know how she made her way from the theater, but a few moments later she was standing on the sidewalk outside. Everything looked wonderful to her: the boarded-up storefront across the street, the garbage clotting the gutter, the grimy marquee of the theater itself. She had a part—she actually had a part! A role to play. She felt like screaming. She felt like calling up Adam and telling him her fantastic, stupendous, incredible news.

It was this impulse that brought her up short. She stood there in front of the seedy little theater and wondered at herself. She wanted to call her ex-husband, of all people? What was wrong with her?

Surely Adam was the last person who'd understand why she was so happy at this moment. And that, in itself, marred her happiness.

Would she never be free of Adam Prescott?

CHAPTER EIGHT

"CONGRATULATIONS," said a voice beside Jen. Absorbed in her own thoughts, she hadn't noticed the man come out of the theater—the man who'd just read with her.

She smiled. "Listen, thanks for what you did in there. You helped me relax and get through it."

The man stuck out his hand to shake hers. "David Fielding. Alias Mark, alias partner in the Jacob Hollings Playhouse. A pretty grandiose name for this dump of ours, but someday I'll have to tell you all about Jacob, our eccentric founder. He deserves a little grandiosity."

So David Fielding was not only an actor, but a part owner of this theater company. And he was playing the role of Mark, the lead in the play.

"Well . . . thanks again," she said.

"Aren't you going to tell me your name? Technically I'm your new boss, although Mary Bess likes to think she's the one calling the shots."

Mary Bess—no doubt the fake redhead. Jen felt as if she'd just plunged into an intriguing new world. She was now officially one of the Jacob Hollings Players. She liked the sound of it—a little grandiosity was fine with her.

"I'm Jen Hillard. It's been nice meeting you, David, and I'll see you tomorrow right at seven—"

"Let me buy you a cup of coffee to celebrate."

She wanted to share her moment of excitement with someone. Foolishly she wanted that someone to be Adam. But he wasn't here. He wasn't part of this new life of hers. That was the way it had to be.

"A cup of coffee sounds fine," she said.

She and David Fielding walked a few blocks to a small Italian restaurant and slid into a booth facing each other. They ended up not only with coffee, but with servings of amaretti cake.

The cake was delicious, but it could have been sawdust and Jen would have eaten it gladly. She felt benevolent toward everything and everyone. She wanted to order amaretti cake for the entire place—except that she and David Fielding were the only ones there. No matter. This moment was what Jen had longed for. She repeated the knowledge over and over in her mind. She had a part. She had a role. She had Eileen.

David propped his elbows on the table. "Tell me what you're thinking. I can't decide whether you look like someone who just got hit by a bus or someone who just won the lottery."

"I feel a little of both," Jen said. "This is my first break. My first acting role."

"Don't get carried away," he warned. "The pay's rotten, and we'll be lucky if we get an audience."

"I don't care. I'll always remember this moment. Where I was, what I was doing." She glanced around so she could set these surroundings into her memory: the carnation pink walls, the potted fig trees, the terra-cotta tiles. Her gaze came back to rest on David, and she realized how extravagant she'd sounded.

"I'm not usually like this," she said quickly. "I'm usually very calm."

He smiled. "Hey, I'm just glad I could be here to share the moment. You're not jaded yet. I like that."

He had a nice smile. His hair was sandy colored, grown long enough to curl over his collar, and he had a slightly ruddy complexion as if he'd spent time out in the sun. He looked young and healthy.

"I'm jaded about enough things," Jen said. "It comes with age. I'm thirty-two, after all."

"Interesting," David remarked, "the way you're already setting up barriers. Very well. I'm twenty-six, Jen. Not all that different from thirty-two."

It took Jen a moment to sort out what was happening here. She'd felt a little attracted to a man other than Adam, and then she'd felt oddly guilty about it. So she *had* tried to set up a barrier right away. She was behaving for all the world as if she'd been disloyal to her ex-husband...

It was ridiculous. She and Adam were through. Finished! No matter that she'd gone to bed with him in Newport only five days ago.

Jen poured extra sugar into her coffee. "I'm just getting into character," she said. "I'm supposed to play the older woman, aren't I?"

David stirred his coffee slowly and contemplatively. "Tell me a little about yourself. I'm curious. You say this is your first role. But you must have acted in college or high school. All of us have stories about our tenth-grade drama teachers."

As far as Jen was concerned, nothing about this conversation was going right. She didn't have any such stories to share.

"I might as well admit it," she said. "I was always too much of a coward to try out for high-school or college plays. I had this dream about being an actress ... but it was always safer just to leave it a dream. And after college, well, I kept letting things get in the way.''

''Something tells me you're making up for lost time,'' David said.

''That's one way to put it.'' All her years with Adam—could she call it lost time? In too many ways, she *had* lost herself in him. She couldn't deny that, but it wasn't something she wanted to talk about.

''You seem to be doing pretty well,'' she said to David. ''You're already co-owner of a theater, and you're only twenty-six.''

''You're doing it again. Making it sound like we're generations apart. It's only six years, you know. As to the fact that I've just sunk all my money into the Hollings Playhouse, maybe I'm crazy, maybe I'm smart. Too soon to tell.''

Jen pushed her coffee mug aside. ''Maybe it's good to be a little crazy. After all, it's crazy to try being an actress at thirty-two—one of these times I really will stop mentioning my age.'' Jen slid from the booth and stood. ''Look, thanks for celebrating with me, David. But I have to get back to work.''

He rose to stand beside her. ''Have dinner with me tonight.''

''You don't waste any time, do you?''

''Not when it counts,'' he said. ''So, what do you say? I'll pick you up at eight.''

Jen paused, then shook her head. ''It's not such a good idea.''

''Let me guess. Those six years again.''

She smiled a little. ''No, that's not it. But I'm . . . sort of involved with someone right now.'' She listened to her own words. What was wrong with her? An agreeable man was inviting her to dinner, and she had to invent excuses. Because that was all it was—an invention.

"Sort of involved," David echoed. "Doesn't sound too daunting. Obviously there's some prevarication going on here."

"It's difficult to explain." Jen wished she hadn't even started. "It's just . . . complicated."

David looked disappointed. "You know you're in trouble when a woman tells you it's complicated. The *C* word. Bad news all around."

Jen couldn't help smiling again. David really was an engaging man. She put out her hand to shake his this time. "I'll see you tomorrow at the theater."

"Fine, Jen Hillard. Tomorrow it is."

They parted at the door of the restaurant, and Jen felt a vague regret. She had a suspicion she was going to like working with David. So why hadn't she accepted his invitation? Such a simple, ordinary thing—going out to dinner with a new man. Why couldn't she just let it be simple and ordinary? Why had she fabricated that nonsense about being involved? Showing poor judgment and going to bed with your ex-husband did *not* constitute involvement. Even if you'd done it twice. . . .

"Damn you, Adam Prescott," Jen muttered under her breath, and then she hurried to work at the deli.

A WEEK LATER Jen sat within a group clustered on stage. For what seemed the hundredth time, she repeated the opening to Act Three, Scene Five.

"'Lisa, dear, I'm only trying to help you. I don't want you to get hurt—'"

"Wrong, Hillard," said Mary Bess for what also seemed the hundredth time. "All wrong. I told you to be nasty. Sour. Insincere. Got it?"

Jen shifted in her chair, her muscles cramped from sitting so long. The theater had no air-conditioning, and she was sticky with perspiration. "I just don't see Eileen as a sarcastic, underhanded person," she said with as much patience as she could muster. "She genuinely cares for her niece. She feels awful that she's attracted to Mark. She's tortured about the whole thing."

"Oh, wonderful. The sensitive routine." Mary Bess pushed lank strands of that improbable red hair away from her face. "Just give Eileen some gumption, all right? She's seen what she wants, and she's going after it."

"Of course she has gumption. Of course she's going after what she wants. But she still cares about Lisa—"

"Hillard, I don't want a dissertation. Just say the lines, and say them the way I tell you."

Jen clenched her hands. All week she and Mary Bess had been working up to this disagreement. Mary Bess wanted Jen to portray her character as lonely, embittered and spiteful. Jen saw Eileen as lonely, impassioned and confused. Every instinct in her told her she was right about this—Eileen needed to be a sympathetic character. At the same time, she knew she wasn't winning any popularity contests with Mary Bess.

David leaned forward in his chair now. "I think we should listen to Jen. The role of Eileen is pivotal. If her tone is off, Lisa and Mark will be off, too."

Mary Bess stared at him. "We agreed that I'm the director on this one—at least, that's what I thought we agreed."

Angela, the nineteen-year-old playing Lisa, slapped her script shut. Everything about Angela seemed pared down. She was slight in build, her hair cropped short, her nails always nibbled to the quick. Put her on a stage, though, and she became bigger than life. She would begin to sparkle, a small gem suddenly magnified. She was a very good actress, and she'd given Jen a few pangs of envy already. "Excuse me, everybody," she said now. "But all we've done the whole night is argue about Eileen, Eileen, Eileen. Can we just get *on* with it?"

"No," said Mary Bess. "We're done for tonight. Hillard, when you show up tomorrow, be ready to do it my way." With that, she left the stage, moving with her usual world-weary air. Angela, after a resentful glance at Jen, stalked off, too. Only Jen and David remained, the lights glaring down on them.

Jen reached up and massaged the sore muscles in her neck. "I didn't imagine it would be like this," she said with a sigh. "I pictured camaraderie, teamwork. Except that I just can't keep my mouth shut when I'm supposed to. I almost feel like Eileen's a real person, and I have to defend her."

"For what it's worth, you're right. This play is going to be hard enough to sell as it is. If the audience can't identify with Eileen, we'll really be in trouble."

Jen glanced at David. "I'm probably opening my mouth again when I shouldn't . . . but I don't quite understand the hierarchy. You and Mary Bess . . ."

"It's your basic power struggle," he said ruefully. "Mary Bess has really had a hard time of it just trying to keep this theater company going. She resents like hell taking me on as an investor, even though she needs me. She doesn't like sharing her authority—yet. She'll just have to get used to it, though. I plan to make some changes."

Jen studied him a little more closely. Most of the time David conveyed easygoing affability, but now and then a glimpse of his determination came through. Like now, for instance. He stood and came around to massage Jen's shoulders in a matter-of-fact way.

"I'm good at this," he said. "Hey, you really are tense. You need to loosen up."

She slipped out of her chair and turned to face him. "Look, David—"

He held up his hands in mock surrender. "I know, I know. Your life is complicated. You're thirty-two. There's some guy you're involved with…sort of. And no, you won't go to dinner with me tonight. Did I cover everything?"

"Just about," she said dryly. Every evening this week after rehearsal, David had asked her to dinner. And every evening she'd given him the same answer: no. Yet it didn't seem to deter him. He was definitely persistent underneath that laid-back manner of his.

Jen stuffed her script into her carryall. She went down the steps from the stage, David beside her. They walked all the way to the door, but then Jen turned and glanced back. It really was a decrepit theater, with its tattered seats and faded curtains. But it still seemed special to her, a place for magic.

"Gets to a person, doesn't it?" David murmured as if reading her thoughts. "Even when I was a kid, I was fascinated by the contrast—the stage all lit up, the darkened theater. I'd sit in the audience in the dark, and it felt to me like those people on the stage were in a different land—a land where I longed to be."

"That's exactly how I felt as a child," Jen said. "I always thought once you stepped onto that stage, it was like going through an invisible door into another world."

They stood together for a moment, sharing a quiet companionship. It was a pleasant feeling, soothing to Jen after the rehearsal she'd just endured. She allowed the moment to draw out a bit, and then she left the theater with David.

Night had fallen, but the air still seemed close. It pressed in on Jen with all the grime and soot of the day. She wished that a giant electric fan could swirl cool air through the city for a moment, chasing away the heat and the dirt.

"So, where would you like to eat?" David asked cheerfully.

"I'm going to eat in my apartment—alone. Thanks, anyway, David."

"Alone. Sounds like the mysterious man you're involved with isn't going to show. Come to think of it, he never shows."

"It's a long story."

"I'm a good listener."

Jen was seriously tempted to give in tonight. Surely it would be enjoyable, sharing a meal with David. Why couldn't she permit herself a little enjoyment?

While she was still debating the matter, a long limousine pulled up at the curb. It was a vehicle Jen knew altogether too well, and it looked completely out of place on this squalid street. Nonetheless, a tinted window slid down and a familiar face peered out. It was the face of Jen's mother.

"Jenna—there you are, sweetheart! I've found you at last." Beth smiled fondly, apparently forgetting that only last night she'd slammed the phone down in Jen's ear yet again.

Jen stepped closer to the car. "Mother...how *did* you find me?"

Beth leaned out the window. "Your Uncle Thomas is having a wonderful time reviving his connections with the theater. He's the one who managed to track you down, dear. Very enterprising of him, I must say. Aren't you going to introduce me to this nice young man?''

David had stepped up to the limo beside Jen, and he held out his hand to Beth. "David Fielding. So you're Jen's mother. It's a pleasure to meet you. I've been wanting to know more about Jen, and I'm sure you can be of assistance.''

"How charming . . .''

Jen frowned at David. Wasn't he being a little *too* charming?

"Jen and I were just trying to decide where to eat dinner,'' he said without missing a beat. "Perhaps you'd like to join us, Mrs. Hillard.''

"I don't think—'' Jen began.

"Oh, if you're sure I won't be an imposition,'' Beth exclaimed, still poking her head out the window of the limousine.

"Of course not,'' David said, portraying the very image of geniality. "Jen and I would be delighted to have your company, wouldn't we, Jen?'' He gazed expectantly at her. Beth swiveled her perfectly groomed head and gazed expectantly at Jen, too. What a pair—David and Beth had known each other only seconds, but already they were a team. It was highly irritating all around.

Jen grimaced, but she didn't see that she had much choice in the matter. She was still worried about how Beth was handling her broken engagement, and now that Beth was right here, Jen had to take advantage of the opportunity to check up on her mother. Of course at the same time she had to tolerate her mother checking up on *her.* What a mess!

"Very well, Mother. Let's all have dinner together.''

"Wonderful," Beth said in a tone of satisfaction. As if on cue, the stiff-faced chauffeur came around to swing open the door of the limousine.

"Good evening, Ms. Hillard," he said to Jen in very correct tones.

"Good evening, Vance," she answered. "How are you?"

"Quite well, Ms. Hillard."

It was a superficial exchange by any standard. Beth surrounded herself by only the most stern, off-putting of employees—people who took their jobs much too seriously in Jen's opinion. When she'd been growing up, all her nannies had been like that: very serious, very correct. It seemed that Beth refused to employ anyone with a sense of humor.

Jen climbed into the limo, followed by David. Immediately she was engulfed in the blessedly cool air of the vehicle. That was one thing about wealth—it was very helpful in matters of climate control.

A moment later the car purred away from the curb, riding as smoothly as if the shocks were cushioned in silk. That was another thing about wealth—its cushioning effect. Jen found it exasperating, but at the same time she couldn't help sinking back into the comfort of leather upholstery. Meanwhile, she and David sat opposite Beth like two subjects summoned before the Queen.

"How delightful this is," Beth said. "Now, you must allow me to be something of a bore and take you to Ramir's, my favorite restaurant. My treat, of course."

Jen winced, for Beth was referring to one of the most exclusive establishments in the entire city.

"Mother, let's do something a little more down-scale—"

"Nonsense, dear. I really am a fuddy-duddy, I'm afraid. Ramir's is the only place I can possibly eat when I'm in New York. You don't mind, do you, David?"

"No, of course not." David seemed to be enjoying himself, glancing from Beth to Jen as if speculating on the undercurrents between them. Jen was starting to feel more than annoyed. She disliked having the two halves of her existence meet up like this. They didn't fit together—not at all.

Only a short time later, however, Jen left the buffered interior of the limo for the equally buffered interior of Ramir's. The ornate surroundings—antique Georgian chairs, plasterwork ceiling, medallion paintings and all— could have been transported straight from an English manor house. Beth seemed completely at home. In fact, the Hillard dining room in Newport bore a striking resemblance to this place—English elegance carted wholesale across the Atlantic.

Jen knew she was being mean spirited, but by this point she didn't care. What was Beth up to, anyway? The woman never did anything without some ulterior motive. Jen sat across from her mother at the table and looked her over carefully. Beth's cheeks were powdered just the right amount, her lipstick perfectly applied, the scarf at her neck folded with precision. Even so, something about her seemed awry. Maybe she was simply too cheery for someone who'd broken off her engagement on the eve of the wedding.

"Now, David, I really recommend the monkfish," Beth said as David settled himself between mother and daughter. "Of course, there is always the calamari, but I've never been very adventurous. What do you think?"

"Monkfish, it is. But please tell me about Jen. She's much too secretive a person."

"She most certainly is," Beth agreed. "If her uncle Thomas hadn't found her out, none of us would know about her acting career. A shame, because we're all proud of Jen. Even Adam, of course."

"Adam," David echoed with a speculative air.

Beth leaned toward him confidentially. "Jenna's ex-husband. Surely you know about Adam..."

"Afraid not," David said, regarding Jen now. His expression seemed purposefully bland.

"Oh, dear, I've put my foot in it." Beth looked pleased. She didn't say anything more, allowing Adam's name to linger evocatively in the air. Jen refused to let her mother's manipulative tactics get the better of her. She perused her menu with great deliberation. It was David who finally broke the charged silence.

"I've never been married myself," he remarked. "Did I tell you that, Jen?"

"Yes, I believe you did."

"Thought so. Sometimes those little details between two people can be important."

Jen glanced over the top of the menu. "David, I've only known you a week."

"Sometimes a week is all it takes," he said seriously, addressing Beth. "I like Jen. I wish I could get to know her better. But she didn't even tell me that she has an ex-husband lurking in the wings."

"In the wings...my, I like that. You really are an actor. But Jenna hasn't always been so reticent," Beth went on. "It's only been this past year, since she left Adam. That's really the way it was, you know. She left *him*. It's all quite a puzzle."

"I'll say." David paused. "With Jen, it's one puzzle after another. For instance, she keeps being mysterious and telling me she's involved with someone, but I never see him around."

"Goodness," said Beth, looking concerned. "A mystery man. I hadn't counted on that."

Jen closed her menu. What she really wanted to do, however, was throttle both her dinner companions. "This conversation is mesmerizing, but I'd like to change the subject—"

"Jenna, who on earth are you involved with?" Beth persisted. "Who is this mystery man?"

"Wouldn't we all like to know," David put in.

The two of them gazed at Jen expectantly. She might have laughed, except that she didn't find this situation amusing in the least. She wasn't about to confess that her ex-husband and the so-called mystery man were one and the same. It would be mortifying, particularly as she *wasn't* involved with Adam. She'd made a mistake with him, that was all. Very well, two mistakes.

Jen picked up her menu again. "I'm ready to order," she said resolutely.

Beth stared hard at Jen, but then retreated behind her own menu. "I really do hope you're going to have the fish, Jenna."

"Nope. I'm going for the chicken terrine." Jen, however, knew it didn't matter *what* she ordered. She doubted that anything she ate would sit well with her this evening.

David and Beth behaved themselves reasonably well throughout dinner. The two of them chatted like old friends—but that was a problem right there. Beth had so easily intruded on Jen's new life, and David seemed to be having a grand time. Apparently Jen was the only one out of harmony.

At last the meal was over. Jen pushed her chair back with relief, but David and Beth prolonged matters. They pursued an involved discussion over who should pay the bill. Finally Jen snatched the bill herself, cringed when she saw the amount—and handed it to Beth.

"Mother, thank you. David, you'll just have to salvage your masculine pride some other way. And now...we're going!"

They left the restaurant, piled into the limousine and drove David to his apartment.

"Mrs. Hillard," he said solemnly, "this has been a most pleasant evening."

Jen's mother beamed. "I should hope so. You really are a very nice young man, but it appears that you have a great deal of competition where Jenna is concerned. Not only do you have the mystery person to contend with, but I warn you that Jenna's ex-husband is not completely out of the picture."

"I've always enjoyed competition—"

"Good night, David," Jen said firmly.

David seemed regretful to cut short his entertainment, but he obliged by exiting. The limo glided forward again.

Jen sank back against the leather cushions. "All right, Mother," she said, with as much self-control as possible. "I know what you're trying to do. You're trying to avoid your own problems with Phillip by poking your nose into *my* life—"

"Forget Phillip. Phillip is history. I can't believe how busy you've been, Jenna. That nice young David is besotted with you, and you've got the mystery man, as well. Tell me who he is. I simply must know."

Jen gave a strangled sort of laugh. The whole thing was hopeless. Somehow, in the space of one evening, she'd managed to acquire an incredibly complicated *and nonexistent* love life.

What next?

CHAPTER NINE

ADAM CLIMBED the steps of his brownstone, keys jiggling in his hand. It was late, and he was damn tired and not in the best of spirits. He'd been brainstorming for days—weeks—and he still hadn't come up with the solution for his newspaper. Perhaps he was burning out, too.

"Yeow."

Adam glanced down and saw a scrap of fur perched on his doorstep. A completely black scrap of fur, like a tuft of night fallen from the sky.

"What the—"

"Yeeoooow." It was a mournful, piercing sound. Adam wondered how something so small could have emitted it. He turned his key in the lock and pushed open the door. The ball of fur bounced right into his house.

Adam swung the door shut, set down his briefcase and surveyed the scraggly kitten now sitting on the hall rug. Two yellow eyes stared back at him.

"Hell," Adam muttered. "Where did you come from?"

The kitten bounded over to him and started rubbing back and forth against his shoe. The message was obvious: *Love me. Feed me.*

A stray kitten. Just what he needed. Unfortunately it was too late to go traipsing around the neighborhood asking if anyone had lost an animal. Except maybe the animal wasn't lost. Maybe someone had abandoned it.

"It takes a real jerk to dump a pet," Adam informed his unexpected guest. The kitten just stared back at him. What was he doing talking to a cat? Maybe he really was losing it.

Adam tried an experiment. He walked down the hall and into the kitchen. The cat skittered along after him. Experiment successful. Somehow Adam had known it would be.

He swung open the door of the refrigerator and found the contents not very encouraging. A couple of beers, stale bread, one wrinkled apple, a jar of mustard. He closed the refrigerator and opened a cupboard, instead. This was more promising: lots of cans. He was always buying canned goods, tossing them into his cupboard and then forgetting about them. One thing about canned food—it didn't spoil.

Baked beans, cranberries in sauce, Chinese noodles...tuna fish. Adam set down a bowl on the floor, dumped half the can of tuna into it and watched the kitten go at it. The animal acted like it hadn't eaten in days.

Adam took the other half of the tuna and made himself a sandwich with the stale bread and the mustard. He'd had better, but he didn't feel choosy tonight. He sat at the table with a beer and his sandwich, loosening his tie. All the modern conveniences surrounded him, although he rarely used them. He couldn't remember the last time he'd even shoved a frozen dinner into the microwave. It occurred to him now that Jen had always disliked this kitchen. She'd complained that it was too modernized. She didn't like the fact that the fireplace in here had been bricked off by the previous owners or that the wooden beams of the ceiling had been painted over.

She'd talked about restoring this room to its nineteenth-century origins, but somehow she'd never gotten around to it.

He wondered if he should have moved after the divorce. In this place he kept bumping up against things that reminded him of his ex-wife. The beach house was the same way, particularly after his last encounter with Jen there. Almost two weeks ago... he'd held her and made love to her. Lord, it'd felt good to have her in his arms again.

Adam stood up abruptly. The kitten had finished wolfing the tuna and sat back a little unsteadily. Maybe he'd given it too much to eat. He took another bowl from the cupboard, filled it with water and set it down on the floor. The cat refused even to look at it.

Adam crossed the hall to the living room. He turned the stereo to a classical station, opened his briefcase and took out the notes he'd jotted earlier today. He frowned at them as he sat down on the couch. Why did his ideas for the newspaper seem so uninspired? He had to come up with something good, and he had to come up with it soon. He couldn't hold off Darnard Publishing much longer. Either he had to sell or find a workable alternative. It was that simple, that difficult.

He'd almost forgotten about the cat. It had followed him and now was trying to scramble up the side of the couch. Adam studied the kitten for a minute, then scooped it into his hand. Tiny claws, impressively sharp, kneaded his skin. The animal started to purr, going at it full throttle. It was like holding an alarm clock wrapped in velvet.

Adam set the cat down at the other end of the couch and picked up his notepad again. He jotted down a few more unsatisfactory ideas. The music on the stereo changed from Mozart to Beethoven, a somber, moody piece that made it difficult to concentrate. Adam stifled a yawn. He stretched his legs out on the couch, not bothering to take off his shoes. He watched as the kitten began creeping along the cushions toward him, yellow eyes blinking. The cat had a shifty expression, as if it knew it was getting away with something. Perhaps not wanting to press its luck, it stopped and plunked itself down against Adam's side. Then it began licking its paws.

"Tomorrow I'll find out where you live," Adam said gruffly. "Or I'll find you a new place. One or the other."

He was talking to the cat again. Not a good sign. The kitten just blinked and went on licking its paws fastidiously. Adam stretched his arms and clasped his hands behind his head. The Beethoven played on stormily in the background, somehow suiting his mood. This time he yawned for real and closed his eyes. The kitten made a small warm spot against his side....

Some time later, the sound of the telephone jarred Adam awake. He opened his eyes groggily. There was no longer a warm spot against his side. Now there was a warm spot against his armpit. A warm, wet spot.

Adam looked down and saw that the kitten had crawled up to nestle between his arm and his chest and gone to sleep there. But that wasn't all it had done. The damn thing had peed on him.

The damp spot on Adam's shirt was a pretty good size. He wondered grouchily how something so small had produced it. And weren't cats supposed to be naturally trained or something?

Not this one apparently. It purred against Adam's chest as if it had found a permanent home. And meanwhile the phone was still ringing. Adam plucked up the cat with one hand and grabbed the receiver with the other.

"Hello."

"Adam, thank goodness!" The voice on the other end of the line belonged unmistakably to Beth Hillard, his former mother-in-law.

"Beth, what's up?" Something was always up when Adam got a call from Beth.

"I know it's late. I wouldn't have disturbed you, but I simply didn't know what else to do. It's about Jenna, you see." She paused dramatically.

"What's wrong? She all right?"

"Yes. Yes, of course. I didn't mean to alarm you. But I'm in New York. I came to see Jenna."

Adam dangled the kitten in front of him. "That's fine," he said. "Just fine—"

"Adam, it is *not* fine. I'm here in my hotel, and all the while I have to think about Jenna living in that...that..."

"Hovel," Adam supplied.

"Exactly." Beth sounded genuinely distressed. "She didn't want me to drop her off at her apartment, but finally she couldn't get out of it. When we drove up to that horrid building, I thought it had to be a joke. But she's really living there!"

The kitten dug its needlelike claws into Adam's hand. "Jen's doing what she wants. You can't change that." He'd change it himself in a minute if he could. He didn't like Jen living in that dump any more than her mother did.

"Adam, that's not all." Beth became oddly breathless. "If it were just this David person, I wouldn't be so concerned. But there's a mystery man, too, and who knows what Jenna is getting herself in—"

"Slow down. What are you talking about?" That was another thing about Beth. She'd jump right into the middle of a subject and expect you to be there already, waiting for her.

"I can't explain, because I don't know what's going on myself. I gather that Jenna keeps putting this David off, but who *is* this mystery man? That's the real question."

The kitten was now attempting to traverse the length of Adam's arm. It occurred to him that Beth was being deliberately scattered at the moment, as if she was trying to entice his curiosity. Well, she'd managed to get the job done. He was curious all right.

"First of all, who's David?" he asked.

"A very nice young fellow who seems enthralled with Jenna. She could do far worse for herself. But you're missing the point. I'm calling you so that you can do something about the mystery man in Jenna's life. Find out who he is, for one thing."

By now the kitten had reached Adam's shoulder and seemed to be settling down for another nap. He thought about Jen. When he'd seen her in Newport, he could've sworn he'd reached the right conclusion. He could've sworn she wasn't involved with anyone. According to Beth, however, men were suddenly coming out of the woodwork.

"Look, Jen doesn't need my interference—"

"You don't believe that any more than I do," Beth interrupted loftily. "You want to interfere, Adam. You can't stand *not* interfering."

He smiled grimly. Beth Hillard, the consummate meddler, had his number. "Right. Look what happened the last time I tried to help Jen."

"What did happen, Adam?" Beth seemed alert.

"Nothing... and it's like I told the uncles. I can't do anything about Jen."

"I never pegged you as someone who would back down at the crucial moment. I'm very surprised."

Beth made him sound like an army deserter. What a ludicrous position to be in: a stray kitten perched on his shoulder, cat pee on his shirt and an ex-mother-in-law asking him to intervene in his wife's love life. Make that ex-wife.

"I'm only asking you to come to New York and make sure she's all right," Beth went on. "I can't stay here forever. I have to get back home to the uncles."

"I'm not going to mess around in Jen's life again."

"We'll see, Adam, we'll see. Good night." She hung up with a decisive click.

Adam stared at the receiver for a few seconds before replacing it. Then he pried the black kitten off his shoulder.

"Yeeeoooow."

"My feelings exactly," Adam muttered. Tucking the kitten into the crook of his elbow, he turned to leave the room. But then his eye was caught by a photograph crammed on the back of a shelf. A framed photograph, showing him and Jen on the sailboat they'd owned when they were first married.

Adam picked up the photo and studied it. In the picture he and Jen had their arms around each other and they were laughing at something. They both looked happy. And Jen...Jenny looked beautiful, her dark hair whipping in the breeze, her face radiant.

Gradually Adam became aware of the music still playing in the background. Brahms now, but just as moody and restless as the Beethoven. The kitten curled itself against his elbow. And Adam just went on gazing at the photograph in his hand.

"Ah, Jen," he said in a low voice, shaking his head. "My Jenny..."

RUSS BILLINGTON looked different today—he had actually dragged out The Suit. In all the time Adam had known Russ, he'd seen him wear it on maybe three occasions, and one of those had been a funeral. The Suit was serious business: shiny, dark blue cloth, jacket buttons straining a little, pant cuffs on the long side as if to make up for the jacket's shortcomings. Russ stood in Adam's office, looking decidedly uncomfortable. Something definitely was up if Russ was wearing The Suit.

Adam leaned back in his chair, waiting. He figured that Russ had something to say, and sooner or later he'd get around to it. Not that Adam particularly wanted to hear it. He'd had a lousy night's sleep for one thing. At three o'clock in the morning that darn kitten had decided to throw a party. It had run up the curtains, knocked over a vase, scattered magazines, batted pencils. Adam had tried offering the animal more tuna, more water, but the only thing the cat had seemed interested in was causing a ruckus.

Something else had kept Adam awake, however. He'd kept thinking about his ex-wife and the men who suddenly seemed lined up before her. Not that it should come as that much of a surprise. Jen was sexy. Sooner or later she'd been bound to have someone in her life—

"Damn," Adam said now.

This single word seemed to inspire Russ. He took a step closer to Adam's desk—but that was as far as the inspiration went. He just stood there again, twitching his shoulders a little as if he couldn't get used to that suit jacket.

"What's on your mind, Russ?" Adam prodded.

"It's been two weeks. You told me to take two weeks off. I took them and now I'm back."

"Ready for work?"

"That's right. Ready for work."

Somehow Adam didn't think it would be that easy. "Why don't you just tell me what the problem's been, Russ? It'll be better all around if you do."

Russ took a deep breath, as if steeling himself for something. "You want to know the problem? Ask...ask Sandra what the problem is."

"What does Sandra have to do with it?"

"Nothing. Never mind. Just forget what I said." Russ's moment of purpose seemed to have deflated as soon as it began. Looking harassed, he turned and left Adam's office, banging the door in what seemed a little like a belligerent afterthought. Russ was making a habit of banging doors lately. What the heck had gotten into him?

Adam punched a button on his phone. "Sandra, would you come in here, please."

A few moments later, his managing editor knocked on his door and poked her head into Adam's office. He gestured to the chair in front of his desk.

"Have a seat."

She sat down with a cautious smile. After the dinner they'd shared a couple of weeks ago, she'd seemed a bit restrained with him. Maybe that was for the best, although Adam missed the relaxed give-and-take they'd shared at one time.

"Russ was just in here. And he seems to think there's a problem between you and him."

Sandra looked perplexed. "I don't know what you mean. I've never had any problems with Russ. Even when I started checking his work more carefully, he didn't seem to hold it against me. What's going on, Adam?"

That was the question on everyone's mind, it seemed. Adam wished he had an answer. He leaned farther back in his chair and observed Sandra. As usual, she looked as if she'd spent some time trying to tame her curly hair; today it was firmly battened down. She sat with her hands clasped in her lap, her ankles crossed neatly, as if someone had once told her this was a ladylike pose. He liked her better when she slouched a little, arms flung out boldly. Sometimes he got the feeling that Sandra Koster was really an outspoken woman by nature, but somewhere along the way she'd acquired a "nice girl" demeanor. Maybe when she was a kid her parents had told her that good girls only behaved a certain way, and she still believed it.

Now, at least, a bit of the outspoken part popped out. "I really hate it when you do this, Adam," she muttered.

"What?"

"When you just sit there and *watch* a person and nobody knows what you're thinking. It's very unnerving. Very off-putting."

"I wonder what the problem is between you and Russ."

She sat up straighter, although she still kept her hands clasped. "There is no problem! I've done everything I can to make Russ feel okay about his work going down the tubes. Dammit, a couple of times I even tried to take the blame for him."

Adam rubbed his mustache. Sandra really did have trouble managing other people. It was a shame, because she was a good newspaperwoman. If only she didn't want people to like her so much.

"Bad idea, Sandra. A big part of supervising people is making them take responsibility for themselves. Let Russ have it. Lean on him."

At last the prim demeanor vanished. Sandra's hands sprang apart and she made a gesture of disbelief. "Give me a break, Adam. Russ may be having trouble on the job, but he's not a criminal."

"I didn't mean it quite like that."

"Well, he deserves some respect."

"Fine. Forget I brought it up."

"Yes, *sir.*"

That was a good sign, Sandra being sarcastic. She got up to leave, but he stopped her.

"Hold on a second." He gazed thoughtfully out the windows of his office to the newsroom. Reporters and secretaries were hunched busily at their computers, no doubt aware the boss was watching. Unnerving one's employees was a good skill to acquire; Sandra could do with cultivating it herself.

Adam stood. "Sandra, the newspaper is yours the rest of the day. Take charge."

"But what about that meeting with the circulation auditor?"

"You'll handle it." He shrugged into his jacket, leaving his beeper on the desk. "You won't be able to reach me. Any emergencies are yours."

She stared at him as if he'd just gone crazy. "Adam—"

"Handle it. You'll do fine."

He left the office—right then, in the middle of the day. He couldn't remember the last time he'd done that. Maybe he was being a fool. Maybe not.

There was only one way to find out.

JEN SLAPPED turkey on rye before she realized she was supposed to be doing pastrami on pumpernickel. She dragged out the pumpernickel bread, dropped a slice on the floor and almost sent a bowl of coleslaw tumbling to the floor, as well. She had to stop rehearsing lines in her head as she worked. The character of Eileen was taking over her life—her thoughts, her dreams. Take last night, for instance. Even after that irritating dinner she'd shared with her mother and David, even after the fuss Beth had made about her apartment, she'd gotten ready for bed, gone to sleep and dreamed about playing the part of Eileen. That was promising. She was starting to get some real insight into Eileen's character. She suspected that Eileen possessed an inner strength that the playwright simply hadn't allowed for. Now, what was the best way to make that inner strength come out—

"Hurry it up back there," Gil called from up front. Jen cranked open a jar of hot mustard. Gil, her boss at the deli, never addressed her by name. She wondered if he even remembered her name. She'd worked here only two months, and she knew she hadn't exactly dazzled anyone with her job skills during that time. But making sandwiches all day wasn't dazzling work to begin with.

Jen's friend Suzanne came dashing behind the counter, ponytail flying as she tied on her apron. "Sorry I'm late," she mumbled. "What do you need?"

"Two Swiss and provolone. A double ham and tomato." Jen tossed a row of sesame-seed buns on the counter, then glanced at her friend. The last couple of days, Suzanne had been edgy.

"Are you okay?" Jen asked. "You seem a little flustered."

"I'm late, that's all."

"You're never late," Jen pointed out. "You're so punctual it's scary." She was trying to make a joke, but Suzanne scowled at her.

"I'm just late, okay? It's not a crime. Let it go."

Jen knew that something was the matter with Suzanne, but she couldn't pursue it right now. This was the most hectic time at the deli, the lunch rush when office workers poured out of the nearby buildings and placed their orders—leaving Jen up to her ears in salami and cheese and buns. It wasn't until well after two that Jen and Suzanne could take their own lunch. They sat in what was jokingly referred to as the employee lounge—a windowless alcove with barely enough space for the one small table crammed inside it. They were too tired to make elaborate sandwiches for themselves, contenting themselves with uninspired ham on white.

"You might as well tell me what's going on," Jen said. "I'll only pry and prod until you do. So save yourself the annoyance."

Suzanne hadn't yet touched her food; she was still busy trying to massage the post-rush kinks out of her shoulders. "I didn't mean to snap at you," she told Jen. "It's just that...I think I'm starting to get involved with someone."

"That's fantastic!"

"No. No, it's not." Suzanne propped her chin on her hands. Usually she appeared calm and in control, but now she simply looked overwhelmed. Her ponytail was a little lopsided, as if even such a no-nonsense hairstyle had proved too much for her to cope with today. "His name is Toby, and he's very attractive, and he's a law student, too. Who else would I have time to meet but another student? This week we got assigned to work on a project together, preparing a brief for a mock trial, except that we kept getting sidetracked talking about all these other things and one thing led to another and...well, last night I actually kissed him when we should have been discussing riparian water rights versus prior appropriation."

Throughout this narrative, Suzanne had looked increasingly miserable. A worrisome situation, indeed, coming from the usually unflappable Suzanne.

"Suzanne, what's the matter? Toby sounds very nice. He didn't hurt you, did he?"

"No, Jen...it's just that...it's just... Oh, Jen, Toby's married."

Jen gazed at her friend. "Married?"

"I don't want to talk about it," Suzanne said, her voice tight. "Because I know exactly what you'll say. You'll say I'm being incredibly stupid and that I should know better and all the rest of it."

"Maybe I won't say any of that," Jen replied gently. "Maybe I'll just listen."

Suzanne stared down at her plate, then nudged it aside, still without touching a bite. "No. I can't talk about it. I just...can't."

Jen hated to see her friend like this. "Suzanne—"

"No, Jen...really. Please."

Jen, despite her concern, had no choice but to let the matter rest.

A short while later they both had to get back to work. The afternoon lull was soon replaced by the predinner rush. People who didn't want to cook a meal this evening streamed into the place, looking for ready-made salads and cold cuts.

They were almost through the rush when Suzanne came hurrying back to the sandwich counter. She seemed a bit more cheerful.

"Jen, there's someone out front asking for you."

"Someone . . . someone for me?"

"Yes, Jen, and he's gorgeous. And I do mean gorgeous. Let's see . . . Chocolate brown eyes. Chocolate brown hair, too, except for some fantastic streaks of gray at the temples. Makes him look like he's known trouble and survived. I like that in a man. And what a body . . ."

Jen gazed at Suzanne in dismay. "I don't believe this. You've just described my ex-husband."

Suzanne raised her eyebrows. "Jen, if that guy really is your ex, I don't know how you ever let him go."

CHAPTER TEN

JEN WAS TEMPTED just to duck behind the counter, hiding out with the Roquefort dressing and the dill pickles. She didn't want to see Adam. What was he doing here, anyway? She'd never told him where she worked!

At last she peered around the counter, but her view of the front room was blocked by the warming ovens. She couldn't see Adam.

"It won't hurt to talk to him," Suzanne said. "He seems very charming."

Adam could definitely be charming, but Jen didn't consider that a plus at the moment. She untied her apron, tossed it onto a stool and walked to the front of the deli. Her momentary urge to hide had vanished. She'd never let Adam intimidate her yet, and she wasn't about to start now.

He was sitting at a small table by the window, eating one of the avocado-and-sprout sandwiches that Jen herself had prepared only a short while ago. Why was it that the sight of him always seemed new to her? She'd look at him, and each time she'd want to memorize all the details about him: the dominant lines of his features, the way his hair waved just so back from his stubborn forehead and, yes, the rich chocolate brown depths of his eyes. It wasn't any different today. She stood for a moment and just gazed at him, learning him by heart all over again.

He glanced at her then, and she couldn't very well stand there goggling at him any longer. She went over to his table.

"Hello, Adam," she said coolly. "Let me guess. Uncle Thomas managed to find out where I work and obligingly told you about it."

Adam gave a shrug that almost seemed good-natured. "I'm the detective this time. I went by your apartment building and spoke to your landlady. She was very helpful—for the right price."

"I'll have to talk to her about that. Maybe she can be just a little less helpful in the future."

Adam nodded sagely. "A good idea. You can't have her giving out information to just anyone for a hundred dollars."

"Adam, I really have to get back to work."

"No, you don't. Your friend Suzanne said you had a fifteen-minute break coming up."

Adam was in good form today—taking charge of everyone and everything as usual. Jen pulled out the chair across from him and sat down. "I'll give you five minutes, that's all. I thought we agreed we weren't going to see each other again."

"You came to that agreement on your own, right after we—"

"No need to get into that. What do you want, Adam?"

"The first thing I want is to finish this sandwich. It's good. Much better than the kind I make for myself."

Jen drummed her fingers on the tabletop. "So...how's my mother?"

Adam had the grace to look a little abashed. "I wouldn't know."

"I'm sure you've spoken with her in the last twenty-four hours. It's just too much of a coincidence otherwise. My mother shows up last night, butting into my life...now you're doing the same thing. Are you actually going to tell me there's no connection?"

He ate a forkful of potato salad. "I'll admit your mother woke me out of a sound sleep last night. But that's not why I'm here."

Jen glanced at her watch. "You have three minutes left—"

"Go out to dinner with me tonight, Jenny."

The way he said her name like that...it sent a warmth shimmering through her. It always had, and that was why she wished he wouldn't call her Jenny anymore.

"I can't."

"Previous commitment?" he asked in a suspiciously casual voice.

"Mother, of course, told you about what she supposes to be my love life."

He set down the avocado-and-sprout-on-cracked-wheat. "So she mentioned some guy named David. And someone else she called the mystery man. Sounds like you have a full dance card, Jen." He gazed at her intently, as if trying to divine her thoughts.

"David is just a friend," she began, and then she stopped herself. What was wrong with her? She was actually trying to explain herself to Adam. Glancing at her watch again, she pushed back her chair and stood. "Your five minutes are up," she announced. "It's too bad you wasted a trip all the way from Boston."

"Dinner—that's all, Jen. I'll wait until you're off work."

She curled her fingers around the back of the chair, remembering what had happened the last time she'd accepted a dinner invitation from him.

"I have a rehearsal right after work."

Adam nodded. "Right. Your uncle told me you'd landed a part. Of course, you could have told me yourself. You have my phone number."

"I didn't think you'd be that interested."

"I'm interested." His gaze continued to hold hers. It took her a second or two to realize she was gripping the back of the chair a bit too hard. She forced her fingers to relax one by one.

"So... I have a rehearsal."

"I'm glad you got a part. I know how much it means to you, this acting thing."

Somehow she always ended up feeling defensive with Adam. The way he called it her "acting thing," there was just something dismissive in his tone.

"No, Adam... I don't think you do know how much it means to me."

"Tell me about it, then. You're the one who's always saying we should talk more." Now he sounded reasonable.

"I used to say that when we were married," she reminded him. "Your timing's a little off. Besides, I don't think you came here because you wanted to have a friendly discussion with me."

"I came so I could invite you to dinner. That's it. You'll have to eat after your rehearsal, won't you?"

"Sorry, Adam. I just can't make it. But tell Mother I said hello." Jen turned and walked toward her workstation, making a supreme effort not to spare Adam another glance. He didn't try to call her back or follow her.

She wondered if it was really going to be this easy to get rid of him.

DAVID FIELDING crouched down low, dragging a chalk string across the wooden floor of the stage. Jen crouched down, too, anchoring the opposite end of the string.

"Mary Bess isn't going to be happy with your changing the layout of the set," she told him.

David kept moving along until he reached the proscenium arch, the wall that acted as a picture frame between the stage and the auditorium. Holding the chalk string taut, he snapped the powdered line. "I'm making things better," he said. "Mary Bess will just have to accept that. You can let go now, Jen."

She released her end of the string, allowing it to go zinging across the stage. She sat back, glancing at her watch. "The others are late. When are we going to get on with the blasted rehearsal?"

David produced a large tape measure now. He stood up as he fed out several feet of it, handing the loose end to Jen, and then he began walking backward, unwinding the tape as he went. Jen felt like an unlucky trout.

"Lay the tape along the floor there," he said. "And then tell me why you're so edgy tonight."

David Fielding was the last person she could talk to about that. She couldn't very well inform him that her ex-husband, aka the mystery man, had shown up in New York today. She couldn't very well say that she'd almost been disappointed when she'd left work and he hadn't been outside waiting for her. No. She couldn't possibly explain the mixture of anticipation and annoyance her ex-husband inspired in her.

David jiggled the tape. "Help me out here."

She laid the tape as instructed. David took a few measurements, recorded them on a slip of paper and started working the chalk string again. Jen once more knelt to anchor the opposite end.

"You still haven't told me what's bugging you," he said. "But I'll take a guess. You don't like the fact that now I know too much about you. I know that you're divorced, that your family's rich, that your mom travels around in a limo and that you don't get along with her very well. It really bothers you that I have so much information on you."

"I'm just trying to work out a few things in my life. I'm not secretive by nature."

"Then tell me about my competition. Give me a fair chance."

Somehow the chalk string Jen was holding popped free and went zinging off toward David. He didn't seem to mind. He straightened, then took a folding chair, placed it across from her and sat down.

"You really are edgy, aren't you?" he said, looking interested.

Jen sat down on the floor, wrapping her arms around her legs. "I'm tired, that's all. It was a busy day at work."

"Okay, you won't talk about yourself, so we'll talk about me," David said obligingly. "Let's see... Did I tell you that last year I almost got engaged?"

"No, you haven't mentioned that yet."

"Well, it's true. I was ready to buy the ring, but Megan decided she wanted to go to Europe, instead. Alone. Depressed the hell out of me—for a while, anyway."

David would do this now and then, throw out some detail of his life for discussion. Jen already knew that his parents had split up when he was ten, that he'd had a lot of girlfriends in junior high but none in high school, that his father had remarried twice while his mother kept waiting around for the perfect man, that he had three sisters—two he was fond of and one he wasn't—that he'd majored in theater in college but had managed a small bookstore to support himself until he'd landed a very successful national commercial in which he'd played a deadpan orchestra conductor. David's life, in fact, was like a large, exuberant painting set out for public display, more and more brush strokes filled in all the time. He was an accessible person and so were his memories. Jen felt herself relaxing for the first time since Adam had shown up at the deli.

"I'm sorry about your engagement," she said. "But you really do seem to have recovered."

"So maybe she wasn't the right woman for me—Megan, that is. But she's all in the past. After her came Gloria."

"Wait a minute," Jen said. "I thought your last girlfriend was someone named Denise."

"Right. But Gloria was post-Megan and pre-Denise."

"Did you throw Gloria over, or was it the other way around?"

"Jen, I've told you I never throw a woman over. Too risky a proposition. I just hang around until they get rid of me. I like seeing you like this, by the way."

He'd stirred her out of her momentary contentment. "How do you mean?"

"Smiling. Enjoying yourself. I've watched you this past week, and it's occurred to me that you don't enjoy yourself a lot."

Now she frowned at him. "What a strange thing to say. Of course I enjoy myself. That's the whole point of my new life."

He propped his elbows on his knees and leaned toward her. "Just the way you say that—'the whole point' of your life. It's like you're frantic, racing around even though you haven't figured out yet where you're going."

Jen had much preferred it when they'd been talking about David, not her. "You don't understand. The problem was before, when I was married and just letting my life slide along. These days I know exactly where I'm going."

"And where's that?"

David had a way of poking holes in things other people said; she'd noticed he seemed to like arguments. He made her question whether or not she really *did* have a frantic attitude. Admittedly she felt as if she had to grab her chance while she could. Now that she was over thirty, she'd learned how limited time could be. She'd learned how rapidly the years could pass, leaving her to wonder what she'd accomplished. So, yes, it made her feel a little frantic at times. That was only normal.

"I thought I'd made at least one thing pretty clear," she said. "Before it's too late, I want at least a shot at an acting career. I'm hoping this play is just the start."

"I was talking more about your personal life," David said contemplatively. "This mystery guy, for instance. What's the deal? Where are you headed with him?"

"I should have known," Jen muttered. "You're just trying to get more information out of me. It won't work, David. This is one subject I'm not going to discuss."

He didn't look deterred, but before he could open his mouth again, Mary Bess and Angela came trooping into the theater. Mary Bess climbed onto the stage and immediately let David have it about the new set markings he'd made.

"What are you thinking? We can't possibly put the living room wall over there! It'll close up the sense of space."

"That's what we want," David said. "A closed space. This is an intimate play. The sets should reflect that."

"Wonderful. Let's just pile the damn armchair on top of the damn sofa."

There was a glint in David's eye—apparently he really did welcome an argument. "As long as you get into the spirit of things. That's all I ask."

Mary Bess wasn't one to back down, either. In spite of the weary persona she liked to put on, she was as tenacious as anyone. She and David went at it for several minutes. Angela stalked off the stage in protest, had to be called back, and at last the rehearsal began. However, since David and Mary Bess couldn't reach any resolution about the set markings, Angela and Jen were constantly second-guessing where to say their lines. Then Mary Bess started in again about Jen playing her part more nastily—all in all, a most stressful night.

When it was finally over, David walked Jen out of the theater. "Invigorating session, wouldn't you say?"

"You seem to think so. I suppose your family was very noisy when you were growing up, and you miss the clamor."

"Actually my mother was a strict disciplinarian and never let us make any noise."

"I suppose you're compensating, then..." Jen's voice trailed off. They'd reached the outside of the theater and she glanced around. Then she glanced around again more carefully.

"You're looking for him, aren't you?" David asked. "The man who never shows up."

"Of course not—" Jen stopped herself. She couldn't deny that she'd been looking for Adam. Somehow she'd imagined he might be out here waiting for her. But that was ridiculous. She'd tried to get rid of him at the deli. She'd succeeded. So why this sense of letdown?

"He doesn't make you happy," David said. "That's what I was talking about earlier—how you don't seem to enjoy yourself very much. It must be because of him."

"Right—the mystery man," Jen said in a caustic tone. "Look, David—"

"If you're going to tell me your life is complicated, I've already heard that part."

"You won't let a person get away with anything, will you?" she said ruefully.

"Not when I'm interested in a person." He moved closer to her and put his arm around her shoulders. It seemed a casual gesture, and she even felt comfortable with David's arm around her. But how comfortable should she get with him, that was the question—

"Jen." It was Adam's voice. Low, deep, seeming to resonate along her nerve ends. She twisted around, at the same time slipping away from David's half embrace.

"Adam..." For a few seconds all she did was gaze at him through the glimmering darkness, while his face remained in shadow. But it wasn't really necessary to see him. She *felt* his presence all through her. He had come to find her, after all. The knowledge filled her with a mixture of anticipation and misgiving. Adam was here beside her, dominating her senses, her emotions....

When the silence threatened to grow awkward, she tried to recover herself. "David, this is...Adam Prescott. Adam, David Fielding."

The men shook hands only briefly, not saying a word, seeming to size each other up. Jen was left to fill another silence. She felt obligated to fill it, anyway. "So... Adam...I didn't expect to see you here." An outright lie.

"My dinner offer is still open."

"So is mine," David put in. Jen glared at him. He hadn't even asked her to dinner this evening. Okay, it was the only night all week that he *hadn't* asked her, but that was beside the point.

She had a choice, though. She could turn Adam down. She could also turn David down. Then she could go home, lock herself in her apartment and study her lines. She could keep company with Eileen, the spinster aunt.

"David, thanks, but Adam and I have a few things to discuss," she heard herself saying.

"Maybe tomorrow," David said.

"Sure. Tomorrow."

David and Adam nodded at each other, and then Jen found herself being propelled across the street to Adam's car. With Adam, she always felt as if she were being swept along in his wake.

As he opened the door of the sedan and she climbed inside, she glanced back to the theater and saw that David was still standing there on the sidewalk, watching. She faced forward again. Adam got in beside her, and a second later they were driving down the street, away from the theater. He didn't speak, and he didn't ask her where she'd like to go for dinner. It occurred to her that if she'd accepted David's invitation, he most likely would have deferred the choice of a restaurant to her. And by now he probably would have been making some joke about having won her favor for the evening. Then he'd no doubt talk a mile a minute about his life or probe cheerfully into hers. Funny. She could surmise all these things about

David Fielding after having known him only a short while.

"Adam," she said, "do you ever wonder what I'm thinking?"

He glanced at her, then concentrated on his driving. "That's a peculiar question."

"Not really. Take tonight, for instance. You came for me even though I told you I didn't want to see you again. Did you do it just because of what *you* wanted? Or did you speculate about what might be going through my head, too?"

He seemed to give this some consideration, not answering for a moment. "This may surprise you, Jen," he said at last, "but I've often wondered during the past year if you're happy, if you're finding what you want. As far as tonight, however, I decided I was going to see you again no matter what you thought about it."

"Hmm."

"You're looking for confirmation that I'm insensitive, arrogant... What else did you used to call me?"

"Dictatorial," she supplied. "And feudal—I think I called you that once, too."

"I remember. Does the opinion still stand?"

Now she was the one who thought things over. "Yes," she said finally. "I'm afraid it does."

When she looked at him, she believed she saw a ghost of a smile. It was difficult to tell in the dim interior of the car.

As Adam maneuvered deftly through traffic, Jen compared him to David Fielding once again. Being with David was like paddling about on a sunny lake. Being with Adam was like hurtling down a dark river, turbulence hidden underneath, the rapids threatening ahead....

"Let me guess where you're taking me," she said. "It will be a restaurant we've never been to together, but it will be very elegant. Of course, you won't even notice how impossibly elegant it is because you're so accustomed to that type of thing."

"You keep trying to pretend that your background is different from mine, Jen. There's a certain snobbery in that, even if you are living in a dive."

"Don't you have something disparaging to say about the theater?"

"Okay—that's a dive, too," he said gruffly. "But I'm still glad you got your break, Jen. And I'd like to see your play."

That was a disturbing thought—Adam watching her perform. Just the thought of his being in the audience someday... it made her feel vulnerable. She didn't really want to think about it.

Even Adam's familiarity with the ins and outs of New York City couldn't prevent them from getting caught in a midtown traffic jam, but finally they arrived at the restaurant he'd chosen. The parking valet took charge of the car, and Adam ushered her inside.

This Japanese restaurant was, indeed, elegant, the walls painted in hues of alabaster and cerulean to resemble a sky of white clouds. She and Adam sat before a low table, surrounded by bamboo screens that created the atmosphere of a *chanoma*—the traditional tea-drinking room of a Japanese home. The austere, clean lines of this place suited Adam. There was in him, after all, a certain austerity, too. Adam might move within a world of privilege and wealth, but he did so without excess. For example, the suits he wore were always the best, perfectly tailored, yet he didn't own many. He enjoyed sculpture, but he had only one or two small pieces—again, the best.

At the same time, he wasn't a particularly neat person at home or work. He tended to surround himself with a clutter of files and books, always to do with his newspaper....

"It's a long drive from Boston to New York," Jen said. "Are you going to tell me why you came all this way?"

"I already told you," he said imperturbably. "I wanted to go to dinner with you. And here we are."

"Right."

"You don't believe me, Jenny?" His voice always went a little husky when he called her that. Could he possibly know the effect it had on her? For her sake, she hoped not.

The food, when it came, was delicious—small, beautifully prepared dishes of shiitake, tempura, soba noodles, siso leaf. But Jen couldn't relax. And Adam wouldn't allow the conversation to be relaxed, either.

"From the look of things, you seem to get along pretty well with this David Fielding," he said.

"It's easy to get along with David. Not that it's really any of your—"

"But I'd like to know something about this mystery man I've heard of."

Jen stifled a curse. The mystery man was starting to have a life all his own. Everyone seemed so curious about him, even Adam.

"You should know by now to ignore anything my mother says. She always exaggerates."

Adam studied Jen across the table. His eyes seemed even darker than usual. "Something tells me that Fielding isn't the real danger. It's this other man, the one you won't talk about."

"Danger. That's an interesting way to put it."

"He's the one you care about, isn't he?" Adam persisted. "You might as well tell me, Jen. You never could keep a secret."

She made a sound that was somewhere between a groan and a laugh and that did not at all adequately express her frustration.

"Just leave it alone," she said. "I'm not going to talk about it to you, or David or—"

"So Fielding is worried about the so-called mystery man, too." Adam looked reflective. "All the more proof."

Jen wanted to yell, but somehow kept her voice at a moderate level. "Proof of what?" she asked. "And why are you suddenly so curious about my love life, Adam? Why now? Just answer me that."

"Tell me about the mystery man," he said implacably.

She set down the rice cracker she'd been trying to nibble on and stared at Adam. And then she surprised herself by giving a nod of acquiescence.

"Very well," she said. "You asked for it."

CHAPTER ELEVEN

"THE MYSTERY MAN is a very difficult person." Jen ate two rice crackers in a row while she marshaled her thoughts. "He keeps his emotions so well hidden that sometimes I wonder if he even has any. Other times...well, other times I know that of course he has emotions. He's just buried them for some reason. He's buried them very deep. He doesn't like to talk about love or how he feels. I think he's afraid to admit that he *can* love. I wish I knew why."

Adam listened intently. "This mystery man...sounds familiar."

"He should." Jen frowned a little. "He's someone I've known a very long time—forever, it seems—and yet I really don't know him at all. When does he feel hurt? When does he feel sad? When is he happy? He doesn't share those things. Most of all, he doesn't share how he feels about me."

Adam stroked his mustache. "A real forthcoming person, your mystery man," he said ironically. "Sounds like he's earned his name. But maybe you should give him a little more credit. Maybe he shows his concern, instead of talking about it all the time."

"You're taking his side," Jen murmured. Talking about the mystery man enabled her to step away a little from her own life, as if she were standing back to watch both herself and Adam. And what did she see? Two people who could never seem to come to agreement on what love meant. Two people with different needs. Jen wanted openness and unapologetic devotion; Adam wanted a partner who could give him a family without constantly probing his emotions. Yes. They were two very different people.

"You know," she said wistfully, "I do believe he's concerned about me, this mystery man. I believe he cares about me in a certain way. But it's just not enough. I want more than his concern. I want... passion. Not just the physical kind, though. I'm talking about emotional passion. But I still don't know if he has that to give me— or any woman. Maybe it's just not in his nature."

Adam appeared to study her very carefully. Did he understand what she was trying to say? With Adam, it was impossible to know. True to form, he kept his deepest reactions from her.

"So what are you going to do, Jen?" he asked. "Will you try to turn this man into your ideal?"

"I don't think you can ever change another person," she said sadly. "It's hopeless to try. If someone can't give you what you need... you just have to leave, no matter how hard it is."

Adam went on gazing at her for a long moment, but he didn't ask any more questions. They finished their meal and left the restaurant. Adam drove Jen to her apartment building, and they made most of the trip in silence.

When they arrived on her street, Jen glanced at him. "I still don't know why you came all the way to New York, but thanks for dinner, anyway, Adam. Goodbye."

"I'm walking you up to your apartment."

"No. Not this time."

"Jen, this is a lousy neighborhood. I'm going to walk you to your door and make sure you get in okay. That's all."

If she remembered correctly, these were almost the exact words he'd used that first time—the night he'd come to tell her about her mother's wedding. The next morning she'd woken up with Adam in her bed—all because she'd allowed him to walk her to her door.

"Forget it," she said. "Good night, Adam. Goodbye."

She hurried into her building and up the first flight of narrow stairs. The elevator was out again, but she didn't trust it much even on its good days. The building had at least one pretense of respectability: plastic lighting fixtures had been installed over the bare bulbs on each landing. Unfortunately the fixtures tended to accumulate dead bugs, which gave the lighting an ethereal, wavering quality.

She hadn't even made it to the first landing when Adam reached her side.

"Dammit—" she began.

"Don't waste your breath. You'll need it for the climb."

They reached the second landing . . . the third . . .

"Jen, would it be so bad if you took some money from your trust fund for a decent place to live? Would that really destroy your independence?"

"This is good exercise."

Fourth story . . . fifth . . . sixth . . .

"Everyone is born with certain advantages and disadvantages," Adam argued. "It makes sense to use what you're given."

"It makes sense to find out what you can do on your own."

Seventh . . . eighth . . . ninth . . .

They were both breathing heavily by the time they reached the tenth floor. Jen was pleased to see that she seemed to be in just as good shape as Adam. She worked the locks on her door. Before she opened it, however, she turned around to face him.

"Okay, you walked me here. I'm safe. You can leave."

"Jen . . ." He took her in his arms, pressing her against the door. They were both still panting a bit, but that didn't stop Adam from kissing her. It didn't stop her from kissing him back. She dropped her carryall and raised her hands to his shoulders. Oh, how she craved the touch and taste of him! Even when he was holding her like this, his lips demanding against her own, his body crowding hers into the rough wood of the door . . . even like this, she could never get enough of what she craved. She could kiss him a hundred times, make love to him a hundred times, and still she would need more.

With a moan born of both desire and despair, Jen dragged her mouth away from his and pressed her face against his chest. "No, Adam," she whispered. "No."

"Lord, Jenny. You know we both feel it. This is why I came to New York. This is why I came for you."

She lifted her head and stared at him. "You came so that you could take me to bed. It's that simple, isn't it?"

His features were taut, his eyes so dark they looked black. "There's never been anything simple about you and me. Not when we were married . . . not now."

"You haven't changed, Adam. You never will. And I'll never change, either. I'll always need something you can't give me." With the only shred of willpower she had left, she turned and slipped inside her apartment. Then she closed the door and shot all the bolts home. Afterward she leaned her forehead against the doorjamb, her eyes tightly closed. She knew that Adam still waited on the other side. She ached to take what he *could* give her, even if it wasn't enough. But she didn't unbolt the door. She didn't open it again. And at last she heard the sound of his footsteps receding down the hall . . . away from her.

THE DRIVE from New York to Boston was a long one, and it was very late when Adam walked into the hallway of his brownstone. He glanced around, assessing the damage. The laundry basket had toppled, spewing socks and shirts, another vase was knocked over, a lamp shade was askew, and several paperback books had tumbled from a shelf to the floor. Adam rummaged through the laundry, picking up a T-shirt covered in cat hair.

The kitten bounded out from the bedroom to greet him, coming to rub its head against his shoe.

"Don't start feeling too much at home," Adam warned. "This is just temporary." He took a tour of the rest of the house, ascertaining that the animal had eaten some of the dry cat food he'd left out, and fortunately seemed to know the purpose of a litter box. Before leaving for New York, Adam had paid a quick visit to a pet-supply store.

Now Adam opened the door into the back garden. The kitten went prancing outside on some feline exploration, but came in a few minutes later. Adam examined the cans of cat food he'd purchased, wondering why they all had names that sounded like extravagant six-course meals: Fisherman's Catch Supreme, Chicken-and-Liver Medley, Beef Morsel Delight. He went with the Medley, dumping half the can into a bowl on the floor. The cat sniffed the stuff and then sat back disdainfully. Adam tried the Beef Morsel Delight next, but that received an even more imperious turndown.

Adam considered the matter for a time, then rummaged through the cupboard and found another can of tuna. He dumped half of that into a bowl. The cat started wolfing it down. Too late Adam noticed that the bowl he'd used belonged to a set that Beth Hillard had given him and Jen as an anniversary gift some years ago. Beth probably wouldn't be too happy to know that a cat was enjoying the very fine china. Jen would undoubtedly be amused. She hadn't taken any of the dishes with her when she'd left. She hadn't taken any traces of their married life.

Adam watched until the cat finished eating. Then he went back across the hall to the living room, turned on the classical station, took off his shoes and stretched out on the couch. The kitten followed him, clambering up the side of the couch and then clambering onto Adam until it found a comfortable spot on his chest. Rachmaninoff played from the stereo, a stormy, romantic piece. Contrary to what his ex-wife might think, Adam recognized romantic when he heard it.

The kitten gazed at him, blinking now and then. Adam gazed back discontentedly. "My mission in New York was by no means successful," he informed the animal. "Then again..."

Here he was, talking to the cat—not that he was getting much of a response. The kitten just settled down on his chest, purring contentedly, curling itself into a ball.

Adam closed his eyes, but it didn't do any good. He could still see Jenny in his mind, the way she'd looked and felt tonight: her gray eyes luminous, her dark hair like satin against his hands, her skin creamy but flushing to rose when he touched her.

But she'd turned away from him. She'd proved to him that he was a fool, after all.

Not that it was any news to him. Hell, why couldn't he just open up to Jen?

DAVID WINGED a large straw hat toward Jen as if it were a Frisbee. "Try that," he said. "Looks like something Eileen would wear."

Jen put the hat on her head, then picked up a 1950s-style hand mirror to study the effect. "No way," she said. "Eileen would see this hat as dowdy. And that's the last thing Eileen wants to be—dowdy. She's very concerned about presenting a youthful image."

"Youthful...youthful..." David muttered like a chant as he disappeared down one of the crowded aisles of this hodgepodge of a shop. Everything was for sale here: vintage clothing, secondhand furniture, antique snuff-boxes, yellowed sheet music, model ships, a collection of Depression glass.

Jen fingered a string of beads. It was her day off from work, and David had suggested this shopping expedition in order to outfit Jen's character, Eileen. David believed it was essential to know what kind of shoes and jewelry and clothes your character wore—even what kind of socks.

At first Jen had enjoyed the idea of bringing Eileen to life with such details. She'd gladly accompanied David here to SoHo, where they'd explored one store after another. This was one of Jen's favorite neighborhoods. She loved the old cast-iron buildings with their generous, airy spaces and grand windows, their elaborate facades of dormers and arches and columns. Normally, she'd be delighted to spend a morning here, but today... today a pervasive melancholy seemed to take her over, a sadness that encroached like an advancing ocean tide. She'd been trying to hold it at bay, yet still it washed through her.

David reappeared with a striped miniskirt. "Youthful," he pronounced.

Jen shook her head. "Eileen is smart. She knows she would look ridiculous if she tried to dress *too* young. She's after something more subtle."

"Subtlety...subtlety..." David muttered now. But this time he grabbed Jen's hand and took her along with him as he went off on another exploration. It felt oddly comforting to hold hands with David, but her instincts told her not to prolong the moment. She slipped her fingers away from his as they came to a rack of summery dresses.

"Here you go," David said, rifling through them. "Pick one of these."

"Don't maul them—they're fragile." Jen lifted one from the rack and surveyed it: a 1930s-style dress that was both filmy and slinky, skirt swirling from the knee downward. It was a floral print that had faded over time, adding to the nostalgia. "Yes," Jen murmured. "Eileen would wear something exactly like this. Sensual but just a little innocent, too. It reflects the way she's starting to feel about Mark. Attracted to him, scared of her attraction, but then not able to think about anything but him."

"Lucky Mark." David seemed about to take Jen's hand again, but she stepped past him. Still carrying the dress, she went to sit on a high-backed sofa with frayed cushions. She glanced at the price tag on the sofa.

"Reasonable. Not that Eileen would ever own a piece of furniture like this. She prides herself on having more sophisticated taste."

David came to sprawl beside her. "I've created a monster," he complained. "All you've talked about today is Eileen."

"I thought that was the whole idea. We're here to get more familiar with Eileen's and Mark's personalities. But you haven't found anything for Mark yet."

"Mark is more Upper East Side. He wants to wear expensive clothes—he only wishes someone else would pay for them. But I didn't bring you here just so you could wallow in Eileen. I thought it was a clever way to make you spend more time with me." David gave Jen an engaging smile. "I figured I had to consolidate my gains after last night. I still can't believe you finally agreed to have dinner with me."

Yes, she'd had dinner with David last night. It had been a pleasant evening, just as this morning had been pleasant and enjoyable. So why had this dreariness assaulted her?

"I wonder which one you're thinking about," David said speculatively. "The ex-husband or the mystery man?"

"Don't start that again."

"Neither one of them has shown lately. But I'm always around. Doesn't that tell you something?"

Jen smoothed out the dress she held. It had been several days since Adam had arrived in town so unexpectedly. Six long days to be exact. She knew she'd done the right thing in turning him away, but she ached inside every night when she tried to fall asleep.

"I think you and I should take things slowly, David."

"That's a hint to back off if I've ever heard one. But taking things slow is always a mistake."

"It's the other way around," she objected. "From the sound of it, you always rush into relationships too quickly. I mean, there was Gloria and Denise and— Who's the other one?"

"Megan. She's the one who left me for Europe."

"Anyway, if you hadn't rushed it, maybe you would have figured out Megan wasn't right for you and you'd have saved yourself a lot of trouble."

David stretched out his legs as casually as if he was sitting in his own living room. "If we did it your way, Jen, people would be so sensible they'd never fall in love. They'd save themselves a lot of pain, but a lot of happiness, too."

"That's not such a bad idea," she muttered. "Not bad at all."

"Are you really such a cynic? Which one made you that way—the ex-husband or the mystery man?"

She suspected David would be happy to have a prolonged discussion about it—he seemed to relish prolonged discussions—but she stood up.

"Let's go buy some more clothes for Eileen," she said.

He rose to his feet, too, gazing at her musingly. "I wonder what it would take to get him out of your head," he murmured, "whichever one it is..." Then, before Jen could protest, David leaned over and kissed her. Right there in the store, he brushed his lips against hers. It was a very pleasant kiss. It didn't overpower or overwhelm. It just felt good—and that was precisely why Jen stepped back so quickly.

David's smile was rueful. "Obviously it'll take more than that to make you forget him."

"David—"

"I wish I could make you forget." For a moment he looked almost somber. Regret stirred in her. Under other circumstances, she might very well have given in to David. But as it was...

As it was, she still had that ache deep inside her. An ache that had nothing whatsoever to do with David Fielding.

THIS COMEDIAN was just plain bad. He was doing a routine about all the ways he'd tried to take control of his son's birth, but it wasn't working. Only a light spattering of laughter sounded through the audience now and then. Adam felt sorry for the guy. Why didn't he move on to a new routine? You had to be pretty bad if you didn't know when to let a joke die and go on to the next one.

At last the comic wrapped things up, accepted an unenthusiastic round of applause and left the stage. Everyone at Adam's table seemed to have a comment. He'd come to this comedy club with his friend Chris Lyons, Chris's date Gabrielle, and Gabrielle's friend Autumn. Technically speaking, Autumn was Adam's date. Lord. He was on a date with a woman—a girl—named Autumn. She couldn't be any older than twenty-two. But she was the first one to speak.

"I really hate it when men do jokes about childbirth," she said. "It just seems so...inappropriate. It always makes me think of high school boys snickering in the locker room."

Adam wondered if Autumn realized that boys in high school locker rooms snickered about anything *but* childbirth. Then Chris spoke up.

"Men make jokes about it because they don't know what else to do. When my daughter was born, joking was the only thing that kept me sane. My ex-wife handled it a lot better than I did." Chris periodically trotted out stories about his former wife and his daughter, neglecting to mention that his ex-wife wouldn't speak to him and he saw his daughter only on major holidays. Chris liked to believe that the family-man image helped to impress new women. Chris went out with new women all the time, but he was pathologically insecure about the venture. At forty-one, he still looked for any edge.

Gabrielle put in her two cents' worth. "I think it's healthy for men to talk about childbirth. Even if they make jokes, at least they're *acknowledging* what women go through. And they're trying to be a part of it." Gabrielle was strikingly pretty, her red hair falling in two perfect arcs on either side of her face. She glanced around the table as if seeking support for her statement.

Autumn, however, looked displeased that her friend had disagreed with her. Chris looked as if he was trying to figure out the best way to get Gabrielle into bed. Then all three of them stared at Adam as if waiting for his pronouncement on the subject of men and bad jokes and childbirth. What was this—a round robin, everybody taking turns with the opinions? But it was the type of thing that happened when you were out with people who didn't know each other very well. Adam and Chris had been friends since college, but Chris had only dated Gabrielle a few times, and Adam hadn't even laid eyes on Autumn before tonight. Why had he let Chris talk him into this?

Everybody was still staring at him, but he didn't have anything profound to say. All he could think about was what he'd do if Jen was pregnant and about to have a child. His child. He'd be scared as hell. Jen would probably be scared as hell, too. And maybe, somehow, they'd get through it together.

Except that Jen had categorically refused to have a child with him. It had gotten to the point where she wouldn't even discuss the subject.

"I think," Adam said, "we should all have another drink."

Autumn gazed at him in disappointment. She seemed determined to prove that she was an intellectual, making sure everyone knew that she was a graduate student in eighteenth-century French political history. She even had the face of an intellectual—pale and serious. But her hair just didn't go with the image. It was fluffy, all blond wisps and swirls. Why, Adam wondered irritably, would a woman work so damn hard to be taken seriously and then give herself fluffy hair?

He knew it wasn't a question he was going to spend too much time pondering. He drank a light beer, sat through another mediocre comedian and then suggested the four of them move on.

Nobody objected, but there was some difference of opinion about what to do next. Chris wanted to try a jazz club, Gabrielle wanted to go dancing, and Autumn voted for a stroll. Adam seconded the idea of a stroll, mainly because he'd been in enough clubs since his divorce to last him a lifetime.

A short while later they were straggling down a neighborhood street, surrounded by magnolia trees and Victorian houses with fanciful turrets and towers, built a hundred years ago by Bostonians on the way up. The two women walked together, while Adam and Chris fell into step behind them.

"Lighten up," Chris told Adam. "What's with you tonight? We're supposed to be having a good time. Don't you like Autumn? Best season of the year, some people say."

Adam suspected that Autumn wouldn't appreciate Chris's humor. Chris could wear thin on you after a while. He was basically well-meaning, but he had a tendency to overdo things. Heir to a banking fortune, he was always in demand for dinner parties and club openings. He rarely turned down an invitation. And somehow he was always getting himself into trouble with women— dating two at a time, or going out with an eighteen-year-old he could've sworn was twenty-five. Society columnists were always happy to follow Chris around, snapping photos of him in the midst of his escapades.

Because of his friendship with Chris, Adam had ended up in a few of the society columns himself. He'd been lonely after his divorce, and so he'd allowed Chris to drag him to dinner parties and such. Chris invariably knew a woman who had a best friend who needed a date—but that was wearing thin, too. Very thin.

"What's the problem?" Chris persisted. "You can't lose spirit. You just have to keep jumping in there." Where women were concerned, Chris subscribed to something he called the cork theory. It was like diving into a swimming pool. Maybe you went under a few times, but you just had to trust that eventually you'd pop back up—like a cork. Chris was an optimist. He was terrified of jumping into that pool, but he kept doing it, anyway.

Gabrielle and Autumn apparently decided it was time to mingle with the males, and Autumn treated the group to a rather involved description of French architectural influences on Boston. Adam felt like he was out with a tour guide. But he only half listened; he was still thinking about the cork theory.

He knew he just couldn't do it anymore. He couldn't keep jumping in looking for a new woman. Tonight had proved that much to him at least.

But where the hell did he go from here?

CHAPTER TWELVE

THE ENVELOPE ARRIVED just as rehearsal finished. A messenger appeared at the door of the Jacob Hollings Playhouse, insisting that he deliver it to Jen and no one else. She took it and before she could even ask a question, the messenger had vanished out the door.

Intrigued, Jen gazed down at the envelope. It bore no handwriting, no clue to its sender, and was made of heavy, creamy vellum. She broke open the seal and found no letter inside. There was only a single theater ticket.

David glanced over Jen's shoulder. "Impressive," he commented. "I wouldn't mind a seat to that show—except that I'd have to stop eating for a week to afford it."

"You're exaggerating." Jen turned the ticket over in her fingers. It was not, however, just any ticket. This one promised admittance to *Quivira,* a very popular musical on Broadway.

"Any idea who sent it?" David asked.

Jen didn't answer. David, impossibly nosy, took the ticket from her and examined it.

"Pretty convenient, I'd say. It's for tomorrow night. We don't have a rehearsal then. It's almost like someone knew."

Jen still didn't speak, lost in her own thoughts. That ticket, arriving in a plain, tasteful envelope, had aroused an unsettling mixture of doubt and suspense in her.

David, meanwhile, went on without any encouragement, "Very interesting. You know, this ticket is almost like...a lure. Someone's just cast a line, and I'm fairly certain you're the fish."

"Don't be ridiculous," Jen said, snatching the ticket back from him. "You have an overactive imagination."

"I don't think so. I suspect I'm right on." David looked her over soberly. "The only question is...will you take the bait?"

THE FOLLOWING EVENING, Jen sat in her apartment, holding the theater ticket and debating whether or not to tear it into pieces. If she was smart, that was exactly what she'd do. She'd tear it into pieces, and then she'd spend a quiet evening at home studying her lines.

But that ticket was so...mysterious. And maybe that was appropriate for a mystery man.

Both doubt and longing surged through her. Surely it had been Adam who'd sent the ticket. But what game was he playing? If she went to the theater, well, it would be as if he'd snapped his fingers and she'd obeyed. Could she allow that?

Jen tossed the ticket down on the coffee table. She took her script, turned to Act Three and began reading.

After a few minutes, she closed her eyes and recited several lines to herself. Then she opened her eyes—and saw that ticket on the coffee table.

Jen stood up restlessly and glanced around her apartment. It might be a decrepit place, but she'd done her best to give it a more homey feel. She'd bought some art posters at a street stall and framed them herself—no matter that the posters had a tendency to slip from their makeshift backings and end up lopsided. She'd also purchased some pressed-wood bookshelves for a very reasonable price and had painted them an attractive shade of oyster white. Not to mention the wrought-iron plant stand she'd happened upon at a flea market, finding that the rust came off quite nicely. . . .

That ticket lay on the coffee table, taunting her. Jen stood still for a moment, debating all the pros and cons of going to the theater. Then she turned and went into her small bedroom, rummaging through her closet. She wasn't sure if the pros had won or the cons. All she knew was that she'd just given in to her longings. She wanted to see Adam again. She had to see him.

The contents of her closet were sparse, but she pulled out the dress she'd intended to wear to her mother's wedding: a coral silk sheath, dramatic in its very simplicity. It would have to do, because she didn't own anything more elegant.

Impatience took over now, a sense of expectancy she couldn't quell. In such a short while, she'd see him again. She would be with him. Adam . . .

Jen stepped into the shower and forced herself to stand under the water for quite some time, in spite of the way the pipes rattled. She hoped that maybe the water would douse a little sense into her. That was all she needed, a little common sense.

Apparently she didn't possess even that. No longer able to tolerate any delay, Jen got out of the shower and quickly dried her hair. Then she swept it up with the pair of turquoise-and-silver combs she'd purchased at another street stall. Finally she slid into the coral sheath. She was on her way out the bedroom door when she hesitated, returned to the bureau and picked up her one small bottle of perfume. She dabbed some on, then wondered if it was too much. The way her pulses had quickened, the perfume would be radiating from her. But it was too late to worry about that. She hurried out to the other room, grabbed the ticket and went down to hail a cab.

A short while later, she arrived at the theater district near Times Square. All the old excitement kicked in for her when she saw the marquees blazing with lights, the dusky sky a backdrop. She still remembered the first time her parents had brought her here on a visit. She'd been eleven, and for some reason the dazzling lights had made her think of carousels—as if she'd been spinning with the magic of it all.

Of course, during the past months Jen had not attended a single Broadway show. On her meager salary, she simply couldn't afford such an indulgence.

The cab deposited Jen in front of the Barrett Theater. She entered the crowded lobby and found herself surrounded by a striking art-deco motif. Egyptian-style friezes wound their way all along the top of the marbled walls, while high above shone a crystal chandelier cut in geometric shapes. It was a streamlined sort of luxury, and the contrast to the scruffy Jacob Hollings Playhouse could not have been starker. Jen stood still for a moment, feeling oddly disloyal to the Hollings Playhouse by coming to this place. And why *had* she come? She began to regret the impulse that had carried her here, and she turned to go.

Then she saw him.

Not Adam...but David. David Fielding, looking handsome in jacket and tie, standing across the lobby a little separate from the other patrons. *David* had sent the ticket?

Jen's first reaction was a piercing disappointment. She'd wanted so much for it to be Adam....

Her second reaction was an attempt to cover up her disappointment. David walked toward her, and when he reached her she managed a smile.

"Very clever," she said lightly. "You really are a good actor. I never would've suspected."

He didn't return her smile. He looked rather grave, in fact. "I was hoping you'd at least wonder. But the whole time you thought it was from him, didn't you?"

"Isn't that what you intended?"

He shook his head. "No. I wanted you to speculate at least a few times about whether or not it was me."

She touched his arm. "David, no matter what, it's a very nice surprise. A romantic thing to do." And that was the irony. She'd been hoping for a romantic gesture from Adam, not David. She'd wanted to ignore the fact that her ex-husband was notoriously *un*romantic.

David still seemed chagrined. "Sometimes you set out to do something and it sounds great in the planning stages. Then when you actually do it...it just doesn't come across the way you'd intended."

Now she smiled for real. "Are you trying to make me feel sorry for you?"

"A little." He began to look more cheerful. "Is it working?"

"Not in the least. But I can't believe I get to see this musical. I took the bait, as you call it, and now I'm going to enjoy myself thoroughly." She tried to convince herself she was speaking the truth, even though the disappointment had settled inside her. The disappointment of knowing that Adam wasn't here, that he couldn't give her what she needed.

David's gaze, meanwhile, traveled over her appreciatively. "You look especially beautiful tonight, Jen."

She ought to be gratified by his attentions. Another man was courting her and being wonderfully romantic and all the rest of it. Why couldn't she concentrate on that, instead of her ex-husband?

She took David's arm as they went through the crowd and into the auditorium. "Thank you, David, for...well, just thank you."

He'd arranged for excellent seats, close enough to the stage for a perfect view, but not too close that the orchestra would be a distraction. As Jen settled into her plush seat, she thought once again of the Jacob Hollings Playhouse with its rows of tatty old velvet chairs.

But then the auditorium lights went down, the curtain went up, the orchestra began to play—and Jen tried to forget everything but the pageantry before her. *Quivira* was the boisterous, appealing tale of a band of Spanish explorers off in search of a mythical city of gold in sixteenth-century Texas. The music was catchy, the acting and singing superb, the story by turns outrageous and touching.

Even as she became caught up in the play, however, she couldn't seem to stop thinking about Adam. She realized how few times she'd attended the theater with him when they were married. He'd spent so many late nights at the newspaper, for one thing. But it had been more than that—a sense that the theater was *her* activity, not Adam's. In what little spare time he had, he enjoyed physical activities such as hiking, riding, tennis. He wasn't one to sit around and watch others perform. And so Jen had gone to plays with friends or by herself.

When the curtains came down at intermission, David glanced at Jen. "Enjoying yourself?"

"Oh, of course. This is fantastic, David. I can't thank you enough—"

"You sound like you're reading a speech," he said. "You know, whenever I'm with you, I feel like there's three of us. You, me...and the guy who makes you unhappy."

"He's not here with us right now," Jen said firmly. "We can have a perfectly good time without him. We *are* having a good time."

"You say that often enough, maybe you'll convince one of us."

Jen gazed at him in exasperation. "Are you always so observant?"

"Generally. But you're easy to read, Jen. Your face is very lovely and very expressive." With that, David escorted her out to the lobby for a glass of wine.

As Jen sipped her wine, she made an effort to concentrate on David. He really did look attractive tonight. Jen suspected he'd taken special care with his attire—she'd never seen him in a jacket before. His sandy hair curled at his collar, and his hazel eyes reminded her of the color of leaves just starting to turn in the fall. And he was so attentive, standing here with her, embellishing his latest argument with Mary Bess in an effort to make Jen laugh. David gave the impression that there was nowhere else he would rather be right now than here in this theater with her. Adam had never made her feel like this, as if she possessed all his attention, all his focus. She'd always pictured his mind as being compartmentalized: one small room in it for her and a quite large room for the newspaper. There was only one activity during which Jen had ever felt she had Adam's complete participation: lovemaking.

She felt the color staining her cheeks, and she couldn't look at David. Even when she was listing Adam's faults, she got herself into trouble.

It was a relief to go back into the auditorium. She and David took their seats, and the orchestra started up again.

Sometime during the performance, David reached over in the most natural way possible and took hold of her hand. For once she didn't pull away. She allowed her fingers to remain clasped in his for several moments. It was a pleasant sensation, holding hands with David in the darkened theater. It was also a comforting sensation. As soon as Jen realized just how comforting it was, she slipped her fingers away from his. She didn't want to be unfair to David; she didn't want to use him for some type of consolation.

After that, she actually managed to lose herself in the musical, and she regretted the moment when the curtain fell for the last time. It occurred to her that going to the theater had been another type of comfort and consolation for her. Was it any coincidence that during the worst times in her marriage she'd attended as many plays and movies as she could?

Now she and David took a cab to her apartment building. The elevator was still out, so they had to climb the nine flights of stairs. And Jen remembered that night a week ago, when she had climbed these same stairs with Adam. They'd been breathless by the time they'd reached her apartment.

And now here she was with another man, reaching her doorway breathless again. Once again she unbolted the locks. And once again a man took her in his arms. David, not Adam. David this time.

She allowed him to hold her, pressing her cheek against his shoulder. And this time her breathing quieted down, became steady and even. Not like the other night . . .

"Jen, can I come in?"

"David . . . it's been a very nice evening, but—"

"Don't say it," he murmured. "It's bad enough that you used the *N* word. When a woman tells you that she had a nice time, you know you blew it."

Jen couldn't help smiling. "I'm afraid you have a streak of melodrama in you. What on earth is wrong with having a nice time?"

"It's like saying you had vanilla pudding for dessert, instead of cherries jubilee. It's like saying you took a nap, instead of going skydiving. It's like saying—"

"Okay, I get the message. But I *did* have a nice time. A great time, even. Does that satisfy you?"

His arms tightened around her. "I'm not feeling exactly satisfied right now, Jen. You see...I think I'm falling in love with you."

This, at last, made her draw back. She studied him in dismay. "David...no. Don't say that. You're always falling in love too quickly. With Gloria and Denise and—"

"This feels different," he said somberly. "The others...sometimes I get the feeling they were just rehearsals and this is the real thing. The big show. Would it be so terrible if I loved you, Jen?"

"Oh, David. Of course it wouldn't be terrible. But I don't know if *I* can love anyone right now."

"Except him." David stated the words flatly, and Adam almost seemed to materialize between them, shadowy but intrusive, like the negative of a photograph.

She closed her eyes. "I don't know if I still love him. I don't want to love him. I shouldn't love him, I know that much for sure..."

She felt the touch of David's lips on hers. "If you'd give me a chance, I'd make you forget him. I'd damn well try, anyway."

She opened her eyes again and gazed at him sadly. "Not tonight, David," she murmured. "Not tonight."

He kissed her again, more thoroughly this time. And it was a good kiss, a nice kiss. Then Jen went into her apartment, shot the bolts home and once again heard a man's footsteps retreating down the hall.

SUZANNE SEEMED oddly keyed up. She sat across from Jen in the employee lounge, creasing a paper napkin over and over in her hands. Her expression, normally so calm and straightforward, was one of suppressed excitement. And, instead of her usual ponytail, she wore her hair loose, allowing it to fall past her shoulders. She'd curled it, and it looked very pretty. Until now, Suzanne had never bothered to style her hair. She'd once told Jen that she'd rather get in an extra ten minutes of studying than fuss with a blow-dryer and curlers. Obviously something had changed her mind.

"Want to talk about it?" Jen asked in a deceptively casual voice.

Now a wariness seemed to take Suzanne over, as if somehow she had to protect herself. "Everything's going fine for me. Really, it is."

"That's great."

Suzanne put another crease in her paper napkin. "That problem I told you about before, well, it's not really such a problem, after all."

"You mean the problem with ... Toby."

Suzanne nodded. "*That* problem. But you see, well, Toby and I ... things have advanced a little. We're more serious now about each other. Quite serious, to be honest. And we've been discussing a lot of things. He's told me how unhappy he is in his marriage and how he plans to ask his wife for a divorce." Suzanne seemed anxious to explain. "The point is that Toby wants to do the right thing. He doesn't want to hurt his wife, but he also knows that things can't go on like this. He knows that a marriage is no good when both people are just pulling farther and farther apart from each other. In the long run, there's a lot less unhappiness involved when you just call it quits. Well, *you* understand."

Suzanne paused. Apparently she wanted confirmation from Jen that divorce made everyone involved healthy and happy. Yet it was so much more complicated than that.

"Sometimes divorce is the only answer," Jen said unconvincingly. She was concerned about her friend, and she had her own questions. Was this Toby sincere? Did he genuinely care for Suzanne? Unfortunately there was no way of knowing.

"Well, anyway," Suzanne said at last, "both Toby and I want to do the right thing. We've talked about how much better it will be after his divorce. Once that's finalized, we can move in together until we've each finished law school. And then we'll think about getting married ourselves. We're not going to rush *that,* of course. Now Toby realizes how important it is to be sure before you marry someone. I want to be sure, too." A glimpse of uncertainty showed in Suzanne's face—just a glimpse, and then it was gone. "I'm already sure that I love him, Jen. That I do know."

Suzanne crumpled her napkin into a ball. "Well, time to get back to work." She sounded embarrassed, as if she regretted revealing so much.

"Look," Jen said, "whenever you need to talk, I'm here. That's all. I'm here."

"Everything really is going fine. I wish you'd believe me." Suzanne took her hair net from her pocket and grimaced at it. "If I don't wear this, the boss'll have a fit. But do you think it will flatten me down too much?"

Jen gazed at her friend. With her hair falling in those soft curls past her shoulders, she suddenly looked much too vulnerable. Jen found herself longing for the old Suzanne—the forthright, studious, ponytailed Suzanne.

"After work, I'll show you a way to brush out your hair that will help," Jen said. "You'll get most of the curl right back."

"Thanks, Jen. I mean it—thanks." With that, Suzanne hurried back to work.

Jen remained seated a moment longer, staring at the crumpled napkin on the table. She knew she certainly wasn't the best person to give advice to someone else, not when it came to matters of the heart.

Ever since taking her to the theater that night, David Fielding had been intent on courting her. He'd been doing a very good job of it, in fact. Although he'd lived in Manhattan most of his life, he liked to pretend that he was a visitor seeing everything for the first time. So far he'd enticed Jen to take the Staten Island Ferry, spend hours in the Metropolitan Museum of Art, spend yet more hours exploring Little Italy and Chinatown and Central Park. But no matter what they were doing together, David always made Jen feel as if it was something fun and special because she was with him. He behaved as if he couldn't imagine being with anyone else, anywhere else. Jen knew how important the Jacob Hollings Playhouse was to David, but he had made his priorities clear: romance first, work second.

Of course, David complained that he hadn't gotten very far in the romance department with Jen. A few brief kisses were all they'd shared, and David made it clear he wanted more.

An attractive, considerate, passionate man was interested in Jen. A man, no less, who talked about everything—his emotions, his life, Jen's emotions, Jen's life. How David enjoyed talking! He'd already told Jen a number of times that he was falling in love with her. But how did *she* feel? Why couldn't she figure out the answer to that question?

Jen swept up Suzanne's crumpled napkin and tossed it into the trash. Here, finally, was her chance to have the type of relationship she needed. A man like David, a man who made you feel special, a man who bathed you in the light of his emotions, didn't come along very often. Any woman who let David get away had to be an idiot. So what was stopping Jen from taking the next step?

It couldn't be Adam. She wouldn't *let* it be Adam, a man who would scarcely admit to having emotions, let alone talk about them. She hadn't heard a word from him since he'd taken her to dinner that evening and expected her to go to bed with him. He hadn't gotten what he'd wanted—so, naturally, he'd disappeared from her life. It figured. Damn him for giving so little to her.

She reached up and repinned her own hair net. The thing always made her feel like someone out of a 1940s movie. But it was also a symbol of her new life, her ability to support herself, to depend on no one else. Certainly not on Adam...

There she went again, thinking about him. That was a mistake. She needed to think about David, instead. Adam was in her past. But maybe, just maybe, David could be in her future. If only she knew—

"Break time's over," Gil hollered from the front of the deli. Sighing, Jen went to mix the three-bean salad.

CHAPTER THIRTEEN

JEN/EILEEN STOOD in front of the chalked square marked MANTELPIECE. "'You're angry,'" she said. "'Haven't you realized yet? It's no use, being angry at Lisa.'"

David/Mark came to stand at the other end of the chalked square. "'Admit it, Eileen. There's one thing you and I have in common. We're both fed up with Lisa.'"

"'Is it all we have in common, Mark?'"

"Wrong," Mary Bess interrupted in a beleaguered tone. "You're supposed to be seductive, Hillard. Not wistful. Never wistful. I thought we agreed—Eileen is trifling with Mark."

"She'd only like to believe she's trifling with him. She won't admit that underneath she's really beginning to care for him."

"Hillard, do you realize how few weeks are left before we actually have to perform this play? And you're doing nothing to convince me that your interpretation of Eileen is the correct one. Nothing."

Jen felt her shirt sticking to her back with perspiration. The air in the theater had become even more stifling than ever now that summer was peaking. And she knew that Mary Bess was right about one thing. Her portrayal of Eileen hadn't been at all convincing. What was wrong with her? She *knew* Eileen should be an intense, passionate woman who attempted to manipulate Mark's and Lisa's emotions out of loneliness while still harboring a genuine need to give and receive love. But whenever Jen spoke her lines, she couldn't seem to bring those complex qualities to life. Instead, she made Eileen sound drab and insipid. No wonder Mary Bess kept turning up the pressure to make Eileen into a bitter, malicious person, anything with a little bite to it.

David had been watching Jen with almost a sympathetic air, and now he seemed to change the subject on purpose.

"The real problem is the set. As a prop, the mantelpiece is going to be too static. We need something more organic."

Predictably this got Mary Bess going. "Great. Wonderful. You want organic? Why not just put legs on the damn mantelpiece and have it run around the stage. Is that organic enough for you?"

David and Mary Bess continued arguing until, equally predictably, Angela/Lisa reacted by stalking off the stage. She had to be placated, as usual, and the rehearsal went downhill from there.

At last it was over. David and Jen were left alone. Jen slung her carryall over her shoulder.

"That was a disaster," she muttered. "David, you shouldn't try to rush to the rescue every time Mary Bess and I have a disagreement. I can handle her on my own."

"It's better if she grouses at me, not you. That leaves you free to handle Angela."

Angela, it seemed, had developed a strong dislike to the character of Eileen in the play, feeling that it took away too much from the part of Lisa—the acknowledged starring role. Consequently Angela also harbored a strong dislike for Jen.

Now Jen blotted the perspiration from her forehead. "I don't know how we're ever going to pull this play off. We're only three actors and one director, but the politics involved are incredible."

"It's a good sign, things going so badly."

She wasn't really in the mood to joke about it. "Let me guess," she said sourly. "Theater superstition has it that crummy rehearsals make for a glorious opening night."

"No. But the way I look at it, things can't get much worse than this. And if things can't get worse, they have to get better."

She smiled. David had a habit of doing that—making her smile at his perverse reasoning. Now he came around behind her, slid her carryall away and proceeded to massage her tense shoulders. Along with all his other positive qualities, David knew how to give an excellent shoulder massage.

"Where shall we eat tonight?" he asked. "I'm in the mood for Greek."

"Hmph. I'm in the mood for pizza."

"So we'll flip a coin again," he said. "Two out of three. You want heads or tails?"

"Last night we had to flip at least twelve times before you agreed that I'd won. Maybe tonight we'll just do your choice."

"You give in too easily, Hillard. Put up a little fight." He turned her around until she was facing him. "Jen . . . on second thought, let's not go out tonight. Come to my place and I'll fix you something to eat."

"You cook, too?" she asked.

"No, but I'm good at throwing noodles into boiling water. A jar of spaghetti sauce, and we're in business."

Jen had never been to David's apartment before. "It's not such a good idea," she said. "Eating in and all."

"Jen . . . what are you afraid of?"

"I don't know."

He drew her close and kissed her. Usually she pulled away after a few seconds. This time she allowed the kiss to continue for quite some time. She tried to lose herself in it. David was a very good kisser, very adept. So why *couldn't* she lose herself in the moment? She was like a swimmer merely testing the water . . .

"Jen, come home with me," he murmured. "It's time, isn't it?"

She pulled away as she pondered that question. She knew one thing for certain. It was up to her whether or not she was going to get on with her life. She'd spent so many years loving a man who couldn't give her what she needed, a man who'd kept his heart closed to her. Now another man had come into her life, someone who was opening his heart to let her in. Maybe it was time to move on.

Jen hesitated another long moment, and then nodded slowly. "Yes, David," she said. "Yes. I'll go home with you."

A SHORT WHILE LATER, Jen sat stiffly in an armchair in David's loft. She felt uncomfortable, ill at ease . . . no, more than that. She felt ridiculous. Whatever resolve had brought her here was fast dissipating. It didn't help that the place was all one large room, no dividers between the living space, the eating space . . . the sleeping space. She stared over at the bed. It was covered by a quilt in cheerful shades of apricot and marigold yellow. And apparently David was one of the few men in the world who actually made his own bed every day. The sheets and pillows were neatly arranged.

Jen wrenched her gaze away, focusing, instead, on other details: the old-fashioned trunk that served as a coffee table, the glass-fronted bookshelves, the rolltop desk with its myriad cubbyholes. Obviously she and David shared the same enthusiasm for antique stores and secondhand shops.

"Nice place," she said at last, trying to sound nonchalant. David was rattling around in the kitchen area, doing something with pots and pans. But then he stopped. He came to sit on the trunk across from her, reaching over to take her hands in his.

"Can't you relax with me?" he asked.

"Not at the moment."

"Okay, so I'm a trifle... unrelaxed, too." His hands tightened on hers. "And I lied, Jen," he said seriously. "I don't have any spaghetti sauce. Never did."

He'd done it again—made her smile. The tension broke a little. "I get it. You lured me here with the promise of spaghetti, and now you're not going to deliver."

David rose to his feet, then drew her up beside him. He kissed her again, more deeply this time. "Mind if I feed you later?" he murmured. "I promise I'll figure out something."

Jen allowed him to go on kissing her. She kept her eyes firmly closed; she had to concentrate on the moment, on what was happening right here. David took a step backward, then another, drawing her with him. Without having to look, she knew he was leading her toward the bed. A bed she would share with a man who wasn't Adam—

"No," she said, pulling away from David. Damn Adam Prescott. Even now he couldn't leave her alone.

"Jen—" David began, a look of concern on his face.

"No, David. Just... no."

WHY WAS THE WORLD suddenly composed of couples?

Adam sat in his favorite bookstore, the one that had decided almost as an afterthought to be a coffeehouse, too. The espresso bar had been crowded into a small corner among the racks of books. Close by Adam's table was a chalkboard on an easel, announcing a poetry reading at nine and a special on mocha almond delight. Adam, however, was drinking his cappuccino heavy on the cream and cinnamon. And, meanwhile, he was watching couples.

A young man and woman browsed together among the biographies, touching now and then. Another couple, a bit older, was engaged in a subdued quarrel in the garden-book section. Adam couldn't hear what they were saying, but he could see the stony expressions on their faces. Yet another couple headed along the nature-book section. The man pushed a baby stroller and the woman carried a diaper bag. They didn't touch. They didn't argue. They just looked tired—shell-shocked, actually— and the baby in the stroller was screaming.

Adam put his cup down. He didn't know what he was doing here. It was only four in the afternoon, and by rights he should still be at the newspaper. But lately his restlessness had grown....

A woman with her hair tied back by a bright scarf perused the travel section. Somehow she reminded him of Jen. Maybe it was because Jen had often swept back her hair like that when she went sailing with Adam. Of course, that had been a long time ago, when they were first married.

Sitting here now, Adam suddenly missed their sailing excursions. He missed the snap of canvas in the wind and the pulse of waves against the hull. He missed feeling the wood of the helm underneath his hands...and having

Jenny nudge him aside good-naturedly so she could take her turn guiding the boat. Jenny, laughing just because she was happy, the breeze tangling her hair even though she'd tied it back, the sun turning her skin a honeyed brown.

She'd loved sailing. If it had been up to her, they would have been out there every weekend. During the first year of their marriage, he'd managed at least two weekends out of every four. And after that, well... When had it stopped seeming so important to please his wife?

Adam made an effort to people-watch again. He saw at least three women searching through the self-help section, a man flipping through the cookbooks, another man picking up a newspaper on the way to the cash register.

So far Adam hadn't been paying a lot of attention to the people buying newspapers. Now he did. The newspaper dump across from him had two bins. The top one held Adam's paper, the *Boston Standard,* and below it were copies of another paper, something with a catchy color graphic on the front page. From here Adam couldn't read the masthead, couldn't tell if it was a local or out-of-state.

He got another cappuccino and kept his eye on the newspapers. Eventually a woman came by, leaned down and extracted a paper from the bottom stack. Not the *Standard.*

It was a minor incident, but it bothered Adam. He kept watching. In the next half hour, three more people had chosen newspapers. Not one had gone for the *Standard.* How many other times had that happened today?

Adam settled back in his chair unhappily. He felt as if his newspaper was being slighted somehow, bypassed, like a country road abandoned when the new freeway comes through. But why should he let that happen? Why didn't he get on the damn freeway himself?

That was it. Of course. Suddenly it seemed so simple and clear. At last he had an idea for his newspaper. Maybe even the right idea.

Adam pushed his cup aside. He took a small pad out of his jacket pocket, flipped to a fresh page and began jotting notes. He lost track of time, letting the cappuccino grow cold. It didn't matter. The idea was taking shape under his pen, looking better all the time. Maybe, at last, he was really on to something.

THE PRESSES THROBBED and rumbled, and Adam leaned on the railing, watching pages of newsprint stream by in a blur. Martin, the pressroom superintendent, nodded at Adam as he went past. Martin had a guarded look. Obviously he knew about the commotion Adam had been causing upstairs the past few days, but was reserving judgment.

Adam got the impression that several of his employees were reserving judgment. That was exactly what he wanted. A healthy dose of skepticism was necessary for planning the major change he had in mind. He needed his staff to throw out all manner of objections to his new idea, bringing up all the problems they foresaw. Recognizing those problems was the first step to solving them.

Three days ago, Adam had informed the investment banking firm of Fowler, Meredith and Company that he would definitely not be selling the *Boston Standard* to Darnard Publishing. And then he'd started the rounds of meetings: brainstorming sessions with the members of his sales and marketing departments, his director of production, his business manager, his managing editor. By now the conference room of the paper had seen a marathon of overtime, with more doughnuts and cups of coffee than anyone cared to count. Adam had his staff discussing strategies from every possible angle. The change he planned for the *Boston Standard* was going to be a monumental job and a monumental risk. But if they did it right, maybe it would also be one hell of a success.

During the past few days he'd felt an unfamiliar exhilaration. He believed he understood why. For years he'd tried to preserve the newspaper as handed down to him by his father, his grandfather, his great-grandfather. There'd been merit in that, and he didn't regret it. But now he was finally allowing himself a new vision of what the paper could be. He was combining family heritage with his own view of the future. It felt good—damn good.

Adam turned and climbed down the metal stairs to ground level. All the rigging that surrounded the presses made him think of an oil derrick. When he'd been a kid, clambering around here had been one of his favorite activities. He'd come to the newspaper building every chance he got. He'd never had any question about what he was going to do with his life.

Yes, even as a boy, he'd preferred to spend more time here than at home. It hadn't been just because of his fascination with the newspaper business, though. A lot of times he'd simply needed to get away from his house, away from all the turmoil there. The accusations, the tears, the reconciliations, eventually the accusations again. His mother and father, absorbed in hating and loving each other, too often as if the rest of the world didn't exist. It had gone on like that until the year Adam turned seventeen. That year, everything had changed....

Why was he thinking about it? Certain memories were useless. You could go back over them in your mind, again and again, allowing anger and guilt to seep from the past into the present. It was a waste. Hadn't he learned that much by now?

Adam walked down the length of the room by the thrumming presses, trying to recapture his earlier exhilaration. But somehow it eluded him.

He'd allowed too many memories.

"YOU NEED FLOWERS."

Adam stopped, balancing a bicycle on either side of him, and glanced at the person who'd just spoken—a scrawny man of fifty or so, surrounded by tubs of violets, roses, tulips, daisies. The flowers gave this grimy New York City street corner a welcome splash of color.

Adam inspected the wire basket fastened to the front of one of his bicycles. He could picture the basket overflowing with violets and roses. The man was right. He did need flowers.

A few moments later, Adam had bought all the roses the vendor had to offer, and most of the violets, too. He took several bills out of his wallet and handed them over.

"I don't have change for this much," the man said.

"Keep it." Adam wheeled his bicycles on down the street. He should have thought of flowers on his own, and it bugged him that he hadn't. He wanted this to go just right.

He was pretty sure he'd thought of everything else. The bicycles were brand-new, top of the line, and he'd even had a bike rack mounted on his car for them. So far his only problem had been finding a parking place close to Jen's apartment. He'd ended up a few blocks away, but he didn't mind. For some reason he liked wheeling the bikes along.

At last he reached Jen's building and hauled the bikes into the lobby, only to see the Out of Order sign on the elevator. He surveyed the first flight of steps. There was no choice in the matter, so now he lifted each bicycle by the frame. The one with the wire basket wobbled for a second or two, and the flowers almost came tumbling out. He steadied it and then began climbing.

On the second-story landing, he got stuck negotiating a tight corner, bicycle tires bumping against the walls. He backed down a few steps, almost lost the flowers again, then finally lugged his two bikes upward. By the fourth floor, he was sweating. By the sixth floor, he was really sweating. These were supposed to be the lightest bikes on the market. They didn't feel light—not anymore.

On the eighth-floor landing he ran into a lady carrying two large tote bags. Bicycles versus tote bags—not promising. Adam pressed against the wall to let her pass. She seemed to get caught in his spokes for a minute there, but at last she made it, giving him a quizzical expression as she squeezed around him.

By the time Adam had reached the tenth floor, he was not only sweating from the exertion but from the lack of air-conditioning in this dive. He supposed it was a good thing he'd worn shorts and a polo shirt. Actually it had been a long time since he'd worn shorts, and he'd almost forgotten he owned any. Shorts were for days off work, and Adam didn't take too many of those. He was glad he'd taken this one. A broken elevator was just a minor inconvenience.

He guided both bikes down the hallway until he reached Jen's apartment. Leaning one bicycle against the wall, he knocked.

There was no answer for several moments. Could he have missed her somehow? He knocked again.

At last her voice came from the other side of the door. "Who is it?"

"Special delivery," he said gruffly, stepping beyond the view of the peephole.

After a pause, he heard her begin to undo the bolts. He got ready, one bike on either side again, and as soon as the door swung open he barreled on through.

"Adam! What on earth . . . ?"

Mission accomplished. He was in Jen's living room, bicycles and all. She stood before him, looking none too pleased about it. Another minor problem—he just had to convince her that, deep down, she was glad to see him.

"Adam, what are you doing here? What's this all about?" She surveyed the bikes with a distrustful expression. Adam surveyed *her*.

She looked beautiful, even in jeans and an oversize T-shirt. He allowed his gaze to linger on her. He thought about kissing her and a whole lot more, and for a minute he debated just dropping the bicycles and taking her into his arms. But then he reminded himself that today he wanted to do things differently from the last time he'd seen her.

"We're going for a bike ride. Central Park," he announced. He propped each bicycle up by its kickstand and indicated the one with the wire basket full of flowers. "This one's yours."

"Oh, Adam . . ." She had a strange expression on her face now, almost a stricken look. "You can't just come charging in like this and expect me to . . . You just can't."

Okay, he was willing to admit that maybe his approach was a little heavy-handed. "Jenny . . . I'm just asking you to come with me. A bike ride, nothing more. We'll spend the afternoon together. What do you say?"

"I can't," she said, her voice suddenly no more than a whisper.

"Why not?" He moved closer to her, which wasn't all that easy considering how much space the bicycles were taking up.

She still looked oddly upset. Then a rustling sound came from the kitchen, and someone stepped out of it. A man, casually munching from a bag of tortilla chips. Adam recognized the guy right off. David Fielding. Jen's acting friend.

Except that maybe he and Jen were a whole lot more than friends.

CHAPTER FOURTEEN

ADAM'S FIRST IMPULSE was to pound David Fielding's face. He didn't think that would go over too well, though. He waited for a second impulse. None came to him. All he could do was stand there, wondering if Jen— his Jenny—was sleeping with another man.

It wasn't any consolation to realize that Jen didn't seem to know what to say, either. She gazed at the bicycle nearest her, reaching out to rescue a pink rose that was about to tumble from the wire basket. David Fielding stepped over and clasped her hand as if to prevent her from touching any more of the flowers. He stared at Adam with an expression that could only be described as combative. Adam had taken a dislike to Fielding the first time he'd met him. Now he'd *really* taken a dislike to him.

At last Adam spoke. "You're right, Jen. I can't just come charging in like this. I made a mistake."

"Oh, Adam..." With her free hand, she gestured at the bicycles. "This is just a little overwhelming."

He had to get out of here before the situation degenerated any further. "Look, I'll have someone pick up the bikes later when your elevator's working."

Jen was back to looking stricken. "You carried them all the way up here?"

He hadn't meant to invoke her sympathy. Sympathy wasn't what he needed right now. What he needed was ... just to get the hell out of here.

"Like I say, I'll have them picked up later." He left her apartment, closing the door after him. He went down the hall and down the stairs—without his bikes.

Without Jenny.

DAVID BALANCED a ball of putty on his nose, then slowly began shaping it. Jen sat across from him, watching in a sort of unwilling fascination. David was making himself up for a benefit performance tonight. This was his third try at creating a new nose. Apparently he was a perfectionist when it came to such matters.

Half the lights on the dressing-room mirror were broken. The other half gave off an apathetic glow. Everything in the Jacob Hollings Playhouse needed refurbishing, dressing rooms included. But David didn't seem to mind. He just kept working the putty, giving his nose a bit of a hump this time.

Jen examined the trays of supplies in front of her: spirit gum, wax, cotton, greasepaint, shading brushes, color palettes, latex, gauze, sponges, scissors, castor oil.

"Quite a collection you have here," she observed.

"When no one wants me to be an actor anymore, I'll become a makeup artist." David finally seemed satisfied with the shape of his nose and proceeded to stipple it for texture.

"I've noticed that acting doesn't seem to ... well, torment you," Jen said reflectively. "You just don't seem to take it that seriously, and I think that's why you enjoy it so much."

"You don't sound like you're paying me a compliment," David remarked. "You sound like you're complaining."

"No, that's not it at all. I admire you for it. With me, I seem to take everything way too seriously. Acting in particular." She sighed. "The harder and harder I try to grasp Eileen's character, the more it escapes me. I'm really starting to worry about it."

David had started in on the greasepaint, but he turned to look at Jen. The humped nose made him appear rather sagacious. "You're definitely not relaxing with the part," he said. "Maybe I'm imagining things, but you've been worse since the bicycle thing."

Jen wished he wouldn't keep referring to it that way— as the "bicycle thing." She wished he wouldn't refer to it at all, but he seemed to have a need to keep bringing it up.

"David, that was almost a week ago. I've tried to put it behind me. You should do the same."

"If you've put it behind you, then why are those bikes still cluttering up your living room?"

"I'm sure Adam will send someone to pick them up soon."

"You seem to like having them around," David persisted. He made the bicycles sound as if they were orphaned children she'd decided to adopt.

"The truth is, I'm hardly ever in my apartment," she said lightly. "If we're not rehearsing, you're always taking me off somewhere. Take tonight, for instance. This benefit where you'll be performing."

David picked up his greasepaint stick and tapped it against his palm. "Sounds like you're complaining again. Ever since the bicycle thing, you haven't seemed quite as happy with me."

"David, will you stop with the bicycle thing?"

"Jen . . . I love you."

He'd never said it quite that way before. It had always been "Jen, I think I'm falling in love with you." But this time there were no qualifiers. It had been a simple, clear-cut "I love you." He sat there with his putty nose, waiting for her to respond, and she couldn't.

"I wish I knew what it would take to get him out of your head," David said at last. "And I wish I knew what it would take to get those damn bikes out of your living room."

Jen felt an ache inside, an ache that was becoming more and more familiar. "Maybe we just need to give it some time," she said quietly.

He frowned. "Are you going to tell me that we're still rushing it? You won't even make love with me—"

"Please, David. Don't start again."

He seemed about to say something more, but then went back to creating his new face. Deftly he shaded lines onto his forehead and cheeks with a brush, then used another brush along his jaw. By now she was aware of all of David's good qualities. He was openhearted and considerate and fun to be with. So why couldn't she take the next step? Why *couldn't* she make love to a man who so obviously cared for her?

Jen picked up one of the fake mustaches from the makeup table and smoothed it in her hand. It was almost the same color as Adam's. If she was completely honest, she'd have to admit that those two bicycles in her living room plagued her with other unanswered questions. Why had Adam shown up so unexpectedly? What had he intended? Had he simply been trying a new method to get her into bed? The take-her-for-a-bike-ride-in-the-park-and-then-seduce-her method? Except, it didn't seem like Adam's style. He wasn't one to use subterfuge. And those flowers . . . those flowers had seemed genuinely romantic. Violets and roses. Somehow she hadn't been able to take them out of the wire basket. They were wilting there, dropping petals all over her floor.

And that brought her to another question. Why hadn't Adam sent someone to pick up the bicycles as he'd promised? It almost seemed as if he was leaving them with her as some sort of reminder. A reminder of what, however . . .

Jen quickly put down the fake mustache. Perhaps none of those questions merited an answer. Whatever Adam had intended that day, it was just too late to find out. Because she'd gone on with her life. She was starting to get involved now with another man. A man who loved her. Only one thing was lacking. Jen had to decide that she loved David back. When she did, well, everything would be settled.

David had finished his makeup job, and it was a bit startling. There were subtle grooves on his cheeks and across his forehead, and even more subtle shadowings along his jaw. It was the sort of face that would do very well for the part of the Edwardian gentleman that David would be playing tonight.

"Just think. You stick with me, Jen, and you could come home to someone different every night."

"No, thank you. I'll stick with the original."

"Do you mean that?" He was suddenly very serious.

"David, let's just take it one step at a time."

"You know you're in trouble when a woman tells you to take it one step at a time," he said in a lugubrious tone.

"I'm not going to feel sorry for you."

"Oh, well," David said, sounding a little more cheerful, "if you're not going to fall at my feet and swear eternal devotion, we might as well get out of here."

A short while later they caught the subway uptown. David enjoyed sitting in the train in his high starched collar, homburg hat and theatrical makeup, already in character as an Edwardian gentleman. But if he expected to draw stares or comments, Jen knew he was bound to be disappointed. The jaded New York commuters took him completely in stride.

He and Jen arrived at the Monarch, a gracious old hotel of umber-colored brick with an ornate facade of Gothic arches. The place was equally gracious and ornate on the inside. Soon Jen was part of the audience in the large hotel banquet room, watching the opening act on stage. David belonged to a troupe of actors who periodically put on plays to benefit different charities. Tonight's performance was part of a fund-raiser for a medical research foundation. And it was a delightful performance—a farcical murder mystery/romance. David portrayed a very proper gentleman caught up in solving the crime.

He was a good actor, there was no denying. He seemed immersed in the role without letting it burden him, conveying the sense that he was quietly poking fun at the character he played. Such an attitude was perfect for tonight's comedy. Jen watched him with a mixture of envy and admiration.

She was a fortunate person, she told herself, to have a man like David in her life. Yes. Very fortunate indeed.

She just had to keep telling herself that.

SURPRISINGLY IT WASN'T always easy to find Boston brown bread in Boston. Sandra, however, seemed to know just the food stall in Quincy Market that would carry it. She led Adam through the crowded aisles until she found it.

"Want some?" she asked.

"Sure."

Sandra had insisted that this particular meal was her treat. Over the past several days, she and Adam had been working such long hours at the newspaper that they'd fallen into the habit of eating together, and Sandra had finally objected to Adam always picking up the tab. Well, it was fine with him if she wanted to pay now and then. Their long hours weren't going to end anytime soon, and they had to have periodic nourishment.

They continued browsing through the stalls, building their meal as they went: bowls of steaming chowder, a plate of oysters, watercress salad. When they couldn't carry anything else between them, they made their way along the brick-paved mall and sat down to eat on a shaded bench.

The marketplace was one of Adam's favorite places in the city. He liked the lively chaos here—the jugglers and magicians, the throngs of people browsing through the shops, the canopied pushcarts offering yet more wares for sale. Except that one of the pushcarts was overflowing with flowers. Daffodils and lilies, tulips and hyacinths...violets and roses. Adam stared sourly at the blooms. He wasn't overly fond of flowers at the moment.

Jen and another man. Why couldn't he get used to the idea? And why couldn't he stop thinking about it? His Jenny—

"Did Bob ever get those demographics to you?" Sandra asked. It took him a minute to focus on her question.

"He handed them over this morning," Adam said. "The figures look promising."

"Everything looks promising," Sandra said confidently. "This is going to work. I know it is."

Sandra, more than anyone at the newspaper, had jumped on the bandwagon of Adam's new idea. She seemed to share his vision as no one else yet had. He was grateful. He needed to work with someone who understood where he was headed. Not to mention the fact that Sandra's enthusiasm served as a tonic to him.

The need to share his ideas, his vision... When he'd lugged those two bicycles all the way up to Jen's apartment that day, he'd had in mind—among other things—to tell her about his plans for the newspaper. He'd wanted to tell her that he intended to transform the *Standard* into a national weekly with a circulation clear across the country. The way Adam saw it, up until now the paper had been attempting to deliver the world to New England. He intended to turn that around and deliver a little bit of New England to the world. And that was what he envisioned: a strong national paper with a Boston flavor. This town represented so much of America's past—a rowdy fight for independence, a proud and colorful heritage. Hell, millions of tourists came here from everywhere all the time. Adam wanted them to be able to open up their newspapers and savor a taste of Boston while they were still sitting at home.

Anyway, he'd wanted to tell Jenny all that. Not that it made any sense. Talking to Jen about the newspaper had always been difficult. During their marriage, she'd increasingly seen the *Standard* as a threat, as something that came between the two of them. So why had she been the first person he'd thought of when he came up with his new plan? Why had he wanted to tell her about it?

But of course he hadn't ended up telling her. He'd barged in on her, seen her with that David Fielding and—

"I'm meeting with the graphic designers this afternoon," Sandra said. "We're going to discuss possible layouts for the new magazine section. If you have any last-minute suggestions, let me know."

"Right," Adam said. "Right." He glanced at Sandra. She seemed more spirited lately, as if all the extra work actually agreed with her. And she was even becoming more assertive. The other day Adam had overheard her arguing with the promotion director about his presentation on direct-mail campaigns. That was a good sign.

"What's all this doing to your home life?" Adam asked now. "You probably never get to see your son anymore."

"Didn't I tell you?" she said, her voice suddenly brittle. "Brian is spending a month on Cape Cod with his father. And the Twit of course." Sandra still referred to her ex-husband's girlfriend as "the Twit."

"Sorry to hear it," Adam said.

"Yeah, well . . . when I talk to Brian on the phone, he always has such wonderful news to share with me. It seems that the Twit makes superb chocolate-chip cookies, and she lets him eat half the dough. It turns out that she's also fantastic at street hockey, and she doesn't mind reading comic books with my son. Brian is always careful to point out that I never make chocolate-chip cookies and that I don't like comic books." Sandra put down her brown bread. She didn't look quite so vibrant anymore, and Adam was sorry he'd brought up the subject.

"Adam . . . you know something?" she said after a second or two. "I think I really have got over the part about my ex-husband and the Twit. I mean, just because she's young and firm and all the rest of it . . . Anyway, as far as I'm concerned, she can have Don. She's welcome to him. But when it comes to my son...that's the part I'm really having trouble with. She's so damn *popular* with Brian. And that somehow makes me into an unpopular old hag."

"You're not an old hag," Adam said. "Even if your son makes you feel like one."

"Gee, that's the nicest thing anyone's ever told me," she muttered caustically. A few weeks ago, she might have apologized profusely for making such a comment. Now she just stared morosely into her bowl of clam chowder.

"I don't know much about children," Adam said. "But I have a feeling that the Twit—your ex-husband's girlfriend, that is—is simply a novelty. Pretty soon your son will be tired of her, and he'll be asking you for chocolate-chip cookies."

"You know, I could always buy that ready-made dough in the grocery store."

"Sure. That's the best kind to eat raw."

Sandra actually smiled. "Thanks, Adam. For cheering me up, that is. I really appreciate it. You can't imagine..."

Sandra hadn't changed all that much; she could still be profuse.

"Hey," he said. "I have to keep you cheerful. Work hours are just going to get worse and worse."

"I don't mind, especially with Brian away." Sandra looked wistful, but then she glanced at her watch and became businesslike once more. "We have to get back. I have that meeting at two, and then you and I need to talk about that story on reform initiatives. I'm still not satisfied with the slant..."

They tossed the remains of their lunch into the trash and discussed the newspaper all the way back to work. Somehow they were still managing to get the *Standard* to press every day while planning for the future—a brand-new future. It ought to be enough for Adam, knowing that his newspaper had a chance.

So why wasn't it enough?

JEN ARRIVED at work a few days later to find an honor bestowed on her: for the first time ever, she would be allowed to mix the recipe for Gil's famous egg cream. Suzanne was assigned to teach Jen the perfect proportions of milk, soda water and Gil's secret syrup. No one knew exactly what was in the syrup. Gil trusted his employees only so far.

Suzanne measured out the ingredients. Her face looked drawn today, her movements too meticulous, too precise, as if she feared that any moment something inside her might shatter.

"Always pour the soda water just so," she said, a forced briskness in her voice. She finished mixing the rest of the ingredients and then gave Jen a sample of the drink to try. It was smooth and creamy, with just the right amount of sweetness and a pleasant tang added by the soda water.

"Delicious," Jen said.

"You know Gil." Suzanne's tone was mocking now. "He says that tasting egg cream is like tasting wine. You have to train your palate so that you can judge true quality."

Jen glanced at her friend. Suzanne's face still had that pinched look, as if she was trying very hard to contain all her difficult emotions.

"How's it going?" Jen asked gently. "We've hardly had a chance to talk lately." Jen knew why that was. Suzanne had purposely avoided talking. She concentrated on her work and never seemed able to take her break with Jen anymore.

"Everything's fine," Suzanne said crisply. "Just fine."

"School going okay?"

"Of course school is going okay. And for your information, Jen, everything's fine with Toby, too. That's what you want to know about, isn't it? Whether or not I'm still seeing Toby. Well, I am seeing him. And everything's fine."

"Suzanne—"

"No, he hasn't asked his wife for a divorce yet. I can understand why he's delaying—I don't blame him. I'm sure it's very difficult to turn to the person you've been married to for five years and tell her that it's over. I'm sure it's very difficult indeed." Without warning, Suzanne seemed to run out of steam. For once she didn't bustle about, trying to avoid Jen. She just stood there, both hands flat on the counter, staring down.

"Suzanne, maybe it's okay to have doubts," Jen said softly. "That happens in any relationship. Wondering if you're doing the right thing, if you're headed in the right direction."

"Why don't you just be honest," Suzanne said, her voice tight. "You think that in my particular situation, I *should* have doubts. That's what you really want to say, isn't it?"

This wasn't going at all well. "I'm not trying to accuse you," Jen said, her voice still gentle. "I'm just saying everyone has doubts."

"You've already judged Toby, haven't you? You don't even know the guy, but you've made up your mind about him. If only you understood how much agony this whole thing is causing him. The last thing he wants to do is hurt his wife or hurt me."

Suzanne looked so unhappy. Jen hated to see her friend like this. If only there was something she could do to help.

"I wish you'd believe me," Jen said at last. "I'm not judging you or Toby or anyone else."

Suzanne was staring downward. Then her face seemed to crumple a little. "Jen... I did something foolish yesterday," she said quietly. "I just couldn't stop myself. I had to see her. I had to see Toby's wife. I had to know what she looked like at least. And so I waited across the street from Toby's apartment. I just stood there and waited."

Jen didn't say anything now. She knew this was another time when all she could do was listen. And at last Suzanne went on, her voice very subdued.

"I was sure I'd be able to recognize her. Toby told me once that she had long red hair, that she was vain about it and didn't like to have it cut. So I kept picturing this beautiful woman, with her red hair... and then she came out of the building. Except that she wasn't really beautiful. She was just... average looking. Ordinary. She walked off down the street..." Suzanne turned to look at Jen. Her face was bleak.

"I try to remember all the things Toby's told me—how he and his wife don't get along anymore, how they have so many problems, how a divorce will be the best thing for both of them. But I just keep seeing her in my mind—Toby's wife with her ordinary looks and her long red hair. And I can't hate her anymore. I try and try, but I can't hate her. What can I do, Jen? Now that I've seen her, what can I do?"

Jen wished she had an answer. But she had no answers for the confusion in her own heart. How could she possibly help her friend?

It seemed that all she and Suzanne had anymore were questions. No answers at all. Just painful questions.

CHAPTER FIFTEEN

ADAM AIMED a feathery yellow dart across his office and almost hit the board. Almost, but not quite. Instead, the dart chipped the plaster wall and fell to the carpet next to several other feathery yellow darts—proof of Adam's less than successful attempts.

"I win," Sandra announced even before she'd tossed her own last red dart. Her throw flew right to the center of the target. Not a bull's-eye, but near enough that it didn't matter. She was good at this. Damn good.

It had been Sandra's idea to nail a dart board up in Adam's office. She'd claimed that an occasional game would help keep their minds alert during their late-night brainstorming sessions. She'd just neglected to mention that she was a hustler at darts. So far Adam hadn't stood a chance.

It was another late night, and Adam had lost another game by a mile. He shook his head and sat down heavily in his chair.

"I've always admired a man who can accept a woman winning at sports," Sandra said, sounding a little smug. "Better luck next time." She went to the board and began removing darts one by one.

Adam leaned back in his chair, feet propped on his desk. "Any inspiration yet?"

Sandra went to sit once more on the old leather couch pushed against the wall. She picked up her notepad.

"How about calling the paper something like the *World Gazette?*"

"No—too generic. We want something catchy, a name people will remember."

"I've been playing around with another idea. How about the *National Standard?*"

"That might have possibilities." Adam rubbed his mustache. "Hell, maybe we should just leave it the *Boston Standard.*"

"I've considered that, too. Or the *New England Standard.*"

It was ironic that the simple matter of a name was tripping them up. So far they'd tackled a multitude of other problems: production costs, distribution facilities, advertising budgets. But they had yet to come up with a suitable name for the revamped newspaper.

"Maybe we should call it a night," Adam said. "I have to go at it with Stan first thing in the morning."

"I don't know why he's being so difficult about everything."

"He thinks we should do endless research reports and test circulations before we launch the new *Standard.* If I followed his calculations, it'd be at least a year before we're ready. I'm afraid we don't have time for that kind of delay. If we have any chance of revitalizing the newspaper, now's when we have to move on it." Adam swung his feet down from his desk. He was more and more aware of the risk he was taking with the paper. He knew how much was depending on this venture—the livelihoods of several hundred employees. Not to mention his own livelihood and his self-respect. Failure with the *Standard* wasn't something he could contemplate.

Sandra doodled on her notepad. "I'm really not all that tired yet," she said. "We can work a little while longer, Adam. As a matter of fact, I'm getting used to these all-nighters.''

"In other words, you don't want to go home."

Sandra tossed down her pad. "I wish I'd never told you. But it's true. That empty house makes me feel so damn lonely. But what can I say to Brian? He's having a lot of fun on the Cape. I can't be the ogre and ask him to come home early, no matter how much I miss him. He says it's the best summer vacation he's ever had. All because of the Twit." Sandra's shoulders seemed to slump. And then tears welled up in her eyes. It looked like she was going to cry again.

Hell. Adam was no good at this type of thing. He liked the easygoing camaraderie he and Sandra had established these past few weeks. He was even getting used to her talking about her ex-husband's twenty-year-old girlfriend as the Twit. But tears . . . He was no good with tears.

Too late. They were already trickling down Sandra's cheeks. She searched through her pockets, found a tissue and dabbed at her eyes.

"I'm sorry. I don't mean to do this. Damn, Adam. It's bad enough losing my husband. But do I have to lose my son, too?"

"You're not losing him."

"Easy for you to say." The tears kept trickling down her cheeks.

Adam went and sat beside Sandra. "You won't lose your son," he repeated. "Nothing can make that happen."

"What makes you so sure?" Sandra's voice was muffled because she had her face buried in her tissue.

"I may not have children, but I was a child once myself," he said, his voice gruff. "Believe me, even when you try to escape from your parents, they're always a part of you. There's no getting around it. You're always someone's son. Long after your parents are gone, you're still their son."

"Oh, Adam..."

He didn't know quite how it happened, but Sandra turned toward him and then she was sniffling against his chest. He brought his arms around her.

"You're just tired," he said. "You need to go home."

She raised her face and gazed at him with bleary eyes. "I look awful, don't I?"

"You look fine."

"No. I look awful. It's really not like you to be flattering, Adam. Don't do it now."

"Okay," he said. "Maybe you do look a little bedraggled."

"Thanks," she said. "For being honest."

Then she kissed him, seeming almost desperate. Abruptly she pulled away. She scrambled to her feet and hurried toward the door. "I can't believe I let that happen. I really can't—"

"It's not your fault, Sandra. We're both a little punchy here. Too much work, too little sleep."

She'd reached the door, only to stop. She stood with her back to Adam, not saying anything. He waited for her to leave. But she didn't leave. Slowly, still without saying anything, she closed the door to the office. Then she crossed to the windows and began rattling down the blinds. There was no one in the newsroom, but she lowered the blinds, anyway.

"Sandra," Adam said. "You should go home, get some rest."

She tugged on a cord, and the last of the blinds clattered downward. Then she came to sit beside Adam. With a look of determination, she placed her hands on his shoulders and kissed him again.

A short time later they both sank down full-length on the battered leather of the couch. For years, Adam had kept the couch in here for the occasional night when he'd worked so late he required a place to stretch out. But he'd always stretched out on his own. This was definitely a mistake.

"Don't stop," Sandra said. "Please don't stop."

He went on kissing her. It was what she seemed to need . . . maybe what he needed, too. Except that his desire was all for another woman . . . a woman with dark hair and smoky eyes. . . .

"Jenny . . ." Adam groaned.

Sandra froze. A second or two later she slithered off the couch. "Oh, no. I've never been so stupid. Never . . ."

Adam felt awkward as hell.

Sandra gazed at him. "I don't care whose name you said. It's just . . . everything. Everything is just . . . everything!" And with that garbled statement, she fled from his office.

"MARRY ME," said David/Mark.

Jen lowered her script. "There's nothing in here about Mark asking Eileen to marry him."

David tossed his own script aside and came to clasp Jen's hands in his. "This isn't Mark proposing to Eileen. This is me proposing to you. Marry me, Jen."

All she could do was stare at him. "You're not serious."

"Totally serious. Marry me, darling."

Jen couldn't believe she'd heard him correctly. She moved away from David and lowered herself into his Victorian rocking chair. She and David definitely shared the same taste in antiques, but that fact wasn't particularly helpful at the moment. Jen rocked back and forth, back and forth. She wished they could just go on rehearsing their parts for the play. Never had she longed so much to immerse herself in the role of Eileen. She did *not* want to ponder marriage.

David, however, was not going to let the matter rest. He sat down on the old-fashioned trunk across from her, looking very expectant.

"David," she said at last, "I have to admit that you've taken me by surprise. If we were rushing things before, now we've just gone into overdrive."

"Give me three good reasons why you shouldn't marry me. No, make that five. Five good reasons."

"For goodness' sake, why five?"

"Just to be on the safe side," he told her. "There's a possibility you could come up with three reasons not to marry me, but no way could you come up with five."

As always he made her smile. "Here's a suggestion," she said. "I won't give you any reasons, and we'll just table the subject. It's much too soon even to be thinking about it."

David reached forward and clasped her hands again. "Jen, don't you know how much I want to do this? I want to spend my whole life with you."

"Oh, David . . ."

His expression turned glum. "You know you're in trouble when a woman starts out a sentence with 'Oh, David.' It's a sure sign you're in for bad news."

"You really do have a melodramatic streak."

"So give me five reasons. That's all I'm asking. Just five reasons why we shouldn't get married."

He was impossible. Now he just sat there looking at her, his hazel eyes clear and earnest.

"Reason number one," she said. "We haven't known each other long enough."

"How long does it take?" he asked immediately. "I realized how I felt about you practically the first minute I met you. And you already know everything important there is to know about me."

She moved her fingers restlessly in his. She couldn't argue the last point. She *did* know the most important thing about David. He wasn't afraid to share all his thoughts and feelings with her.

Jen rocked a little faster. "Reason number two," she said. "I'm too old for you."

"Those six years again, Jen? I thought we'd left that behind us."

"Reason number three," she said. "I don't see how I could possibly fit marriage into my life right now. There's too much going on."

"Marriage would actually simplify things between us. You could move in here with me."

"No," she said firmly. "I've gone that route before. I won't do it again. If you and I got married, we'd have to find a place that belonged to both of us."

He looked hopeful. "Are you saying yes?"

"No." Jen slipped her hands away from his. She stood and crossed to one of the windows. It was dark outside, but she could see into the lighted windows of another apartment building across the street. She saw a woman nestled into an armchair, reading. A woman alone. It was a peaceful, refreshing sight.

"Reason number four," Jen said. "We haven't even made love yet—"

"Through no fault of my own."

"And reason number five," Jen said firmly. "I'm sorry, David, but I'm still sorting through my feelings about us. I need more time—"

"It's him, isn't it? Always the ex-husband. Why did you divorce him if you can't get him out of your mind?"

Jen swiveled around. "Believe it or not, what I'm talking about doesn't have anything to do with Adam. It's about you and me." She paused, but she knew that sooner or later she had to bring this up. She wasn't doing either herself or David any favors by keeping her frustration to herself. "We have something we need to resolve," she went on. "Sometimes I feel a little crowded, David. I need a bit more breathing room. Last night was a perfect example. I wanted to attend my acting class— alone. You were offended. I tried explaining that I simply need a little time to myself, for my own pursuits . . ."

"You went to the class," David said, his tone almost self-righteous. "I didn't try to stop you."

"I wouldn't let you stop me," Jen said as calmly as possible. "You just have to understand. One of the big reasons I came to New York was so I could have a life of my own. I can't give that up."

"Come off it, Jen. If it weren't for Prescott, you wouldn't be telling me any of this. You're inventing excuses."

Jen took a deep breath. "How can I convince you this has nothing to do with Adam? David . . . haven't you heard a single thing I've said?"

"I've heard," he muttered. "And I've observed a few things. Such as the fact that you still have two bikes in your living room, and one of them is dripping dead flowers all over the rug."

Jen couldn't deny the ever-intrusive fact of those bicycles. Just as she couldn't explain why she hadn't called

Adam and demanded that he have them removed from the premises. Nor could she explain why she hadn't tossed out all the shriveled roses and violets.

"David, leave Adam out of this. You're missing the point. It wouldn't matter who I was involved with, I'd still want a certain amount of space." She didn't mention that, between her and Adam, there'd been too much space. Was there no happy medium? With Adam she'd known distance, and with David she knew togetherness and then some. Was she asking too much from life, wanting just the right balance?

David stood. He stuffed his hands into his pockets, somehow managing to look both mournful and belligerent at the same time. "I wish I could knock the hell out of your ex-husband. And I wish there was some way you could think about me—only me."

Jen realized he really hadn't heard a word she'd said. Perhaps her confused feelings in regard to Adam were a problem, but she and David had a problem entirely separate from that. He just couldn't seem to see it.

"David . . . you're so even tempered about acting. But when it comes to love . . ."

"When it comes to you, Jen," he said in a low voice, "I'm so in love I can't think straight. You're trying to make me feel like that's a crime. But tell me, is it really such a crime, the way I love you? Is it really so bad?"

ADAM HAMMERED in another piece of wood, then stood back to inspect his handiwork. The item he was constructing had started to look like a mutant coat rack. Admittedly he'd gotten a little carried away. But after all, this was his first foray into the art of carpentry.

The kitten had discovered a new game. It rolled on its back, batting at Adam's pant legs. He glanced down at it. The animal had filled out a little. It had grown. All that tuna.

Adam studied the cat, then inspected his wooden creation once again. "Staple a little carpeting on it and it'll be a decent scratching post, I suppose. But don't get any ideas, cat. It's going with you when I find you a home."

The kitten didn't seem perturbed. It just went from batting Adam's pant legs to tangling its claws in his shoelaces.

Adam set down his hammer and rubbed at the crick in his neck. He glanced at the clock and saw it was almost midnight. Normally he'd still be at the newspaper. But the last few nights... well, the last few nights he'd been working late hours at home, instead of at the office.

He and Sandra had been trying to go about business as usual, but the tension between them was thick. Needless to say, they hadn't competed at any more games of darts.

He felt pretty damn bad about what had happened. It had been a big mistake. But it *had* happened, and he didn't know what to do to change it.

He went into the kitchen and pulled a beer from the refrigerator. The cat skittered along behind him, a puffy ball of black fur. Adam sat down at the table, popped open the beer and took a long swallow. The kitten jumped onto a chair and then onto the table. It sauntered over to Adam.

"Down," he said without much conviction. The cat licked a drop of beer that had landed on Adam's hand, its tongue raspy. Apparently satisfied, it curled up on the table and started to purr.

Adam's thoughts drifted to Jen. He wondered what she'd think if she knew he'd said her name while kissing another woman. Somehow he didn't imagine she'd be flattered.

He glanced at the clock again. What was she doing right now? Was she with David Fielding? Probably. It seemed she had everything squared away. New career, new man—everything in place.

Maybe he was supposed to be happy for her. Maybe he was supposed to congratulate her on making a life away from him. But he didn't feel congratulatory right now. Not toward Jen—and certainly not toward himself.

He drained the rest of his beer and reached around the cat, bringing his laptop computer toward him. He booted up the computer, then selected the file labeled PROJ-2 from the screen. He contemplated the latest figures of projected advertising volume for the *Standard*. National advertisers would be especially important now.

But Adam stared at the figures without really seeing them. He was thinking of Jenny again. What would it take to get her out of his thoughts?

The kitten invented yet another new game, pawing at the empty beer can until it clattered over onto the floor. The cat looked pleased with itself, almost gloating.

"Glad somebody's happy." He was talking to the cat more and more. He had to do something about that.

The telephone rang. He pushed back his chair and went across the hall to answer it.

"Hello."

"Adam! I'm so glad you're there. I simply didn't know where else to turn." It was the unmistakable voice of his ex-mother-in-law. He should have known.

"What's up, Beth?"

"I called too late, didn't I? Really, Adam, I wouldn't have called at all, but I just didn't know what else to do. You can't imagine—"

"Beth, just tell me what the problem is, and I'll see if I can help."

"I knew you wouldn't let me down!" she exclaimed. "You never have before. You've always come through."

"Is this about Jen?" he asked suspiciously.

"Of course not! Why ever would you think I'd be calling about Jenna? This is about me, Adam. A matter of quite some urgency. Can you come to Newport tomorrow evening? I wouldn't ask, except that it really is very important."

He was still suspicious. Obviously Beth didn't intend to tell him what the problem was over the phone. She was plotting something. He had no doubt about that.

"I need you here, Adam." The uncertainty in her voice got to him then. Always before, Beth had been the dauntless matriarch, sure of her own position, guarding her principles imperiously. But tonight she just sounded uncertain. This was definitely something new. Adam hesitated only another second or two.

"I'll be there," he said.

JEN LAY SPRAWLED OUT on the floor of her apartment, trying to pretend she was relaxing on an ocean beach. This was an exercise her acting teacher had suggested for counteracting nervous tension. Jen had been experiencing quite a bit of that lately. The character of Eileen still eluded her. Whenever Jen rehearsed her part, she felt as if she was watching Eileen recede farther and farther away, like someone running off into the distance. And Jen couldn't catch up no matter how hard she tried.

It didn't help that David had invested the character of Mark with an injured pride. Ever since he'd asked her to marry him, he'd been behaving that way—injury alternating with a sort of martyred dignity. It meant that now Mary Bess yelled at both Jen and David. And Angela kept stalking off the stage in disgust. Rehearsals were horrible.

Jen wiggled her legs and tried to imagine that she was sinking into soft white sand. But maybe imagining a beach scene was a mistake. It reminded her of the beach house and the hours she'd last spent with Adam there...

She opened her eyes. Another mistake. Because now she was looking up at the spokes of a bicycle wheel.

The only place on the floor with enough room to lie down was right between the two bikes. And even as she lay here, a dry rose petal drifted down onto her face. Was she imagining it, or could she still smell its perfume?

Jen gently pressed the rose petal against her skin. A wave of yearning washed over her, sudden and unexpected. She couldn't define it, refused to try. She only knew that it left her with a sorrow as poignant as the wilted petal she held against her cheek.

The telephone rang. Who on earth could be calling at this hour? It was after midnight. Jen straightened, only to bump her head against the wire basket on the bike closest to her. At last she made it to her feet and snatched the receiver up on the fourth ring.

"Hello," she said apprehensively.

"Jenna! I'm so glad you're there. I simply didn't know where else to turn."

"Mother, what's wrong?"

"I know I'm calling too late. I'm sorry I disturbed you, dear. I just didn't know what else to do."

"Are you all right? Are the uncles all right?"

"Uncle William and Uncle Thomas are fine."

"Mother, please don't keep me in suspense."

"I need you to come to Newport tomorrow. It's rather urgent. And it's not really the type of thing I can explain over the phone."

Jen didn't like the way her mother sounded. There was an edge to Beth's voice, as if she was just barely managing to keep herself under control.

"I think you'd better tell me what's wrong," Jen said firmly.

"Jenna, do this for me. Just come to Newport. I can't face the situation alone."

"What situation?"

"I just hope you can make it. Goodbye, dear." Now Beth sounded forlorn. And she hung up before Jen could say another word.

Jen set the receiver back down slowly. She'd have to turn her schedule completely upside down in order to travel to Newport tomorrow. She'd miss work and rehearsal at a time she could ill afford to. And maybe this was just another of her mother's schemes.

Or maybe her mother really needed help. Unfortunately there was only one way to know for sure.

CHAPTER SIXTEEN

A GREAT-UNCLE anchored on either side of her, Jen made a sedate turn around the back terrace of the Hillard mansion. The honeysuckle along the trellis was neatly clipped, the herb garden trimmed in tidy patches of lemongrass, sage, white-flowering chive. Everything on the Hillard estate was like this—orderly, groomed, kept within parameters. Even the bay-leaf shrubs were confined to wooden planters, as if it might be dangerous to let them spread their roots willy-nilly in the ground.

"I must admit I'm puzzled," said Uncle William on Jen's right. He sounded peeved. "Beth has not confided in me, and I don't understand what suddenly has her in an uproar."

"I believe I can guess," said Uncle Thomas on Jen's left, sounding purposefully bland. "It's not that difficult, Will."

"Unlike you, I don't go poking my nose into other people's personal concerns."

"You should try it some time. You would find your life less dull."

"Dull—my life's not dull."

"Dull as beets."

"Uncles, please. I think you both have fascinating lives," Jen said. "In fact, I couldn't take any more liveliness from either one of you."

"A true diplomat," said Uncle Thomas.

"Jenna always knows how to put you in your place, Tom. That's why she should come back to Newport."

"Hah! It's you, Will, who's been put in his place. Besides, our Jenna is going to make a very successful career for herself on the New York stage. What does she want with two old codgers like us?"

Jen squeezed Thomas's arm. "I want the two of you to go on being my meddlesome uncles, that's what."

"Jenna, Tom is the one who meddles. Please bear that in mind." William seemed a little put out, so Jen squeezed his arm, too.

"You're both exactly the type of uncles I need." Since Jen's last visit to Newport, the two old gentlemen seemed just a little frailer to her. Uncle William, in his old-fashioned vest and cuffed trousers, Uncle Thomas, dapper in pinstripes. Both of them were slightly stooped, as if shrinking in on themselves. Being with the uncles now, Jen felt torn between her two lives as never before. She needed to be in New York; she needed the independence she'd found there. But she also felt the tug of loyalty toward her family. She realized that she missed her dear, exasperating uncles more than she'd been willing to admit.

"Fine evening for a stroll," remarked a deep voice from the other side of the terrace. Jen and the uncles stopped, then slowly pivoted around like a chain of ice skaters. And there was Adam, coming toward them. Jen had suspected he'd be here, but the sight of him still affected her. She clung to the uncles as if they were supporting *her,* not the other way around.

Adam, moving dynamically, as if nothing could ever stand in his path, the lines of his features obstinate. His dark hair sprang back from his forehead with those hints of silver, and his dark eyes captured hers with that intense, uncompromising gaze.

"Adam, my boy," said Uncle William. "Now that you've arrived, perhaps we'll find out what's going on. Why is Beth in such a swivet?"

"I'm afraid I don't know any more than you do. She's ready for all of us to convene in the library—that's the only information I have." Even as Adam spoke, he continued to survey Jen. She tried to be cool, indifferent, but she could feel her face heating.

"Will," said Uncle Thomas to his brother, "all you have to do is ask me what's going on and I'll tell you."

"Hah. You don't know any more than the rest of us. I refuse to humor your idle speculations."

"Your problem, Will, is that you speculate too little. You won't use your imagination."

"I have a perfectly healthy imagination."

"I don't see any signs of it."

"Critical discernment is not your most well-developed faculty, Tom."

As the uncles continued to needle each other, Jen propelled them forward a little at a time. They made their way into the house, Adam going ahead to usher them through the sliding wooden doors of the library. Jen's mother was standing at the head of the carved oaken table. Looking unusually nervous, she gestured for everyone to take seats around her. Jen carefully deposited each uncle in a chair, then sat down herself. Adam sat on the other side of the table, directly in Jen's line of sight. He seemed to have no qualms about perusing her. What was he thinking? What was he feeling? Jen wondered if she'd ever know. Unfortunately she continued to experience an uncomfortable awareness of Adam's every move. She frowned at him and tried to concentrate on the proceedings at hand.

Now Beth lowered herself into a chair. She folded her hands on the table, but didn't speak. She seemed to be waiting for something. Maybe she was just trying to prolong the aura of suspense. If so, she was doing a good job of it.

Beth had certainly chosen an imposing setting for this gathering. The library was one of the more impressive rooms in the house, with its high ceiling, wealth of mahogany bookcases, tall windows and swagged curtains in heavy crimson. It was always a place that had made Jen feel overwhelmed: hundreds and hundreds of volumes intended only for Hillard eyes.

Beth continued to sit in silence at the head of the table, ignoring the way the uncles were muttering to each other. She looked as if she'd taken even more care than usual with her appearance today, wearing a dramatic red coatdress. Perhaps that had been done for effect, too; the color of the dress matched the crimson of the curtains, making Beth seem very much a part of this grand room. But there was still that nervousness about her, and Jen had the impression that her mother might spring up and bolt from the library at any second. It was, as Uncle William had declared, all quite puzzling.

The doors to the room slid open again, and now Phillip Rhodes entered. This was a surprise, Beth's ex-fiancé making an appearance. Phillip nodded gravely to all present and sat down opposite Beth. The uncles were both momentarily speechless, as if not sure how to respond to this new development.

Phillip himself seemed perfectly collected. He'd always been a background sort of person, a foil to Beth's flair. For years he'd overseen a very successful real-estate business, but he'd recently taken early retirement to devote himself to a career as an amateur naturalist. The study of botany was Phillip's greatest enjoyment, and Jen suspected he actually liked plants more than people.

"Thank you all for being here," Phillip said. "As you may not be aware, Beth and I have recently reopened discussions concerning our situation. Now we've reached a possible solution, but find it necessary to consult each of you in regard to the matter. You in particular, Adam."

Jen found her gaze drawn inevitably back to her exhusband. Adam's pose was relaxed, and he looked no more than politely interested. It struck her then how fitting this gathering was to the Hillard tradition. Beth and Phillip, instead of solving their problems in private, had convened a family council in order to do so. And, of course, Adam Prescott was included in the family. The whole thing was proceeding like an executive board meeting. Phillip at one end of the table, Beth at the other, the rest of them sitting in between like support staff—not a state of affairs particularly conducive to romance.

Now Beth spoke, sounding a little stilted, as if she'd practiced her words before the mirror but hadn't fixed on the proper delivery. "Phillip and I have thoroughly discussed out situation. We agree that, if our marriage plans are to proceed, we must find a solution to our living accommodations. Phillip, for reasons previously stated, refuses to relocate to the Hillard premises." Beth paused. Her hands were pressed tightly together, and she sounded even more stiff as she went on speaking. "However, as Jenna and Adam once pointed out, perhaps it is advantageous for any marriage to start on neutral territory. Phillip agrees with that assessment. At the same time, he realizes I do not wish to abandon my family."

Jen studied her mother closely. Beth didn't appear glad to be saying any of this. If a reconciliation was in the works, why didn't she appear happy? What was really going on here? But before Jen had a chance to wonder any further, Phillip took up the topic again.

"Adam, this is where you come in. Your parents' house has been vacant for some years now. It has occurred to Beth and me that we might purchase the home from you and refurbish it for ourselves. It would be neutral territory, so to speak, for both of us. Yet the house is also close enough that Beth will be able to keep an eye on the uncles whenever she chooses. It seems an ideal compromise, but of course we must lay the matter before you. The decision to sell is entirely yours."

Adam no longer evinced only a polite interest. He looked thoughtful, perhaps even a bit troubled. "You've taken me by surprise," he said. "I don't know what to say. I'll have to think it over—"

"Absolutely," Beth said. "We want you to take all the time you need. There's no rush. And we want Uncle Thomas and Uncle William to think the matter over. You, as well, Jenna." Beth stared anxiously at Jen. She almost seemed to be hoping that Jen would throw out some objection to the idea.

"Will and I can take care of ourselves," Uncle Thomas said. "Beth, you should live wherever you please. Hawaii, Tahiti, the Bahamas. But moving right next door— that's much too prosaic."

"Prosaic," repeated Uncle William in a scoffing tone. "I should like to have Beth close by. Jenna, too. Life is quite adventurous enough here in Newport. No one needs to go flitting off to the Bahamas."

"Will, when was the last time you had an adventure? And I don't mean the time you ran off to Boston and wrote your novel."

"Please refrain from discussing my novel, Thomas."

"It's your favorite topic, even though you won't admit it."

The family meeting had degenerated. The uncles continued to quibble, and Phillip and Adam moved to a corner of the library for their own discussion. Jen took advantage of the opportunity to grab her mother and ferry her down the hall to the sun room. This was one of the least imposing rooms in the house and therefore Jen's favorite. Latticed windows on three sides allowed the evening light to pour in. Potted ferns and geraniums hung from the indoor pergola, creating the sense of a garden bower. Jen prodded Beth onto the wicker chaise lounge, then perched beside her.

"All right," she said. "Out with it. Why on earth have you let Phillip talk you into this if it's not what you want?"

"Jenna, whatever gives you the—"

"Cut the act, Mother. Out with it."

"First, Phillip has not talked me into anything," Beth replied with some asperity. "But when he contacted me a few days ago to discuss a rapprochement, of course I felt obliged to listen. And the idea is very sensible."

"What's wrong, Mother?"

Beth leaned her head back on the chaise. "Is it so obvious that something's wrong?"

"You've gone to a great deal of effort to make it obvious, starting with your phone call last night. Apparently Phillip isn't picking up on the clues, but I am."

Beth sighed, without drama for once. "Jenna, I'm so glad you came. I wonder if anyone else would understand what I'm going through." She straightened. "You see, I was so happy when Phillip finally came to see me the other day. He'd put his silly pride away for once. How could it not mean a great deal to me?"

Jen refrained from mentioning that Beth herself possessed a considerable amount of pride; why hadn't *she* been the one to make the first move?

"Go on, Mother," Jen said patiently.

"Well, anyway, Phillip came up with this idea about buying the Prescott house, and I let myself get swept along at first. I was just so relieved to have Phillip back I suppose I wasn't thinking very clearly. But now..."

"Is there something about that house you dislike?"

"No, no, of course not. Alex and Grace Prescott were dear friends of mine. It would almost be a way to honor them, making their home come to life again. Goodness knows Adam hasn't been able to face the task."

"What is it, then?" Jen persisted.

Beth suddenly looked despondent. "Jenna...this isn't the easiest thing to confess, especially to one's own daughter. But I'm...afraid. Afraid of getting married again. Terrified, if you want to know the truth."

Beth Hillard, usually so in control, usually so adept at manipulating other people's lives. This very same Beth Hillard, admitting that she was afraid.

Jen reached out and patted Beth's hand in an awkward gesture. She wasn't used to comforting her mother. "I didn't realize. I had no idea."

"Well, neither did I, not for a long time. I tried to ignore all the signs. Jenna, your father and I had a very good marriage, but it wasn't perfect. Sometimes I needed more than he knew how to give. I never told you this because I wanted his memory to be special to you. I didn't want to ruin that."

Jen stared at her mother. "What was it he couldn't give you?"

Beth smiled wistfully. "Haven't you guessed? It's the one thing you've always wanted from Adam. A deeper love. A passion that goes to the soul."

Jen had never heard her mother talk like this. Could it be that she and Beth were actually alike?

"I wish you'd told me about this a long time ago," Jen said softly.

"How could I? Don't you understand? I tried to hide it from myself. It's one thing to need a certain type of love, quite another to acknowledge it. And I was truly devastated when your father died. He was a good man. A man, in fact, very much like Phillip. Dependable, kind...undemonstrative."

"I believe I *am* beginning to understand," Jen said. "You're afraid that your second marriage will be a repeat of the first."

Beth made a small grimace. "It sounds so callous in a way, as if I'm somehow disparaging your father's memory..."

"I know how much you loved him. Nothing can change that. But you've started to be honest with yourself, Mother. I don't think you can stop now."

"How can I want more than I already have? I've been a very fortunate woman. I was married to your father, and the Hillard family accepted me as one of their own. Now Phillip, a wonderful man, is willing to make compromises in order to marry me. And I have you, the great joy of my life! How can I possibly ask for more?"

Jen restrained her own rueful smile. Beth was getting a little carried away again about the delights of motherhood.

"Maybe it's not wrong to want more. Take it from me—the longing for the love you're talking about won't go away by itself. It's much better all around to deal with it."

Now Beth was the one who patted Jen's hand. "I so wanted Adam to give you that type of love. I always believed, deep down, that he *could* give it to you."

"Mother, we need to talk about you," Jen said firmly. "There's only one solution. You have to go to Phillip and tell him what the real problem is."

"I'm not ready for that yet."

"You'd better get ready, and soon. What if Adam agrees to sell the house? You can't just go along with it."

Beth jumped to her feet. "Jenna, you must go talk to Adam. Right now. Immediately. Tell him that he has to delay his decision as long as possible."

"This is ridiculous," Jen protested. "Talking to Adam isn't the solution. Talking to Phillip is."

"Jenna, please. Do this for me. No need to tell Adam all the details. Just ask him to wait before he makes up his mind. And then I'll be able to think about the rest of it."

Jen would have protested further, but she believed she understood her mother's turmoil. It was scary, all right, contemplating the idea of telling a man exactly what you needed from him. You could very well find out, once and for all, that he *couldn't* give it to you. That had happened to Jen with Adam, and it still hurt. It hurt even after all this time.

Jen stood up and gave her mother a kiss. The scent of Beth's perfume washed over her—the wistful scent of rose petals. Yes, she and Beth had more in common than she'd ever realized.

"I'll go talk to Adam for you. As long as you admit that what you really need to do is to sit down with Phillip for a heart-to-heart."

"I think I've admitted quite enough for one day," Beth said, recovering some of her fight. "Go, Jenna."

And so Jen went to find her ex-husband.

THE STONE WALLS of the Prescott villa shone like topaz in the waning light of evening. The house presided over its own vast lawns. Unlike the Hillard grounds, however, these were not immaculately kept. The grass was shaggy; Jen knew that a caretaker only came once every few weeks to mow.

She went up the curved drive and climbed the steps to the front door. When she'd emerged from her conference with Beth, Adam had already left the Hillard house to come here. Jen hesitated, debating whether to knock. The door was unlocked, however, and in the end she simply went in.

She glanced first into one room, then another. All the furniture was covered in drop cloths. So many shrouded forms. It was sad. That was how this house had always felt to her, as if a sadness were trapped inside like a ghost that couldn't escape.

She found Adam in the drawing room. He stood motionless, gazing at the portrait of his parents that hung in a dim alcove. He didn't turn or acknowledge Jen's presence in any way. At last Jen came to stand beside him, and she, too, gazed at the portrait of his parents. Alexander and Grace Prescott, captured forever on canvas, looking into each other's eyes so devotedly.

"They were very much in love, weren't they?" Jen murmured.

"Do you really think that?" Adam asked, and the harshness in his voice startled her.

"Yes," she answered. "I know I was only a child when your father died, but I remember him and your mother together. And my own mother used to tell me stories about them—the perfect couple." Only now did Jen understand why sometimes Beth had almost sounded envious recounting those stories. Perhaps Beth saw in the Prescotts' devotion to each other what had been missing in her own marriage.

"How little you know of the reality," Adam said, his voice still harsh. "It's always been like you, Jen, to cast a romantic glow on everything. It prevents you from seeing what's really there."

Something in his tone was unfamiliar. It took her a moment to identify that something as anger. Adam was notoriously self-contained. Coldly disapproving, yes. Angry, no.

Now he paced the room restlessly. "I can't understand why your mother and Phillip want to live here. There are too many damn memories."

"Perhaps for you," Jen said carefully. "Phillip, I'm sure, merely sees it as a convenient solution to his problems. As for my mother, the truth is, she's not really sure she wants to live here at all. She sent me with a message. She'd like you to wait on your decision, Adam, until she really has time to think it through."

He looked irritated. "Maybe I'm missing something. In one breath she announces she wants to buy this house. In the next she announces she doesn't?"

"Something like that. It's a long story."

Adam continued to pace. He seemed worked up in a way she'd never witnessed before.

One set of curtains in the room was partially open, but that didn't dispel the murkiness here. Jen shivered a little even though she wasn't cold and went to open the curtains further.

"Don't do that," Adam said, and now she heard a hint of pain in his voice. Just a hint, but it was there. She remained by the window, very still.

"Adam . . . what did you mean when you said I knew so little of the reality? Tell me."

"Some stories shouldn't be told."

"No. You're wrong about that. Today my mother shared some things I wish I'd known years ago. But she's been smothering her emotions. It wasn't until now that they finally came out. I think you smother your emotions, too, Adam."

"Leave it alone, Jenny." His voice was rough, but he'd called her by that private name, Jenny.

She crossed to him and placed a hand on his arm. She could feel his muscles tense. "Something's going on," she said. "It's something to do with this house, isn't it? But what *is* it, Adam? Don't shut me out this time. Please don't shut me out." She heard the pleading in her voice. She'd pleaded with him many other times, and it hadn't been any use. He'd always closed himself off from her. She hadn't been allowed to share whatever pain or sorrow he'd suffered in the past. Why should today be any different?

His silence defeated Jen. She dropped her hand from his arm and turned away. It was then that he spoke, and this time the pain in his voice deepened.

"Lord, Jenny, I hate this house. I hate it. Yet I've never let go. Maybe I can't. That's the worst of it— maybe I just can't let go."

CHAPTER SEVENTEEN

THE SHADOWS in the room thickened, the draped furniture looming eerily here and there like so many shipwrecks in a mist. Adam stood with his head bowed.

"The perfect couple," he said, his voice grating. "Yes, my parents could be the perfect couple when it suited them, when they wanted to put up a front. But here in this house...things were different. No pretense. They argued—a lot. They tried to hurt each other. They knew how to do it, too. After years of marriage, they understood each other's weaknesses."

Jen touched his arm again. "Adam, I had no idea. I'm sorry."

"Don't be. I found a solution. I just got the hell out of here whenever I could. I probably spent more time at the newspaper than my father did." Adam pulled away and resumed his pacing.

"You know what's funny?" he said after a moment. "The worst times weren't my parents' arguments. The worst were the reconciliations. For a while everything would be fine. They'd be enthralled with each other, as if they were trying to make up for all the hurt they'd inflicted. But I always knew that would change, sooner or later. Another confrontation. Accusations, recriminations. More accusations...my mother's tears."

Adam returned to the portrait of his parents. It was obscured by a veil of shadows and dust. "A good likeness," he said sardonically. "The way they're looking only at each other. Even when they were fighting and lashing out, they were absorbed in each other. I felt like an outsider most of the time—an outsider who didn't want to be anywhere near either one of them."

Jen rubbed her arms. She felt a chill that seemed to come from somewhere deep inside her. Unable to stand still any longer, she went to one of the shrouded forms and pulled off the sheet. Revealed in the evening gloom was a small table, the top intricately laid with a marquetry pattern of shell and ivory. A beautiful mosaic, hidden all these years. Too much had been hidden in this house—ugliness more than beauty, it seemed.

"Adam, when your father died—"

"Enough, Jen." The warning in his voice was clear, but she didn't heed it.

"There's more, isn't there? I know there is. You have to talk about it."

"No." He uttered only that one word, but Jen heard the heaviness in his voice. He bowed his head again, there in the gathering night.

Jen went to him then. This time she was determined he wouldn't pull away from her. She wrapped her arms around him and held onto him as tightly as she could.

He remained there, head still bowed. But he didn't lift his own arms to hold her in return.

SUNLIGHT GLINTED on the water. Adam stood at the helm of the boat, welcoming the ocean breeze. He'd forgotten how good it felt to be out here like this. A little sailing seemed just what he needed. The amazing thing was that he'd actually convinced Jen to come along. It had taken some doing, but finally he'd persuaded her.

He glanced at her now. Apparently she hadn't lost any of her skill. She was expertly tending the jib sheets, allowing the boat to work with the wind and glide smoothly through the water. She'd tied her hair back with a scarf, but dark strands had still come loose to whip around her face. In a sleeveless T-shirt and denim shorts, she looked damn alluring. He was sure, however, that wasn't her intention. At the moment she was frowning slightly, apparently lost in her own thoughts.

Finally she glanced at him. "This isn't the same as the *Anna Lee,*" she said, referring to the boat they'd owned when they were first married. "The feel isn't right."

"A rental never feels just right." He thought back on the sailboat they'd once owned together. Jen hadn't wanted anything new—she'd wanted a boat already seasoned by the ocean. And so they'd bought the *Anna Lee* secondhand, with its old-fashioned name and its honey-colored wood mellowed by ocean spray. He'd thought Jen had loved that boat—yet eventually it had been her idea to sell it. He hadn't questioned her decision then. He was only questioning it now....

He was thinking too much about the past. It wasn't doing him any good. Last evening, for example, when he'd dredged up all those memories about his parents, what had been the point? It was done with. It couldn't be changed, so why had he talked about it? He could only be grateful that he'd stopped himself before telling Jenny the rest of it. He hadn't told her the worst. Well, he could be grateful at least for that much.

And here he was now with Jen, a dazzling sky arching overhead, the cobalt ocean spreading out before them. It was precisely the atmosphere needed to obliterate those useless memories of his.

When it came to Jenny, however, certain things couldn't be obliterated.

"How's it going in New York?" he asked.

"Just fine." Her voice sounded a little too clipped.

He thought about what he wanted to say next, but he didn't know how to make it come out right. "Look," he began awkwardly, "that time I showed up with the bikes—"

"It was a nice idea. Just bad timing." She sounded awkward, too.

"Are you serious about this David Fielding?"

Her hand yanked a little, and she brought the jib in too tight. Quickly she corrected it, then glanced at Adam again. "David's asked me to marry him. I guess that means it's serious."

This wasn't what he'd wanted to hear. Hell, what *did* he want to hear? With Jenny, he was never sure.

"Set the date yet?" he asked.

"For crying out loud—no, of course I haven't. Do you honestly think I'd jump into another marriage just like that?"

"I don't know what you'd do, Jen. I've never quite figured you out . . . but you're thinking about marrying this guy, aren't you?"

She sighed. "Yes. I guess you could say I am. David is very . . . nice."

Adam didn't like the way she'd said that. What was so great about this guy, anyway? He told himself he wasn't going to ask, but then he did. He heard himself say the words out loud.

"What the hell is so great about this guy?"

Jen looked exasperated. "Adam, do you really want to get into it?"

As a matter of fact, he didn't, but somehow that seemed beside the point. "It's as good a subject as any."

"Well, *I* don't want to get into it. All I know is that I should have left for New York this morning. What am I doing?"

"You're here with me, enjoying yourself."

"Dammit, Adam, I'm not enjoying myself. Because you've closed yourself off from me again. I can feel it— just like a door slamming in my face."

Adam stared into the distance, watching the bright yellow sail of another boat drift across his line of vision. "Fielding, I suppose, doesn't make you feel like that."

"He's completely the opposite of you. He never shuts himself off."

Adam didn't say anything. He turned the boat straight into the wind, then came about, the boom swinging over. There wasn't any need for words between him and Jen. She handled the jib as expertly as ever, and now they were sailing on a new tack. All accomplished through unspoken communication. Didn't that count for something?

He tied off the helm and went to sit beside Jen. The boat rocked a little, and his knees bumped hers. He reached out and tilted her chin, drawing her toward him. Her gray eyes were lovely—and unexpectedly sad. Before he could kiss her, she slid away from him and went to take the helm, gripping the wheel with both hands.

"Jenny—"

"Making love won't solve anything, Adam. It never has with us."

"I wasn't planning to seduce you on the boat." Actually it was a provocative thought, making love to Jen as they sailed under a sun-streaked sky. It was something they'd done a few times before. . . .

"I wonder if you'll ever understand," she said, and he still sensed the sadness in her. "Last night, when you were talking about your parents, you actually shared something with me, something real. But it scared you, didn't it, Adam? You dislike the fact that you exposed your emotions to me. So you've pulled back. Will you ever understand that maybe it's okay to be a little vulnerable?"

He didn't have an answer for that question. Maybe he didn't have any answers at all for Jenny.

JEN HONKED as the line of cars in front of her slowed. Not that it would do her any good—the stream of traffic into Providence was endless. It had been like this almost the entire way from Newport.

"Jenna, dear," said her mother from the back seat, "it really isn't polite to honk. My chauffeur never honks, you know. I don't see why you wouldn't let him drive us."

"Mother, it was Vance's bowling night. Besides, now and then it's good to experience something besides a limousine."

"What do you think, Adam? Don't you think my chauffeur should have been the one to drive? Vance *is* a very good driver, you know."

"I believe it," said Adam from the front passenger seat. "But Jen likes being in control—or so I've learned."

Jen's eyebrows drew together. Adam's presence was an unwelcome distraction. His presence, in fact, had been a distraction all day. In the first place, she never should have agreed to go sailing with him this morning. It had evoked too many memories of other mornings, long ago, when they'd sailed on the *Anna Lee*. That was the one thing they'd been able to share—a love of sailing. Adam had been a mystery to her in so many ways, but never on the sea. The *Anna Lee* had seemed their own unique haven.

But as the years passed, somehow Adam found less and less time to go sailing with her. The *Anna Lee* had ceased to be a haven. Instead, it had become a relic of an all-too-brief happiness.

Now Jen honked again, loudly and deliberately, as the traffic came to a complete standstill.

"Really, Jenna. You almost ran into that man's bumper."

Jen struggled to control her exasperation. "Mother—"

"It looked awfully close to me. What do you think, Adam?"

"Let's just hope there was no exchange of paint," he said with a grin.

It was never Adam's way to be tactful. With traffic at a standstill, Jen found her glance straying to him. He seemed overpowering in this little car—the English roadster, which was the most modest vehicle in the Hillard collection. His head almost touched the top of the car, and his thigh was right next to Jen's, only the stick shift between them. He gazed back at Jen, and his eyes seemed particularly dark. What was he thinking? And why did he have to look so virile and stubborn and attractive all at once?

"Jenna, dear, I believe that now certain motorists are honking at *you*," Beth said from the back seat.

The traffic was moving again, and Jen pressed her foot on the gas. The car jolted forward, none too smoothly. What was wrong with her? She had her mother in the back seat, yet she'd been gawking at her ex-husband.

"I can't stop wondering what this is all about," Beth said. "Phillip calling me up and insisting I go to Providence. He made it sound so urgent."

"It's certainly a puzzler," Jen agreed. "And why did he want Adam and me to come, too?"

"I really can't say, dear. But I should think you need to change into the other lane."

Jen gritted her teeth and purposefully stayed in the lane where she was. "Mother, did you get a chance to discuss that thing with Phillip?"

"What thing, dear?"

"You know..." Surely her mother was being purposely dense.

"If you ladies would like to talk about something private, just pretend I'm not here," Adam suggested in a helpful manner.

"Never mind," said Beth. "Adam will have to know the truth sooner or later. And the truth is, Phillip and I have a great deal more to resolve than the simple matter of living accommodations. Last night, at Jenna's urging, I explained this to Phillip. I told him in no uncertain terms exactly what I needed. To be precise, I told him I wished to be swept off by him. Swept off, so to speak, on a white stallion." Beth paused dramatically.

"A white stallion," Adam echoed.

"You get the idea," Jen said.

"Oh. Romance," he answered doubtfully.

Jen tried to ignore him. "Mother, what did Phillip have to say to all this?"

Beth sighed. "Nothing." There was that forlornness in her voice again. "He just looked rather concerned. And then he told me, very politely, that my orange shrubs were in danger of sooty mold. And then he left."

Jen almost smiled. How like Phillip to revert to botany in a moment of crisis.

"Well, he did call you today. That's an encouraging sign."

"I'm not at all sure that it is," Beth declared. "This sudden urgency of his—telling me to be at the airport in Providence as soon as possible. It's all very surprising, and I don't like surprises."

"Excuse me, Beth," said Adam. "How can you want romance and yet no surprises? Don't the two frequently go together?"

This was sufficient to confound Beth into silence for a few moments. Jen, however, had something to say.

"I don't know that I agree with you, Adam. Sometimes when a man tries surprising a woman, he's just doing what *he* wants to do. He's not taking her emotions or needs into consideration."

"I see. Fielding, then, he doesn't try to surprise you."

"Actually one time he did." Jen thought about the theater ticket. That had been a surprise all right. There'd been only one problem. She'd wished so very much for it to be Adam's surprise, not David's.

"Anyway," she went on. "I don't see why we're discussing David. Or romance or any of it—"

"You're the one who brought up the subject of romance," Adam pointed out. "I'm just trying to learn a little about it."

"I hardly think so—"

"Don't you believe I'm capable of any romance, Jenny?"

Her gaze strayed to him again. Was that amusement she saw in his eyes? Or was he serious? Those two bicycles he'd hauled up to her apartment—that had certainly been a surprise. But romantic, she couldn't say. With Adam, who *could* say...

"Jenna," said her mother from the back seat, "fascinating conversation, dear, but this time you really are tailgating that nice blue car in front of us. I should like to get there all in one piece, you know."

For Jen, it was a decided relief when they finally arrived at the airport. She pulled right out onto the tarmac, as per Phillip's instructions. And there was Phillip himself, coming to open Beth's door with a flourish. He assisted her from the car, ignoring the bewildered expression on her face.

"Madam," he said, "your white steed awaits."

BETH LOOKED DAZED. No wonder. It wasn't everyday that your ex-fiancé whisked you into a chartered jet and flew you off to Las Vegas to be married just like that. Technically it may not have been a white steed, but it had been a white plane—close enough. It was certainly a surprise. It was certainly romantic. Jen couldn't deny either one of those. Now Beth stood at the altar of this small wedding chapel, Phillip by her side. Of course the wedding chapel probably wasn't to her mother's taste. It was done up entirely in pink: pink walls, pink chairs, pink carpet. Even the flowers massed everywhere were pink: dahlias, begonias, carnations, daisies. All pink.

Come to think of it, Jen was feeling a little dazed by the whole thing herself. As maid of honor, she stood beside her mother tonight. Adam, the best man, stood beside Phillip. Filling the chairs behind them were many of Phillip's and Beth's friends; Phillip's chartered jet had taken on quite a load of passengers, including almost everyone they knew from Newport. When Phillip decided to do something romantic, well, apparently he went all the way.

"Do you, Phillip Henry Rhodes, take Beth Marie Hillard to be your lawfully wedded wife, to have and to hold, to love and to cherish all the days of your life?" The woman performing the ceremony was rather tall and gaunt, and she didn't look good in pink. But that was just a minor detail.

"I do," said Phillip. He was starting to look dazed, too, as if the magnitude of this adventure was only now starting to sink in.

"Do you, Beth Marie Hillard, take Phillip Henry Rhodes to be your lawfully wedded husband, to have and to hold, to love and to cherish all the days of your life?"

Beth seemed incapable of speech. She just stood there, an awestruck expression on her face. The silence was starting to become noticeable. Jen wanted to offer her mother moral support, but couldn't think of a discreet way to do it. She ended up giving Beth a nudge, and that seemed to do the job.

"Oh! Yes... yes, of course. I mean... I do!"

"I pronounce you husband and wife. You may now kiss the bride," said the tall lady in pink.

Phillip embraced his wife as pink helium-filled balloons were released into the air. Then the newly married couple went down the aisle, arms linked. Jen and Adam followed—their arms not linked. The wedding guests trooped after them.

Phillip had rented practically the entire hotel where the chapel was located. Everyone congregated in the ballroom, and the band struck up a waltz. Phillip escorted his new bride onto the floor, Beth still looking a bit awestruck. She'd asked for romance and perhaps received more than she'd bargained for.

Jen sank down at one of the tables, frowning at the pink napkins, the pink mints and the pink crepe-paper streamers.

"What's wrong, Jenny?" Adam asked as he pulled out a chair beside her. "This is supposed to be a celebration. Aren't you happy about it?"

Desultorily she chewed one of the pink mints. It tasted like chalk. "Of course I'm happy. As long as my mother is happy."

"You don't look happy."

"You know, Adam, there are lots of beautiful women here. Don't let me slow you down."

"I can't neglect my duties," Adam said. "I'm the best man, remember? That means supervising the rest of the wedding party."

"Supervise somewhere else, Adam." She propped her chin in her hand, unable to explain the melancholy drifting over her. Maybe weddings always made her feel this way. They were occasions where so much was promised, so much expected of the future. But could the future ever live up to all the hype?

"Perhaps if you get your feet moving, your mind will follow." Adam drew her to her feet and out onto the floor. Another song had started and several couples were dancing. Adam pulled Jen close. She knew she ought to resist him. Certainly she ought to resist the romantic music, tinged with its own sweet melancholy. But then she found her hands moving up over Adam's shoulders, her cheek pressed against his. Being in his arms brought magic. It also brought torment. Because she would always require more than he could give her.

She felt the provocative silkiness of his mustache against her skin, and reluctant warmth spread through her. Adam knew how to hold her when they danced—just as he did when they made love. But why didn't he know how to do it at other times? Last night, at his parents' house, he hadn't been able to hold her....

She closed her eyes, wishing she didn't feel that ache inside, an ache of desire and disappointment that only Adam seemed able to inspire in her. But she didn't let go of him. She just twined her fingers in his hair and went on dancing, wishing the music could go on forever.

The song ended, of course, the rhythm of the music dying down. Jen clung to Adam just another moment.

"You two certainly seem to be having a good time," came the cheery voice of Beth Marie Hillard Rhodes.

With a start, Jen opened her eyes and pulled away from Adam. Her mother seemed to be making a recovery. Beth no longer looked dazed. She looked...sparkly. There was no other word for it.

"Excuse me, Adam, while I borrow my daughter for a moment." Beth propelled Jen off a little way, leaving Adam to talk with the groom.

"Mother, is everything going all right? Is this what you wanted?"

"Goodness, dear, Phillip could not have done a better job of sweeping me off my feet! I never imagined he had it in him. Not that it's easy for him, either, you know. He'd much rather be at home, inspecting his Swedish ivy for leaf rollers. The fact that he would do all this for me..." Beth gave a tender little smile. "Well, I have my answer, Jenna. Even when Phillip decides to lose himself for hours in his greenhouse, I'll never again doubt his love for me."

"I'm glad for you, Mother. Very glad."

Beth gave Jenna a quick hug. "You were right all along, dear. I just had to ask Phillip for what I needed. Now if only you and Adam—"

"Mother, it's not always that simple."

"Isn't it, dear?"

"No, Mother, I'm sorry to say it isn't. Sometimes you ask for what you need—and the other person just can't come through for you."

Beth seemed ready to protest, but it was time for the toasts. As best man, Adam raised the first glass.

"To Beth and Phillip. May their lives together always be filled with . . . surprises."

No one could accuse Adam of wasting words. He was looking right at Jen as he spoke, his expression seeming to carry some sort of challenge. She turned away from him and picked up her own glass of champagne.

Unfortunately the rest of the toasts weren't as concise as Adam's. They became progressively more long-winded and silly. The bridal couple began sneaking toward the door.

"Wait!" someone exclaimed. "What about the bouquet? You can't leave without throwing the bouquet!"

Beth glanced down at the cluster of begonias and dahlias still clutched in her hand. She gazed around the ballroom. And then she hurled the bouquet into the air—straight toward Jen.

CHAPTER EIGHTEEN

JEN AWOKE to the smell of warm flesh and stale champagne. She yawned, then winced at the pounding in her head. She tried to convince herself she was dreaming. It had to be a dream—the gust of snoring close to her ear, the masculine hand resting possessively on her thigh . . .

Jen sat up straight, her head pounding all the more. Her heart seemed to pound in a tempo to match. A sense of foreboding engulfed her. What had she done? Oh, dear Lord, what *had* she done?

She stared at the sleeping form next to her. Adam—his chocolate brown hair rumpled on the pillow, his mustache fluttering just a little as he went on snoring in that restless manner of his.

Her sense of dread growing, Jen glanced around the room. What she saw wasn't reassuring: the near empty bottle of champagne on the heart-shaped nightstand, the bouquet of begonias and dahlias tossed onto the floor, the discarded clothes strewn everywhere, the flocked wallpaper with its pattern of hearts.

Stomach clenched in dismay, Jen scrambled out of the bed. She grabbed her crumpled dress and miscellaneous underwear, then hurried into the adjoining bathroom. She examined the place a bit wildly. Heart-shaped soaps, heart-shaped mirrors. Even the damn sinks were heart-shaped.

She splashed water on her face, then started to tussle with her clothes. Somehow her bra had become tangled in Adam's briefs. Cursing, she finally managed to yank on her bra, underpants and slip. Her dress looked awful, but she yanked that on, too. Then she sat on the edge of the tub and instructed herself to breathe very calmly, very evenly. It had to be a dream. Dear Lord, please let it be a dream.

Very well, she'd had too much champagne to drink last night. So had Adam. That part she was willing to admit. But the rest of it—surely it couldn't really have happened. Adam couldn't really have swept her off her feet and carried her into that wedding chapel. And the tall lady in pink surely hadn't performed another ceremony. "Do you, Jenna, take Adam..."

Jen moaned out loud. She left the bathroom and went to stare at her ex-husband still slumbering on the bed. Except that maybe he was no longer her ex. Maybe she really had done the unthinkable. Maybe she'd actually remarried him!

Jen gazed at him a moment longer, with all the heartache and longing and confusion inside her. Then she grabbed her shoes from the floor, took one more glance at Adam—and fled.

WHEN ADAM AWOKE, his head felt like it was stuffed with wads of cotton. He sat up slowly, grumbling to himself. It took him a moment to remember where he was—some cheesy room in a Las Vegas hotel. Except that, last he remembered, Jenny had been nestled here in the sheets beside him. Jenny, with her dark hair tumbling around her face, her eyes the soft warm color of cinder.

She was gone, though, elusive as a dream. Adam couldn't decide whether he was sorry or relieved not to find her beside him. He swung his legs over the side of the bed, wincing. Now he felt a clanging in his head. It seemed he'd celebrated Beth's and Phillip's wedding just a little too much. *Oh, my God.* Maybe that wasn't the only wedding he'd celebrated.

No! No... He had to have imagined the whole thing. He sure hoped he'd only imagined it. Adam tried to hold on to that thought while he scouted the room for his clothes. Pants, shirt, socks... Where the hell was his underwear?

He found it at last in the bathroom, hanging neatly from one of the towel hooks. *That* he didn't remember.

A few minutes later he prowled around the hotel room again, looking for his shoes. He found them under the bed and sat down to put them on.

He ended up just staring at them. His head was starting to clear. Maybe he'd been a little drunk last night, but this morning he was cold sober. And he could no longer ignore the truth.

He'd really gone and done it this time. He'd gone and married his ex-wife.

JEN/EILEEN walked in front of the chalked square marked MANTELPIECE. " 'No,' " she said. " 'This isn't a good idea.' "

David/Mark stepped very close to her. " 'Yes,' " he said. " 'You've been waiting for me to do this.' "

" 'I never wait, Mark. Not for anyone. Not for anything.' "

" 'Maybe I'm the one who's been waiting.' " David/Mark took another step closer, then placed his lips against Jen/Eileen's. She sprang away from him.

"Wrong," said Mary Bess in a weary tone. "All wrong. You're supposed to kiss him back, Hillard."

"I think it would be a little more realistic if I didn't...if Eileen didn't kiss Mark at all. I mean, wouldn't that be better for the scene? Think about it."

"Hillard, you're supposed to kiss him. And then you're supposed to go to bed with him!"

"Technically speaking, of course," Jen said hastily.

"Mary Bess," David put in, "Jen and I are going to take five. You don't mind?"

"Of course I don't mind. Why would I mind? Just because we're opening a week from tonight, and nobody has a damn clue about what we're doing here—"

Angela/Lisa slapped down her script. "I've had it. This time I've *really* had it."

David took Jen off to one of the small dressing rooms, where mildew spotted the walls and a dead cockroach lay feet up in the corner. The atmosphere fitted Jen's mood at the moment, so she didn't protest. David closed the door, sat her down on a bench, and then stood back to survey her.

"Mind telling me what's going on? You've been avoiding me ever since you came back from visiting your mother two days ago. You won't go out to eat with me, you'll barely answer my phone calls, and during rehearsal you won't even look at me. Darling, what's wrong?"

Jen wished fervently that he wouldn't call her darling. She'd been waiting for just the right opportunity to tell him her problem; that she'd flown to Las Vegas, had too much champagne and then married her ex-husband. She really did want to tell him about all that, but somehow the right opportunity hadn't presented itself. This certainly wasn't it.

"Look, David, after rehearsal...we'll talk. Not now."

"When a woman tells you not now, you know you're definitely in trouble."

"Put a lid on it, David."

He looked injured. "You won't even let me come near you. What have I done, Jen?"

"It's nothing to do with you. It's just...oh, it's a mess, that's all. I've made a monumental mess of my life, and I have no one to blame but myself."

She still couldn't believe she'd done it. What had possessed her? She couldn't just blame the champagne. Some craziness in her had taken over, and she'd done absolutely the worst thing possible. She'd married Adam Prescott for the second time around.

Jen couldn't stop herself from leaning against the makeup table and burying her head in her arms. If this action bore any similarity to an ostrich burying its head in the sand, she chose to ignore the fact. She'd been so overwrought since returning to New York she'd barely rested or slept at all. She hadn't eaten much, either, what with her stomach being clenched all the time. Somehow it didn't help matters that her "new" husband had made no effort to contact her during the past few days. The last time she'd seen him, he'd been snoring in a rumpled Las Vegas hotel bed. She'd caught a commercial flight back east, rather than have to face him again. She'd inflicted the worst sort of pain and humiliation on herself by marrying the man. But it hurt all the more, knowing that Adam hadn't made even one effort to contact her. Never mind that she had made no effort to contact *him*.

David stroked her hair in a comforting manner. "You know you can tell me anything, don't you? Whatever's wrong, I'll understand."

Jen believed that David's understanding was going to be just a little stretched by what she had to tell him. She straightened and did her best to compose herself.

"David, I will tell you about it. But first we have to go out there and rehearse, try to pull this play together somehow."

He didn't look convinced, but he went out on stage with her. They ran through a scene with Angela/Lisa. It went fairly well, although Mary Bess still complained about Jen's interpretation. But then they came back to the scene that was the prelude to seduction between Mark and Eileen. This time Jen managed to remain completely still when David/Mark kissed her.

"Wrong," said Mary Bess, "all wrong. You're supposed to be savoring the damn moment, Hillard. You finally have Mark right where you want him. You're not supposed to stand there like a block of wood. Get the idea?"

They did two more run-throughs. But Jen just couldn't do it. She couldn't respond to David's kiss. Or Mark's kiss, or whoever the heck the kiss belonged to. She didn't know anymore. She just wanted the wretched rehearsal to be over.

At last it was. Jen and David were left alone, but that of course only presented Jen with another difficult situation. How did she tell him? How did she explain something she couldn't possibly understand herself?

They stood on the stage, facing each other, the stifling heat of the footlights upon them. Jen blotted the perspiration from her forehead.

"David . . . I'm sorry . . ."

"Maybe you shouldn't tell me," he said abruptly. "Maybe this is something I don't want to hear."

"I wish I didn't have to say it—"

"No, Jen." He stepped toward her, just as he had when they'd rehearsed their scene. He looked worried and suddenly quite a bit younger than his twenty-six years. "Don't tell me. For just a little while, let things be the way they were before. Just pretend that everything is perfect."

"Oh, David, it never was perfect for us," she said gently. "You know that. I wish it had been, though. I wish somehow it could have worked out."

Every emotion always showed on David's face. It was one of the reasons he was such a good actor: his ability to express the nuances of emotion even without words. And right now what he was feeling was painfully clear to Jen. She saw the hurt she'd inflicted on him.

When he took a step closer and kissed her, Jen didn't pull away. It was a kiss of farewell. She knew it, and surely David did, too—

"Still rehearsing? Or is this the real thing?" came a voice from beyond the footlights. Adam's voice. Jen twisted from David's arms with a gasp as Adam strode to the bottom of the steps leading to the stage. He stopped there. Even though Jen was looking down at him, he seemed the one in command at the moment. Hands in the pockets of his elegant trousers, the sleeves of his shirt rolled halfway up his forearms—effortlessly in command, that was the impression he gave. His face certainly betrayed no emotion beyond amused interest. If the line of his jaw looked a little tense, and if that was storminess she detected in his dark eyes, well, maybe she was just imagining those things.

Jen curled her fingers into her palms. She almost would have preferred Adam to come barging onto the stage, claiming his wife from all usurpers. What would it take to really shatter his control?

She wasn't sure of her own control. Her pulses had quickened from the moment she'd first heard his voice. It took everything she had just to gaze coolly back at him.

"How long have you been here?"

"Long enough," Adam remarked. "And it seems to me you're playing two fields, Jen. Could get a little wearing for you."

Jen flushed. "I'm not playing at anything," she said sharply. "And I was just about to inform David of our...episode in Las Vegas."

"So that's what they call it nowadays. Times have changed since our first go-round."

"Las Vegas," said David. "What's this about Las Vegas?" He glanced from Jen to Adam, then back to Jen. Now his expression was belligerent.

Jen took a deep breath. "David, the fact is...Adam and I got remarried a couple of days ago." There. At last it was out.

David's face registered shock and anger in quick succession. "Married? What the—" He shook his head. "No. This has to be some kind of joke."

Seeing his anger was almost a relief. "Believe me," Jen said, "this isn't something I expected to do. It just...happened."

"That's right," Adam said. "It happened. So now you can leave, Fielding."

David stared at Jen for a long moment as if still hoping it was a joke. She didn't know what to say to him. Maybe there was simply nothing more to be said. At last David turned. He went down the steps, brushed past Adam without looking at him, walked up the aisle of the theater and then disappeared from view.

Jen suddenly felt drained. She sat down on the floor inside the chalked square marked ARMCHAIR. It was only one week away from opening night, and even the sets weren't ready. A sense of unreality engulfed her. What was she thinking? At the moment, the least of her problems was whether or not an imaginary character named Eileen ever got her living room furnished.

Adam climbed the steps onto the stage. Hands still resting casually in his pockets, he walked from one edge of the proscenium arch to the other. He paused to examine the ropes and sandbags heaped together in a jumble. He also examined the tattered canvas drop left over from some long-ago production, and he raised his eyes to inspect the beams and pulleys hanging high above. He seemed to be taking a leisurely tour of the stage—and meanwhile Jen's life was in chaos.

At last Adam sat down beside her. He looked her over as if she were just one more theater prop.

"I suppose it's a good thing I came in when I did," he said. "For being a married woman, things were getting a little cozy up here, weren't they?"

She knew Adam was trying to goad her. Worst of all, he was succeeding. Jen drew up her knees and wrapped her arms around them. "Don't be crass, Adam. I've hurt David rather badly."

"So tell me, Jenny. Why didn't you marry him, instead of me?"

She had other questions on her mind, such as why she couldn't think straight whenever Adam was near her like this. He leaned back on one hand, his manner still casual. Unfortunately there was nothing casual about Jen's reaction to her *new* husband. She gazed at the strong lines of his features and felt a heat that had nothing to do with the glare of the theater lights.

She made an effort to concentrate on the subject of David. "The truth is, if I had any sense... well, I would have chosen him over you."

Adam nodded thoughtfully. "Let's see... You like him because he never shuts up. I seem to remember you saying something to that effect."

"Those weren't exactly the words I used." She tightened her arms around her knees. "Believe it or not, Adam, I enjoyed being with a man who actually knew how to open up to me. A man who wasn't afraid to talk about his emotions or his thoughts. I need that in my life. It's something you can't seem to give to me."

They stared at each other. And this time, at least, Jen knew there was no mistaking the storminess in Adam's eyes. Leaning toward her, he captured her mouth with his. It was an impertinent kiss, seeking and demanding a response. Jen wanted to resist. Dammit, why couldn't she resist?

But already her lips were pliant, accepting. She held her hand against his cheek, needing to touch him any way she could.

It seemed Adam knew just what to do after that. He knew how to tantalize her by brushing his lips against the corner of her mouth, then deepening the kiss all over again. A sensual game of retreat, advance, retreat again, until he compelled Jen to make her own urgent claims. Now she was the seeker, the one who demanded a response. He complied willingly, but still he tantalized and enticed. Still he commanded her senses.

When at last they broke apart, Jen was breathing raggedly, the stage lights seeming to burn into her. Adam's eyes were so dark they were almost black.

"Jenny," he said huskily, his own breathing uneven. "Jenny..."

She was trembling. And she could no longer deny the truth. No one else could make her feel this way. Not David, not anyone.

Because she loved Adam. She loved him completely, hopelessly. She'd tried to build a new life without him, but it hadn't worked. She could never escape her love for him.

And so she'd married him again. It hadn't been the champagne. It hadn't been just a wild impulse. She'd known, deep down, that she had no other choice but to belong to him.

The knowledge brought with it a terrible pain. Because Adam Prescott, her husband, could never truly love her in return.

JEN'S SNEAKERS made no sound on the polished oak floor. For a second or two she felt like a burglar who'd broken into this luxurious apartment. But she held the key to the apartment firmly in her hand. She had a right to be here.

She did a circuit of the spacious living room one more time. The hand-painted Chinese wallpaper was patterned in a graceful design of flowering branches. All the moldings were carved in an elaborate Baroque style, and the creamy marble pillars flanking the doorways were exquisitely veined. Because there was no furniture, the room was revealed in all its stately beauty.

Jen went to the window and gazed out over Central Park where the treetops were clustered in a vivid cushion of green. This was the Upper West Side, where everything about life was cushioned. And this was where Adam now expected her to live.

She perched on the window seat and turned the key over and over in her hand. Adam amazed her. Not long ago, he'd actually agreed with her when she'd declared that her mother and Phillip needed to start their marriage on neutral territory. But now, on his own, he'd chosen this apartment in Manhattan, deciding that he and Jen would live here. When they weren't spending time at his brownstone in Boston, of course.

Jen squeezed her fingers around the key. It was happening all over again. It had been less than a week since that ill-fated trip to Las Vegas, but already Adam had begun to take charge of her life and bend it to fit his own. This luxurious apartment was only one indication.

With an effort, Jen forced herself to relax. She set the key down beside her, then leaned her forehead against the cool glass of the window. Unbidden, the events of last night came back to her.

Adam had shown up at her shabby little apartment without notice. At first she'd been happy to see him. She'd shared her simple dinner with him: canned vegetable soup, bagels she'd brought home from the deli, a pint of cherry-cheesecake frozen yogurt. In a way, sharing that meal so unexpectedly had been romantic. And then... well, then she'd made love with her husband. She'd given herself up to the magic of his embrace. The magic hadn't faded until afterward, when they'd lain spent together in her bed, and once again Adam had seemed to gaze right past her.

Now Jen pushed herself off the window seat. She could no longer bear to sit still. She paced through the rest of the elegant apartment. The master bedroom was quite grand, with its Palladian windows and its balcony overlooking the park. This, of course, was where Adam expected her to sleep with him. He'd no doubt choose a king-size bed, where they wouldn't even have to touch after making love.

She folded her arms against her body as if that would somehow contain her ache of need and longing. Try as she might, she couldn't forget how it had been to wake up in her own small bed early this morning, only to find that Adam had already gone. He'd left something on her bureau, however—a folded slip of paper with a terse message about the new "home" he'd acquired. Inside the slip of paper had been the key to this apartment. Why not just leave money on her bureau the way he had the first time? Payment for services rendered.

Jen couldn't stay here any longer. Beautiful as this apartment was, she detested it. It was too grand, too spacious, too elegant. She hurried toward the door.

However, she made the mistake of glancing into one more room. This one was clearly a nursery. A quaint border of fairy-tale figures had been painted along the walls: a pensive princess, a plump dragon, a knight on horseback.

Did Adam expect this room to become *their* nursery? But Jen already knew the answer to that question. He wanted children. He wanted someone who could carry on the Prescott tradition, the Prescott name. No doubt he still believed that Jen would be a suitable mother to his future children. She was, after all, a Hillard. She had all the proper credentials of heritage and background. Once again, it appeared that she and Adam had formed a family alliance. Nothing more, nothing less.

"No," Jen whispered, her throat tight. She turned away from the room and its impossibly naive fairy tales. "No, Adam..."

He wasn't here to listen. But when had he ever listened?

This time she walked straight to the front door of the apartment. She didn't even stop to pick up the key she'd left on the window seat. She just got out as quickly as she could.

CHAPTER NINETEEN

"I'M IN PARIS! Jenna, dear, can you believe it?"

"Paris," Jen echoed groggily, squinting at the clock by her bed. It was four o'clock in the morning New York time. She sank back against the pillow, cradling the phone against her ear. "Mother, I hate to ask this, but what on earth are you doing in Paris? You're supposed to be honeymooning in California."

"Well, that's just the thing. There we were, walking along the beach in Carmel when Phillip asked me what I thought was the most romantic city in the world. Naturally I said Paris—and the next thing I knew, Phillip whirled me off to France. Isn't that incredible?"

"Actually it is."

"Phillip won't stop being romantic, Jenna. It's the most amazing thing. He's taken the ball and run with it. I never know quite where I'm going to end up." Beth sounded a little frazzled.

"Mother...are you all right?" Jen asked. She finally had her eyes completely open. Beth's phone call had woken her from the first good night's sleep she'd had in a while.

"Of course I'm all right. I'm in Paris, aren't I? With Phillip. What more could I want?" Beth did seem on edge.

"Be sure to get some rest," Jen said, stifling a yawn. "There's only so much romance you can take at one time."

For a moment the line went quiet, filled with nothing but transatlantic static. But then Beth spoke again, her voice muffled, as if she was cupping the receiver to avoid being overheard.

"Well, that's just it. All these grand gestures can be a little exhausting. Poor Phillip—he has a dreadful case of jet lag. He's not accustomed to all this travel. Before, his idea of a trip was to go down to the garden center to check out the latest shipment of cucumber seed."

Jen smiled. "Still . . . Paris *is* the most romantic city in the world."

"In other words," Beth said tartly, "I shouldn't complain when I get what I ask for."

Jen's sheet was tangled around her legs. She tried futilely to straighten it. "The problem with the Hillard women is that we want perfection. Romance in just the right dose. Not too much, not too little."

"Speaking of which, dear, how are you and Adam getting along?"

Jen tensed. Her mother had made quite a leap just now. "I don't see what Adam has to do with anything."

"Stop hedging, Jenna. I saw how well the two of you were getting along at the wedding. Why not admit it?" It really seemed to perk Beth up, talking about someone's romance besides her own. But Beth didn't know the half of it. She didn't know what had happened after she and Phillip had left on their honeymoon.

Jen sat up in bed, rubbing her hair. What was the use of trying to hide the truth? Beth would learn about it sooner or later. Might as well be now.

"Mother...I suppose there's something I should tell you. While we were in Las Vegas, Adam and I...well, we happened to, um...visit the wedding chapel ourselves. On the spur of the moment, so to speak." Jen winced just at having to say the words out loud. Now there was more static on the line.

"Jenna," Beth said, sounding doubtful, "are you telling me what I think you're telling me?"

Jen grimaced. "I'm certainly not going to spell it out for you any further."

"Married...goodness. Put Adam on." Beth sounded shocked—Jen had expected exaltation.

Jen hesitated, staring at the empty pillow next to hers. "Mother, most of us on this side of the ocean are still asleep. At least, we'd like to be asleep. Besides," she added in an acid tone, "Adam isn't here."

"I thought something was amiss. Jenna, where on earth is he?"

Jen wished she'd never started this. She should have known better. Even from Paris, Beth knew how to cause a stir.

"He's probably at home, Mother. His own home—in Boston. And if he has any sense, *he's* asleep."

"At home? His home? What kind of marriage is this?" Beth demanded. "Why, it's not right, Jenna. Not right at all."

"Tell me about it," Jen said more bleakly than she'd intended.

"Dear me," Beth muttered. "It really isn't right. Something has to be done. Something, indeed...Good-bye, Jenna."

"Mother, wait—"

But Beth had already hung up. The telephone line buzzed uselessly.

Jen plunked the receiver back into place. She was wide-awake now. She slipped out of bed and padded into the living room, almost tripping over one of the bicycles there.

"Ouch." She switched on the light and sat down on the couch to examine her stubbed toe. She'd finally disposed of all the dead flowers in that wire basket, but both bicycles remained, taking up most of the space in the room.

Jen gazed at them for a long time. The one with the wire basket was a pretty shade of lavender. The other bike, somewhat larger, was slate black. It looked powerful and dynamic next to its more delicate companion.

Suddenly a wave of hopelessness washed over her. She pressed her hands against her eyes and slumped back against the couch.

Her mother had asked the right question—the only question that mattered.

Just what sort of marriage was this?

THE REFRIGERATOR was ringing. Why the hell was the refrigerator ringing? Adam opened the refrigerator door and searched the shelves for a can of tuna. Only there was no tuna. None at all. This lack of tuna seemed to annoy the two yellow eyes peering over Adam's shoulder. No tuna...annoyed eyes...and still the damn refrigerator just went on ringing and ringing...

Adam jerked upright in bed, sending the kitten tumbling with a wild "Yeoow!" It took him a moment to realize that the entire tuna incident was a dream—just a damn dream. The disapproving eyes, however, seemed real enough—evidently the kitten had been sleeping on Adam's stomach again and didn't appreciate such a rude awakening. And the ringing was quite real. It was the telephone.

Adam groped for the bedside lamp with one hand and picked up the cat with the other. He dumped the cat on the floor, scowling at the clock as he grabbed the receiver.

"This'd better be good," he said.

"Adam, thank goodness you're there!" Beth Hillard Rhodes exclaimed into his ear.

"I don't know where else I'd be at four-fifteen in the morning," he grumbled. "Beth, is everything all right? You're supposed to be on your honeymoon."

"Isn't that where *you* should be?" she asked. "On your honeymoon?"

He opened his eyes more fully. The kitten had jumped back onto the bed and was sneaking along the blanket. "So... you heard."

"Paris is a beautiful city for a honeymoon, Adam. Have you considered Paris?"

He rubbed his face. "Beth, it's a little more complicated than that."

"Why aren't you with her, Adam?"

That was the question of the year, but he didn't know the answer. Where Jenny was concerned, there were no answers, only questions.

"It's a long story," he began.

"I'm not in the mood for stories," Beth said sternly. "I just want you to go to her, Adam. Go to her, and for once give her what she needs."

The kitten had crouched low now, slinking along as if it thought it could pull a fast one on Adam. He frowned at it. "Maybe we could discuss this some other—"

"She needs romance," Beth went on inexorably. "Not too much, not too little. Just the right amount."

"You make it sound like some kind of damn recipe."

"Just go to her, Adam. Don't let her get away from you this time around." With that, Beth hung up, allowing him no chance for rebuttal.

Adam replaced the receiver. He bunched up his pillow and tried unsuccessfully to get comfortable. By now the kitten had climbed onto his stomach again. It didn't seem to have any trouble finding a comfortable spot.

"Don't get too many ideas," Adam warned it. The cat didn't pay any attention; it just started to purr.

Adam switched off the light and lay there in the dark with the cat on his stomach. According to his ex-mother-in-law—correction, his *new* mother-in-law—the solution was simple. Give Jen some romance, in proper proportions, and that would do the trick.

Somehow he didn't think it was that simple. He and Jen weren't agreeing on much of anything right now. He'd found a decent place for them to live in Manhattan; she didn't like it. He wanted her to quit her lousy job; she refused. That was just for starters. Jen kept saying he had to "open up." But somehow that just made him want to clam up. Did she actually need someone who ran off at the mouth? Someone like David Fielding?

That was another thing. It bothered the hell out of him that Jenny was still rehearsing that play with Fielding. Apparently she saw him every day. And apparently she was supposed to get pretty friendly with him on stage. Adam didn't want her getting friendly with the guy—on stage or off.

He turned over, punching his pillow again. "Yeow," protested the cat, tumbling off Adam's stomach. In spite of everything, a pervasive sense of loneliness settled over Adam . . . a loneliness for Jenny.

He just wished it was that simple.

JEN DRAGGED HERSELF into the deli. She hadn't been able to go back to sleep after that call from her mother. She felt tired and depressed, the day seeming to stretch out gloomily before her. Eight hours of work, then another rehearsal where David, in all his wounded dignity, would do his best to make her feel even guiltier....

Right now she'd have liked to return to her apartment and crawl back into bed. However, the prelunch rush would be starting all too soon, and Jen put some corned beef on rye.

Suzanne came striding into the work area. She gave Jen a quick nod, pulled on an apron and began assembling the ingredients for Gil's famous cheese blintzes. Jen herself was not yet allowed to do blintzes, but she watched Suzanne start mixing the batter. There was something different about Suzanne today. She had a resolute expression on her face, but that wasn't all. The ponytail was back. No more carefully styled hair—just that no-nonsense, matter-of-fact ponytail.

"Suzanne," Jen said, "want to talk about it?"

Suzanne worked a spatula around the large mixing bowl. "There's not really anything to talk about."

"I think there is," Jen said quickly.

Suzanne let go of the spatula as if she'd suddenly lost her energy. She looked unhappy, but very calm. Maybe too calm. "I broke it off," she said. "I ended it with Toby. It didn't feel right anymore—perhaps it never did. So I ended it."

"I'm sorry," Jen murmured.

Suzanne's face tightened for a moment. "All I know is that it's over."

Jen wished she could say something comforting to her friend. But she had a feeling it would take Suzanne some time to get over this.

"You had the courage to end it," Jen said at last. "Give yourself some credit for that."

Suzanne shook her head. "It was just a choice—a choice I had to make." She closed her eyes for a few seconds, then opened them again. "I only have one thing left to do—stop loving him."

"Yes . . . I know." Jen had learned too well how tenacious love could be, and how unreasonable.

"Adam?" Suzanne asked gently.

Jen nodded. "Adam."

"Want to talk about it?"

Jen attempted a light tone, but she wasn't successful. "I think you covered all the territory," she said. "I love him. It hurts."

"What a pair we are." Suzanne actually managed a wavery smile. "Me in love with a married man, and you in love with . . ."

"Me in love with a man I marry too often," Jen finished grimly. "Maybe someday I'll see the humor in that, but not now. Definitely not now."

"Think we could make a bigger mess of our lives if we tried?" Suzanne asked, her own voice rueful.

"Not likely. But, Suzanne, there's at least one good thing in all this."

"What's that?"

"Your ponytail's back. And believe me, that counts for a lot."

Russ Billington was wearing a new shirt. In fact, it looked just a little too new, still marked with creases as if he'd taken it straight from the package. First The Suit and now a new shirt. What was going on with the guy?

"Have a seat, Russ," said Adam, leaning back in his chair. Russ just went on standing in the middle of Adam's office, his attitude defensive.

"I don't understand why you want to see me. I haven't made any more mistakes. My work's been fine."

"Relax," said Adam. "And sit down." He waited until Russ finally sat, not that Russ did so with any show of goodwill. He lowered himself into the chair across from Adam's desk, and then sat there with an uncooperative expression on his face.

Adam didn't have much tolerance left for this type of thing. The deadline was fast approaching when they'd be issuing the first edition of the revamped *Standard*. He didn't need more distractions. It was bad enough that he'd gone to Las Vegas last week and ended up with a reluctant wife for the second time around. Jenny seemed to object to every single thing he did. Hell, that apartment on Central Park West was a real find. He'd heard about it through a friend of a friend. Technically it counted as neutral territory; neither he nor Jen had ever lived in the damn place. And it was in New York—Jen's town. So why wouldn't she even consider moving in there? She couldn't keep hanging on to that dive where she lived now—

"You did want to see me," Russ prodded sourly.

Adam made an effort to concentrate on the matter at hand. "It's true your work's been better these past few weeks, Russ. But you still don't have the same drive or enthusiasm you had before. With all the changes going on here, I need everyone to give a hundred percent. Maybe even two hundred percent."

"I'm doing my best," Russ muttered, "under the circumstances."

"What circumstances? Last time you made it sound like Sandra was the problem—"

"She is." Russ's words were barely audible.

"Fine. I'll call her in here and we'll straighten this out." Adam reached for the intercom, but that made Russ jump to his feet.

"No!" He began to pace in great agitation.

"Spit it out, Russ."

"I like her—Sandra, that is. I like her a lot."

Adam stroked his mustache. Somehow this was the last thing he'd expected. "Have you told her how you feel?"

"Of course not," Russ said immediately, as if Adam's question was insane. Not that Adam had any great desire to discuss Sandra at the moment. After what had happened with her that night, right here in his office—Lord, that had been some error in judgment. No doubt Russ would agree if he knew about it.

Russ and Sandra—Adam tried to picture it. Somehow he couldn't. Then again, he was no expert in matters of romance.

"It might not be such a bad idea to clue Sandra in," he said at last. "You could ask her out on a date, that sort of thing."

"She'd turn me down flat," Russ said. "No way can I ask her. No way."

It was obvious that Russ needed a little help in this situation. Make that a *lot* of help. No wonder the guy was still a bachelor.

"Listen," Adam said, "if you don't find out how she feels, you're not going to know any peace. You have to get this out in the open." Adam listened to himself with a sense of unreality. What was he doing now—counseling the lovelorn? Advising someone to open his heart to a woman?

Russ just shook his head in a defeated manner. "I already know how she feels about me. She doesn't like me."

This was as bad as trying to unravel a snarl of yarn. "Has she said she doesn't like you?" Adam asked impatiently.

"She doesn't have to say it. It comes through loud and clear."

Adam tried logic. "Russ, Sandra's always pleasant to you."

"She's that way to everybody."

Adam gave one last try. "You're just imagining she doesn't like you. The only way you'll know for sure is to ask her out. Sometimes you just have to go for it, Russ. And who knows? Maybe the two of you will hit it off."

Russ was starting to look harassed now. "She'll say no," he mumbled. "Of course she'll say no." With that, he left Adam's office. At least this time he didn't bang the door after him.

Still, Adam didn't think he should switch to a career as a matchmaker.

Adam glanced over the advertising figures in the latest printout. It appeared that more than a few accounts were interested in going national with the *Standard.* Good. Adam's personal life might be shot to hell, but at least he had advertisers.

Somehow the thought didn't cheer him up. Finally he punched one of the intercom buttons. "Sandra, mind coming in here?"

She appeared in prompt, businesslike fashion, armored with a notepad. "I was just about to come in, anyway. I need to discuss that new column with you. I've been thinking we should call it something like 'Round about New England,' and each week we'd have vignettes on different parts of the region. We could profile one of the old mill towns, that type of thing. Go for the nostalgia angle, but we'd want to be a little hard-hitting, too. Anyway, tell me what you think."

There was definitely fallout from their encounter on Adam's office sofa. At the moment, Sandra was making every effort not to look at the sofa. She also wouldn't look at him. It had been this way ever since that night.

"Sandra, mind closing the door?"

She stiffened. "Adam, I don't really think—"

"We have to talk about it sooner or later."

She gripped her notepad in both hands. Then, her back held rigidly, she went to the door and swung it shut. Afterward she sat across from Adam's desk, balanced on the very edge of the seat.

"Let's get this over with," she muttered. "I'll start. It was a big mistake, and I think that's all we need to say about it."

Adam didn't like doing this any more than she did. But she was a damn good employee, and somehow he wanted to get things right between them again. Maybe it was impossible, but at least he had to try.

"Is your son back from Cape Cod?" he asked. Start with a neutral topic and work from there. Maybe that was the best tactic.

"Yes," she said tersely. "He's back."

So much for that. Hadn't he learned anything in the journalism business? When you're interviewing someone, never ask a question that can be answered with a simple yes or no. And that was how this felt—like a very difficult interview.

But then Sandra smacked down her notepad. "It's just so humiliating. I've never done anything like that before. Every time I look at you I'm mortified, Adam!"

At least now she was talking about it. That was progress. "I feel the same way," he admitted. "But I'd like it to be over and done with. I'd like us to go back to the way things were before."

"That's not going to happen," she said emphatically. "We talked about our personal problems. We went out to eat, just the two of us. We were trying to be friends." She looked pensive. "Maybe we both needed that friendship for a while. But we can't try it again."

She was right about that much. And every time they *had* shared a meal or a conversation, Adam had been wishing she was Jenny. Some friendship.

"Adam," Sandra went on in a careful voice, "I might as well tell you this. I've been thinking about looking for another job. Maybe that's the only solution here."

"I hope not," he said quietly. "You're one of the best people on this paper. I'd hate to lose you."

"You should know I'm thinking about it, though."

Adam wanted to talk her out of it, but it was a decision she had to make for herself. There wasn't really much else to say.

"Listen, the new column—sounds promising. We'll profile a mill town for the first issue. Lowell is a possibility. A lot of good history there."

"Maybe I can take a run up to Lowell this weekend," she said. "Start gathering material. Brian would enjoy the outing with me. And of course I'll take someone along for photographs. Corie's probably the best choice. I'll check it out with her." She stood, businesslike once more. "Anything else, Adam?"

He thought it over. "Actually... I do have a suggestion. Instead of Corie, why not take Russ along this weekend?"

She frowned. "Russ? I need a photographer, not a reporter. I'm going to write this column myself."

"Right, right...but I have a feeling Russ is looking for a new challenge. And you know he can handle a camera."

"Well, yes, but—"

"It might be wise to have two perspectives for the column," Adam said. "Like I say, it's a different kind of piece for Russ. Might be just what he needs."

Sandra seemed to think this over. "Russ..." she murmured speculatively. Then she smiled a little. "I could use the help, what with the work load around here. I'll tell Russ to be ready first thing Saturday morning."

"Fine," Adam said. "Just fine."

CHAPTER TWENTY

JEN WAS PETRIFIED. A mere five minutes from now, she was expected to walk out onto the stage of the Jacob Hollings Playhouse and actually pull off the part of Eileen. No more rehearsals. It was for real this time. Opening night. And so Jen was petrified literally. She stood in the wings, stone still, convinced she wouldn't be able to move at all when the time came. Five minutes to the first act. She wasn't ready!

David appeared beside her. "So far not much of an audience," he said lugubriously. "I was afraid of this. The play could sink before it's even begun."

"Somehow I don't find that reassuring," Jen muttered.

He surveyed her with an aggrieved expression. "It could have been so different," he said. "You could have been with me, Jen, not your ex-husband. Then we wouldn't give a damn what happened to the play. We'd have each other."

"David . . . please don't do this. Not here. Not now."

"I can't help it," he said. "Every time I look at you, it takes me back. I think about the time I kissed you on the ferry. Or the time I kissed you in that antique store. Or the time—"

"David, stop." Jen's palms were sweating. Her throat was dry. She felt light-headed. What if she forgot her lines or lost her voice? What if she fainted?

"I can tell I'm getting on your nerves," David said. "But I can't stop. I don't know how I'm going to walk out on that stage and pretend you're someone named Eileen. I've been an actor for a long time, Jen, but I think this one's beyond me."

"David," Jen whispered fiercely, "I know you want me to realize just how miserable I've made you. Believe me, the message is getting through. But for right now . . . zip it!"

David looked injured all over again. He was perfecting that look by the hour. Jen didn't know how much more of it she could take. How were they ever going to carry off this play?

Unfortunately there was no time left to worry about it. The tattered velvet curtains of the Hollings Playhouse rose and the lights sprang to life. Angela was already on stage, lounging in an armchair, feet dangling over the side. It was actually a real armchair, not just a chalked square marked on the floor. Somehow all the props had ended up ready on time, after all.

Angela/Lisa looked perfectly comfortable on stage, lolling as she glanced about the set. With just a few subtle techniques, she portrayed all the necessary nuances of emotion. Her smile was that of someone secretly satisfied with herself; her leisurely posture conveyed the inner confidence that was so much a part of Lisa's character. Angela was a damn good actress. Far better, it seemed, than Jen could ever hope to be. This thought didn't do wonders for Jen's confidence, which was already as tattered as the theater curtains.

Angela/Lisa lazily changed position, stretching a little. Jen's cue! And it was just as she'd feared. She was frozen. She couldn't move.

David nudged her forward. "You'll do great," he murmured. "Go out and knock 'em dead, Jen."

She gave him a startled glance; *now* he'd decided to be encouraging? But his words seemed to do the job. At least she was walking out on stage, placing one foot in front of the other.

She couldn't see the audience beyond the footlights. It didn't matter, though; just knowing people were out there was enough to send a jolt of fear through her all over again. Was Adam part of the audience? He knew this was her big night, of course, but had he come? Wondering about it caused her as much apprehension as anything. But she was supposed to deliver her opening line. Why wouldn't her mouth open?

Angela/Lisa gazed at her expectantly. Jen still couldn't get the words out. She knew what she was supposed to say, but she seemed to have forgotten the mechanics of speech. This was dreadful. It was terrible. She was going to disgrace herself entirely—

Angela/Lisa did something quite unexpected then. She gave Jen a friendly wink. It was the first time she'd evinced even a hint of camaraderie. But that was what this was all about, wasn't it? In spite of the wretched rehearsals, the arguments, the misunderstandings—Jen and David and Angela were in this play together. They could make it work, the three of them. Jen wasn't alone. Suddenly she found her voice.

"'Lisa,'" she said, "'shouldn't you be doing something?'"

"'Something like what, Aunt Eileen?'"

"'Anything. You can't just sit around all day—'"

"'Mark will be here soon. Then I'll be doing something, won't I?'"

Things weren't going too badly. Maybe they were even going okay. Jen started to loosen up a little. She just had to stop taking everything so seriously. So maybe she wasn't going to stun anybody with her acting ability tonight—she could live with that. As long as she really didn't forget her lines, and as long as she gave at least a hint of Eileen's character. No matter what, she *knew* Eileen—a woman on the far end of middle age, an intense, passionate woman doing everything she could to combat her own loneliness—welcoming her niece into her home, loving that niece even as she grew more and more jealous of Lisa's youth and beauty and self-assurance....

David/Mark came onto the stage and the complications began to unfold—aimless Mark caught between self-involved Lisa and self-tormented Eileen. Jen forgot about the audience. She even forgot to wonder if Adam was out there watching her. She just let herself get caught up in the story.

They made it through the first act, then to the middle of the second. Time seemed to race, and Jen could only hope she wasn't rushing her lines. But they were halfway through now. Surely she would make it the rest of the way.

Then came the moment in Act Two when Eileen was supposed to kiss Mark, and Jen found herself faltering. This was *David* she was supposed to kiss, a man who still professed to be in love with her. And if Adam did happen to be watching... She couldn't possibly pull it off. She couldn't pretend any longer that she was Eileen.

She had that awful sensation again, the one that had plagued her through so many rehearsals. It was as if she were watching the character of Eileen recede farther and farther from her, almost about to vanish. And Jen couldn't catch up, couldn't grasp Eileen ...

David/Mark stepped closer. Jen/Eileen walked in front of the mantelpiece. "'No,'" she said. "'This isn't a good idea.'"

David/Mark took another step toward her. "'Yes,'" he said. "'You've been waiting for me to do this.'"

"'I never wait, Mark. Not for anyone. Not for anything.'"

"'Then maybe I'm the one who's been waiting.'" David placed his lips against Jen's. She froze. Oh, dammit, she *knew* Adam was watching. She could feel it. And she was just going to stand here, as stiff and unconvincing as a washboard. She was going to ruin the play, after all.

And then it happened. Somehow Eileen came back to Jen. She knew just what to do, just how to act. She lifted her hands and placed them on David's shoulders, returning his kiss. Except that she didn't think of him as David anymore. He was Mark, her niece's boyfriend. Eileen felt guilty for kissing him, but she was also determined to take her chance with him while she could. The lights faded—end of Act Two.

And now it was the final act. The triangle of Mark and Lisa and Eileen finally disintegrated. In the last scene, Eileen was alone, rejected by her lover, rejected by her niece.

The set was empty except for Jen/Eileen. She sank into the armchair, facing stage right, and gazed off into the distance. "'I don't need either one of them. I don't need them at all.'" She bowed her head, the lights faded, and the curtains came creaking down.

Applause sounded from the audience. It wasn't overwhelming, but still, it was applause. Jen, Angela and David did a curtain call—more applause, growing a bit in enthusiasm. And then Angela, undeniably the star of the show, took a curtain call on her own. Now the applause really got enthusiastic, with a "Bravo!" or two thrown in for good measure. And that was fine with Jen. All she knew was that she'd made it through the play.

A happy and triumphant Angela actually gave Jen a hug. Then Angela gave David a hug. And then David gave Jen a hug.

"You did it," he said. "You were really good. And I'm not just telling you that because I'm in love with you."

"David..."

"I know. You're a married woman now. And you want me to zip it." He released her, giving her a sorrowful smile. David really did have a melodramatic streak. He was also endearing, in spite of those melodramatic tendencies. Jen felt a stirring of regret. Why couldn't she have fallen in love with David? It would have been so convenient. So safe.

Mary Bess came across the stage. She looked as world-weary as ever, her dyed red hair pushed back haphazardly from her face. She surveyed Angela, David and Jen.

"None of you embarrassed me completely," she said grudgingly at last. "But you, Hillard...you just had to play the part your way, didn't you?"

Jen gazed back steadily at Mary Bess. "Believe it or not, I tried to play it both our ways."

"Hmph." It wasn't exactly approval from Mary Bess, but it wasn't disapproval, either.

Jen retreated to her dressing room after that, but she was not to be alone. The uncles had traveled all the way from Newport for her opening night, and now they converged on her.

"Congratulations, my dear," said Uncle Thomas. "I knew you would be a star someday."

"Tom, I believe I am the one who has always encouraged Jenna in her artistic endeavors," said Uncle William.

"You, Will? You never even knew our Jenna wanted to be an actress."

"I am speaking of artistic endeavors in general."

"If it'd had been up to you, Jenna would have stayed in Newport forever and never made a success of herself," Uncle Thomas pointed out, a troublemaker's gleam in his eye.

"I want her to come home where she belongs, but I am still very proud of her," Uncle William said in a starchy voice.

Jen hugged each of them in turn. "If the two of you will stop arguing long enough, I'll tell you how much it means to me that you're here." She truly was delighted to see her troublesome, snowy-haired uncles. They were her family, and the occasion wouldn't have been the same without them. She finally understood that family would always be important to her. Living away from Newport this past year had taught her at least that much.

But even as Jen spoke to her uncles, she couldn't help looking past them to the door of the dressing room. She kept hoping and fearing that Adam would show. Had he come to the play at all? Maybe it would be better if he hadn't....

The person who next appeared at the door, however, was none other than Beth Marie Hillard Rhodes, beaming on the arm of Phillip Henry Rhodes, her new husband.

"Mother!" Jen exclaimed in surprise. "I thought you were in Paris. What on earth...?"

Beth gave her a rose-scented embrace. "I couldn't very well stay in France when you were having your debut, could I? You were wonderful, by the way, dear. Not that I would have expected any less. You're my daughter, after all."

"Thanks, Mother," Jen said wryly. It occurred to her that perhaps she had inherited any acting talent she had from her mother—the consummate manipulator of emotions.

"Besides," Beth went on importantly, "I couldn't possibly stay in Paris when it's so clear you need my help with Adam."

Speaking of manipulation...

Jen struggled with the mixture of fondness and annoyance that Beth always seemed to provoke in her. "I think Adam and I will just have to work out our problems on our own, Mother."

"Nonsense—"

Beth was prevented from saying more because Phillip stepped up to congratulate Jen himself.

"You did an excellent job tonight. You should be proud of yourself," he said solemnly. Then he lowered his voice. "I can possibly arrange to fly your mother to Rome for a few weeks. I understand that's a romantic city, too—"

"I can hear you," Beth said imperturbably. "Phillip, it's no use. I shall meddle in my daughter's life no matter where you whisk me off to." Now Beth was the one who lowered her voice confidentially as she leaned toward Jen. "I believe I have finally convinced Phillip that we can be just as romantic at home as abroad. We can go for strolls together, watch old movies, that sort of thing. Small-scale romance, so to speak. Of course, we will be quite busy in the next few months, refurbishing the Prescott home. Adam has decided to sell to us—but of course you knew that."

Jen hadn't known. Adam hadn't shared that rather important piece of information with her. There was so much he didn't share.

"Well, we must all get out of here and leave Jenna a few moments of peace," Beth said, looking rather mysterious. "Come along, Uncle William, Uncle Thomas. You both need to sit down."

"I'm hardly an invalid," grumbled Uncle William. "You don't need to mollycoddle me, Beth."

"Speak for yourself, Will," said Uncle Thomas. "I like to be mollycoddled. Mollycoddle away."

"Tom, if you are trying to be snide about my choice of words..."

The small, shabby dressing room seemed oddly lonely when everyone had finally exited. Adam hadn't shown, of course. Jen had refused to ask her family whether or not he'd even come. She'd refused to put herself through the humiliation of asking.

She sat down in front of the makeup table, melancholy dampening her excitement about the play. It was only now that she noticed flowers had been delivered sometime during the evening. A crystal vase stood on the table before her, filled with a lovely cascade of yellow, pink and lavender blooms. Jen stared at the flowers, not quite daring to hope. Had Adam sent them? She snatched the card lying nestled in the arrangement and scanned it eagerly.

"My love endures, though you belong to another," read the card. "Darling Jen, to your happiness always. D."

Jen crumpled the card. Why did David have to keep behaving in this extravagant manner? Very well, she knew she'd hurt him, but he was turning himself into a martyr.

That wasn't what really disturbed Jen, though. She couldn't believe that once again she'd longed for something to be from Adam—only to find out that it was from David, instead. When would she stop hoping for all the things Adam couldn't give?

"Hello, Jenny."

She twisted around and saw him standing in the doorway. Adam, looking very elegant and commanding in a herringbone suit. Her heartbeat quickened absurdly. She placed a hand to her throat as if that would somehow restrain her wayward pulse.

"Let me guess," she said as coolly as possible. "My mother sent you back here."

He came into the room. "Beth likes to think she's orchestrating the world, but I'm actually here of my own volition."

"Well," she said stiffly, "did you enjoy the play?"

He didn't answer for some moments. He just gazed at her, his expression unreadable. What secrets did he really hide behind his dark eyes and obdurate features? Would he ever allow Jen to know?

"I thought you were sufficiently convincing in the role," he said at last. Trust Adam not to overstate the case. She didn't have to worry about flattery where he was concerned.

"Thank you, I suppose."

"You were particularly convincing in the scene where you kissed Fielding."

"You're not going to start that again, are you? I'm playing a part. What happened between David and me is finished. If you can't realize that, then you don't know me very well at all. I've always been faithful to you. That hasn't changed, even though what we have can hardly be called a marriage." Her tone was more bitter than she'd intended. She twisted around again to face the pocked mirror. Taking a tissue, she began the process of wiping off her stage makeup. She needed a task to keep herself occupied, anything to prevent her from showing Adam how much he affected her. How much she cared...

He came to the table and picked up the crumpled card she'd thrown down. He read it.

"Fielding just won't give up."

Jen felt compelled to defend David. "He's just being...theatrical."

"He's being a jerk," Adam stated flatly.

For reasons she couldn't quite explain, anger stirred inside her.

"At least David isn't afraid to admit he feels things. And if he gets carried away with what he feels...well, at least he feels deeply enough to *get* carried away!"

"As opposed to me, of course," Adam said. "You believe I never get carried away."

"I don't just believe it—I know it." That melancholy settled deeper inside Jen. She knew Adam's passion only when he held her in his arms and took her to bed. Why couldn't he give her the deeper passion she craved?

He studied the vase with its arrangement of yellow, pink and lavender blooms. "I wanted to send you flowers of my own tonight," he said gruffly. "But I couldn't do it. I damn well couldn't celebrate you and Fielding up there on the stage—"

"Adam, David isn't the problem between us. When will you realize that?" Jen gave up the pretense of trying to keep busy. She pushed away the box of tissues and gazed at her reflection in the mirror. Her face was still streaked with makeup here and there, and she looked strangely mournful.

Adam pulled over a chair and sat down next to her. "Somehow I think Fielding *is* the problem," he said. "I think, no matter what you say, that you keep comparing me to him. You've set him up as some cockeyed standard."

Jen felt that ache inside her, the one that had been with her for such a long time now. It had everything to do with Adam—nothing to do with David. But how could she make him understand?

"Adam," she said carefully, "David isn't the man I want. I tried to make him be the one . . . but it just didn't work."

"I'm not the man you want, either . . . am I, Jenny?"

The ache inside her seemed to constrict her heart. All she longed to do right now was go into Adam's arms and tell him yes—yes, of course he was the man she wanted. The only man she wanted! But then everything would be the same as it had always been. Adam leading, while she followed. Her life revolving around his, her love for him growing all the more, while he refused to love her in return.

Jen turned away from him. She turned away from the mirror, too, so that he wouldn't be able to see the yearning betrayed in her reflection. Did he understand what her silence meant? She couldn't know. She clenched her hands tightly in her lap and kept her face averted.

He shifted restlessly. "What will it take to make this marriage work?" he asked, sounding almost impatient. "We can't afford another failure, Jen."

She wondered if he saw it only in those terms—failure or success. Didn't he view his newspaper in much the same way? Something that could be measured through cost analysis—a certain amount of expenditures, a certain amount of profits. No doubt that was how Adam analyzed their marriage. Did the benefits outweigh the costs...

Jen still refused to look at him. She knew she couldn't gaze into his eyes and still have the courage for what she needed to say.

"I can't go back," she said in a low voice. "I can't let our marriage be what it was. You have to offer me more, Adam. You have to decide you're really going to share a life with me. You have to give me as much as I'm willing to give you. Most of all, you have to let me into your heart. I can't accept anything less."

Adam was silent for a while, but then, "You make it sound like an ultimatum."

How coldly he could speak, allowing no emotion to surface in his voice. Well, she had to be cold now, too. She had to be strong.

"It is an ultimatum. No compromises this time, no half measures."

She clenched her hands even more tightly, waiting for his answer. This was his chance to give her what she required—maybe his last chance. But would he take it? *Please,* she prayed silently. *Please, Adam, be who I need...*

His answer came. No words were necessary. He simply stood, remained very still for a moment, and then he walked from the dressing room. He closed the door after him, the only sound the slight click of the latch.

Jen was left alone—just as Eileen had been alone at the end of the play. But this time the emotions Jen felt didn't belong to an imaginary character.

This time her heart was truly breaking.

ADAM DUMPED a load of carpet remnants on his living-room floor. Apparently the cat thought this was a new game, and it pounced on a scrap of blue shag. Adam picked up another scrap of rug and tried wrapping it around a stem of the bizarre wooden tree he'd built.

"Some scratching post," he muttered. "Who the hell ever said I could be a carpenter?"

The cat paid no mind and now attacked a piece of chenille carpet. Adam crossed the hall and pulled a light beer out of the refrigerator. The kitten scampered at his heels. Opening a can of tuna, Adam forked half of it into a bowl and tossed the rest into the fridge. Then he sat down at the kitchen table and popped open his beer.

"I don't care what she says," he told the kitten. "This has something to do with Fielding." Adam had finally given in to these one-sided chats with the cat—especially since he'd gone to see Jenny in that play. Bring out the tuna, and he automatically had a captive audience.

"Anyway," he went on, "she probably does have a thing for that guy. I'd like to knock his head off." Adam's voice sounded hollow to his own ears. This past day or two, he'd been doing his best to ignore the truth, but it still haunted him. Jen had a lot of complaints about him. Maybe they were tied up with the way she felt about Fielding. Maybe not. But the fact remained she wasn't happy with Adam.

The kitten licked its bowl in a fastidious manner, then attacked Adam's socks until he scooped it up onto the table. Then it batted a paw at Adam's beer can.

"I'm a damn fool," Adam said. "Jenny needs something from me, and I don't know how to give it to her. I don't know how to be what she wants. Can you figure that one out?"

The kitten rolled over and stuck all four paws in the air. Adam scratched its stomach. He felt lousy. Without

Jenny, that was just how he felt. But there was something else, and he finally had to admit it.

What if he tried to give Jenny what she wanted and it wasn't enough? What if, no matter what he did, he couldn't be the man she needed?

"So I'm a damn fool," he reminded the cat. "And I'm also scared as hell."

CHAPTER TWENTY-ONE

SOMEONE WAS RAPPING on Jen's door. She pulled the pillow over her head, determined to ignore it. She was exhausted. Last night was the fourth night in a row she'd performed the role of Eileen. Staying in character, building the emotions necessary throughout the play, required far more from her than she ever could have imagined. Today, thank goodness, was her day off from the deli. She needed to sleep. She did *not* need to answer that obnoxious banging at her door.

Whoever it was wouldn't let up. A knock would come, then a pause, then another knock. It was almost getting into a sort of rhythm.

Muttering invective, Jen finally crawled out of bed. She pulled her robe over her baggy T-shirt and stalked into the living room.

"Who is it?" she called grumpily.

"Special delivery," came a very identifiable voice from the other side of the door. The voice of Adam Prescott—her husband.

Jen froze. She couldn't possibly let him in. If she did, she'd lose the little equanimity she'd been able to achieve these past few days. It would be the worst thing she could do for herself.

"Jenny, I need to talk to you."

"Why?" she demanded. "Why now?"

"Why not now?" he countered.

Jen hesitated. Adam was so close, just on the other side of the door. But physical proximity wasn't what she needed from him. If she was smart, she'd leave all the bolts firmly in place. She'd go back to her solitary bed and hide under the pillow again.

"Jenny," he murmured.

Why did he have to say her name like that, his voice lingering on each syllable with just a trace of huskiness...

She undid the bolts and opened the door a crack. She peered out.

Adam stood there, gazing back at her. His expression was intense, his dark hair a little rumpled as if he'd been running his hands through it. She felt herself go weak inside with the longing to touch him. A tingling went through her, as if only near him did she truly come to life. It wasn't fair, his coming here like this, disrupting her once more. She clutched her robe around her, wishing desperately she could just shut the door again.

"What do you want, Adam? What's this all about?"

"You'd better let me in. I have something to tell you, Jenny," he said with determination. "Make that a lot of things."

She hesitated another moment and then reluctantly pulled the door open wider. That was all the invitation Adam needed. He came into her apartment, walked around the bicycles and sat down on her couch. He still looked very intense.

"Have a seat," he said. Only Adam could barge in here and tell her to have a seat as if he owned the place. He fished in the back pocket of his pants and brought out a rather creased slip of paper. He opened it and glanced over it with a frown. "I have a lot to say," he repeated. "Number one—"

"You brought a list?" she asked in disbelief.

Now he looked disgruntled. "Yes, I have a list. It's not every day I go spouting off at the mouth, and I thought I could use a little help. Sort of a cheat sheet. Is that so bad?"

Jen was confused, battling any number of stubborn hopes. At last she went to perch on the far end of the couch. "I suppose I'm ready," she said. "I can't help being curious about all this."

He rattled his list, then studied it for a long moment. "Hell," he said, sounding disgusted. "It isn't going to work. I'm no good at this, Jenny. I came here so I could do what you're always asking. I came here to open up. I just don't know how to go about it."

Those stubborn hopes of hers were growing stronger. "Maybe I could help," she said. "Maybe you could show me the list, and we could go from there."

"Maybe." He didn't sound convinced, but he handed the sheet of paper to her. She examined it carefully. Adam's writing was aggressive and hard to decipher, a fairly accurate representation of his character. Several words had been crossed out, others jotted in. She examined it a moment longer, then glanced at him.

"There's only one problem," she said. "For the life of me, I've never been able to read your handwriting. Maybe if you could just . . . start at the beginning."

He balanced his elbows on his knees and gazed broodingly at the floor. He seemed to be thinking things over.

"The beginning . . ." he echoed. "I don't know where that is. Lord, Jenny, all I can think about right now is the year I turned seventeen. So long ago... It should be done with. It should be finished. I was just a boy... but I'm forty now. A different person. Hell, at least I should be different."

Jen listened. She heard the pain in his voice—the pain he was struggling so hard to stifle. Just as he was clearly trying to stifle the seventeen-year-old boy he'd once been.

She wanted to reach out to him. But some instinct warned her not to speak, just to listen.

"I was seventeen," he said, his voice very low. "Everything changed that year. My mother was diagnosed with cancer. That only made the problems between my parents worse. They didn't know how to face her illness, how to pull together against it. My father started spending more and more time away from home, flying in that old seaplane he loved. He was trying to escape, I suppose, just like I'd always tried to escape that house. Then his plane crashed."

Jen had only been nine at the time of Alexander Prescott's death, but she could still remember standing on the front lawn early one morning with her parents and her great-uncles, all of them shocked because they'd just learned the news: Adam's father had crashed in his plane, dying instantly.

Adam stood up abruptly. He glanced toward the door as if he wanted more than anything to leave. Jen had to force herself to stay seated where she was, letting Adam decide what he would do.

"Jenny," he said, his voice very heavy now, "I felt so damn guilty. There'd been times I'd wished both of my parents would go away, disappear somehow, then my mother became ill and my father died. I kept thinking that if I'd just done something differently, he'd still be alive. She wouldn't be sick."

Adam's features tensed, as if he were still struggling to keep all the pain inside. "My mother would be lying there in the house—in her sick room—and she'd call for me. She'd send the nurse away, and call for me, instead. Of course I went to her—I always went. How could I not? She was my mother. She was sick. She was dying. I remember the smell of that room. Lord, Jenny...all the cleaning, all the disinfecting in the world, couldn't hide that smell—the smell of sickness, of dying. As if her soul were decaying right there before me. Her soul, not just her body."

Adam sat down again. He stared straight ahead, and when he spoke his voice was now carefully devoid of all emotion. "She wanted me to be there beside her. She wanted me to tell her about all the good times, all the wonderful times we'd had as a family. Happy memories, that was what she wanted to hear. I tried. God, I tried. But there were no happy memories. So my mother let me know the good times had happened before I came along. She told me that she and my father had been very happy—but only before me. I can still hear her voice. Plaintive. Angry. Asking me why I'd come between them. Why I'd made them hate each other. Over and over, she asked me that, demanding an answer. What answer could I give her? When I couldn't listen anymore, I'd leave. But she'd call for me again. The next day, and the day after. And I'd go to her again. She was my mother. I had to go to her."

Jen felt a chill deep inside. How little she had known of Adam's family. Images of Grace Prescott flashed before her eyes: a frail woman, sinking into her illness. A delicate woman, it had seemed. Yet she had lashed out at her only son, blaming him for her suffering. Perhaps she simply hadn't been strong enough to blame herself. How terrible to be so weak that you would turn on your own child. Adam was right. Grace Prescott had been sick in her soul, far more than in her body.

"Day after day," he said now, his voice still expressionless, "day after day. For a year it was like that. A year until she died. I'd never realized how many days there were in a year—all those days to wonder if it'd been my fault. Wondering if everything bad in my family somehow did revolve around my existence..."

Jen could no longer restrain herself. She went to Adam. She sat close beside him and wrapped her arms around him as tightly as she could. He was motionless for a very long moment. But then he brought his own arms around her, holding her close.

"God, Jenny," he said, his voice thick, "can you imagine what it feels like to be glad when your mother finally dies—relieved that she's finally gone? And then to know more damn guilt because of it."

"It's all right," Jen whispered. "It's okay. You're not to blame for anything that happened." She was trying to comfort the seventeen-year-old boy in Adam, the boy he'd once been. Maybe that was impossible. He was a man now, maturity forged on that long-ago pain. She didn't know how much she could help. But she went on holding him, anyway, and being held in return.

They stayed like that for a very long while, wrapped in each other's arms on the couch in her shabby little apartment. Finally Adam gazed at her. The tenseness in his features was still there.

"I'm sorry, Jenny, for what I put you through. After my mother died...it seemed I'd had enough emotion to last a hundred lifetimes. I guess I had to protect myself somehow. And so I never gave you what you needed. I shut myself off. I'm still shutting myself off."

"No," she said, her own voice trembling. "No, you're not. You're here with me now. You came to me, Adam.

Whatever happens from now on, you came to me. If you could just tell me one more thing—''

"I love you, Jenny. I love you with all my heart. Do you know how much it scares me to say that?''

She closed her eyes and rested her head against his chest. Oh, what a journey it had been. She felt as if she had traveled all her life just to hear him say those words.

"What happened with your parents—it won't happen with us," she said softly. "I promise you that. You can let go with me, Adam. You can trust me.''

He lifted her chin and gazed at her fully. "To think I almost lost you," he said, that huskiness back in his voice. "I've been so damn stubborn, so determined not to let down my guard... It's not going to be easy, learning how after all this time. Will you have patience with me?''

"Yes. Oh, yes, as long as you love me," she said fervently.

"I love you, Jenny. Lord, I always have. I just wouldn't admit it. Can you forgive me for that?'' His eyes were very dark as he continued to gaze at her.

She placed her fingers tenderly against his lips. "No more guilt," she said, "not between the two of us. I love you, Adam. I've loved you all my life. And now I love you even more—''

He captured her lips with his own. It was a kiss of promise, of renewal.

It was a kiss between husband and wife.

EPILOGUE

JEN LAY in her husband's arms, warm and replete. He smoothed the damp tendrils of hair away from her face.

"That was great," he said. "It always is with you, Jenny."

She reached up and teasingly stroked his mustache. "We just happen to be very good in bed together. What can we do about it?"

"Just stay in practice—that's all I can say."

Jen smiled softly. "You never look away anymore."

Now Adam gave her a quizzical glance. "I'm not sure I know what you mean."

But maybe there wasn't really any need for Jen to explain. Somehow, during this past year of their "new" marriage, it had happened naturally. Adam would make love to her, and afterward she would still see all the love in his heart showing in his eyes. Just as she was seeing it now.

Not that revealing his emotions came easily for Adam. He still withdrew from time to time behind the wall he'd found necessary to build in his childhood and beyond. But he and Jen were working on taking down that wall bit by bit. Maybe they would be working at it the rest of their lives. That would be all right, as far as Jen was concerned. She knew that she was safe and cherished in her husband's love, even when he couldn't always express it.

"Yeow."

Jen peered over the edge of the bed at the spoiled, glossy black cat. A pair of yellow eyes stared at her accusingly. "Okay, okay," she grumbled. "I'll feed you, Sidney." But she sat up rather too quickly, and a wave of nausea washed over her. Grimacing, she held her stomach.

"Eat a cracker," Adam advised. "Isn't that what the doctor told you? Lots of crackers."

She smiled at him wryly. "Between you and my mother, this pregnancy is going to be a doozy. I'm getting so much advice I hardly know which way to turn."

Adam placed his hands possessively on her shoulders, kissing the nape of her neck. "As long as you're okay, I think I'll live through the experience."

"People have babies all the time," she began, but then she dropped the front. "I might as well admit it," she said with a sigh. "I'm terrified of the whole thing. In a little more than six months, Adam, you and I are going to be looking into the face of our son..."

"Or daughter," he said, kissing her nape one more time.

"If you keep that up, the cat is never going to get his tuna."

Adam looped his arms gently around her, cradling her against his chest. "I'm nervous, too, love," he murmured. "Think we can make it through together?"

"Yes. I think we'll manage somehow." She took a cracker from the plate beside the bed and began to nibble. She was feeling better already. Very well, morning sickness wasn't entirely to her liking—*that* was an understatement—but she already had a suspicion the whole thing was going to be worth it. A child who would be hers and Adam's...

They had enough love to share, of that she was sure. During the past year, her husband had done a very good job of showing her just how much love they had between them.

"Yeow!"

"Okay, Sidney," Adam said. "Breakfast." He pulled on his khaki shorts and led the way to the kitchen, the cat slinking along behind him. Jen pulled on her robe and followed a moment later. She paused in the living room, glancing around at the clutter. In the corner were propped two bicycles for rides in Central Park. The one with a wire basket was a pretty shade of lavender, and the other was slate black. Jen liked having the bicycles right here, but she told herself that one of these days she'd get around to organizing the rest of the place. She was still a rotten housekeeper. So was Adam. But a little at a time, they were redecorating this Greenwich Village town house they'd purchased together. And, whenever they had a chance, they worked on the brownstone in Boston, too. It was still quite difficult to get Adam into an antique store, but Jen was doing her best.

She went to stand at the window, allowing the summer sunshine to wash over her. What a complicated life she and Adam had chosen to live! Two homes to juggle, along with the beach house, two careers—and now a baby. But somehow they'd manage it. They'd come this far. The *Standard* was really starting to thrive as a national paper. Adam worked long hours, but not nearly as long as he had during their first marriage. He was getting better at delegating authority and making compromises so he and Jen could be together.

Jen pressed her forehead against the window, smiling ruefully now. She was getting better at making compromises, too. It had just taken her a while to realize she, too, needed to make a few changes. She'd finally quit her job at the deli, accepting that independence came in many shapes and forms—accepting, also, that she only had so much time in the day. If she wanted to have time for her marriage, see her family in Newport, continue acting classes, go on auditions, go sailing with Adam on the *Anna Lee II*, then something had to give. She still maintained her friendship with Suzanne as well.

Her acting career wasn't quite everything she wanted it to be yet, but she'd always known it would be difficult. After her role as Eileen, she'd managed to snag only a bit part in a play that had folded after a week. But she kept working at it. She needed to act. It was a part of her. And her husband had faith in her. Maybe he wasn't the type to indulge in flattery, but that meant she could always trust his comments on her acting ability.

And that was her husband, the second time around: a man she could trust with her heart, and her hopes.

While Sidney ate his tuna, Adam moved to stand beside Jen at the window, linking his fingers through hers. "Happy?" he asked.

She squeezed his hand and looked up into his eyes. "Yes," she said. "I'm happy."

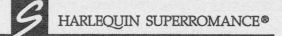

THREE BESTSELLING AUTHORS

HEATHER GRAHAM POZZESSERE
THERESA MICHAELS
MERLINE LOVELACE

bring you

THREE HEROES THAT DREAMS ARE MADE OF!

The Highwayman—He knew the honorable thing was to send his captive home, but how could he let the beautiful Lady Kate return to the arms of another man?

The Warrior—Raised to protect his tribe, the fierce Apache warrior had little room in his heart until the gentle Angie showed him the power and strength of love.

The Knight—His years as a mercenary had taught him many skills, but would winning the hand of a spirited young widow prove to be his greatest challenge?

Don't miss these **UNFORGETTABLE RENEGADES!**

Available in August wherever Harlequin books are sold.

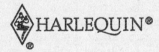

HARLEQUIN SUPERROMANCE®

Four men of courage
Four special men
Four men who'd risk anything
For the women they love

Next month, meet the fourth of our Strong Men!

Major Nick Apostalis is used to danger. A member of the Canadian peacekeeping force, he'd been assigned to some of the world's most hellish places. But none of his tours of duty prepared him for the hell he's going through now that Kara Hartman has disappeared from his life.

Kara knows he'll try to find her but she also knows he won't be prepared for the secret she's carrying...

Watch for PEACEKEEPER, Harlequin Superromance #655 by Marisa Carroll. Available August 1995 wherever Harlequin books are sold.

4SM-4

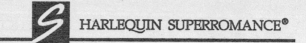

The Dunleavy Legacy
by Janis Flores

For more than a century, the Dunleavy name stood behind the winners of horseracing's most prestigious prizes. The family's wealth and fame was recognized in the most powerful circles.

But times are different now, and the new generation of Dunleavys is about to claim its legacy. Meet the three grandchildren of Octavia Dunleavy, matriarch of the family, as they deal with old feuds and jealousies, with family pride and betrayal, in their struggle to restore the Dunleavy dynasty to its former glory.

Follow the fortunes of Carla, Nan and Seth
in three dramatic, involving love stories.

#654 DONE DRIFTIN' (August 1995)
#658 DONE CRYIN' (September 1995)
#662 NEVER DONE DREAMIN' (October 1995)

This eagerly awaited trilogy by critically acclaimed writer Janis Flores—a veteran author of both mainstream and romance novels—is available wherever Harlequin books are sold.

FLYAWAY VACATION SWEEPSTAKES!

This month's destination:

Glamorous LAS VEGAS!

Are you the lucky person who will win a free trip to Las Vegas? Think how much fun it would be to visit world-famous casinos... to see star-studded shows...to enjoy round-the-clock action in the city that never sleeps!

The facing page contains two Official Entry Coupons, as does each of the other books you received this shipment. Complete and return all the entry coupons—**the more times you enter, the better your chances of winning!**

Then keep your fingers crossed, because you'll find out by August 15, 1995 if you're the winner! If you are, here's what you'll get:

- Round-trip airfare for two to exciting Las Vegas!
- 4 days/3 nights at a fabulous first-class hotel!
- $500.00 pocket money for meals and entertainment!

Remember: The more times you enter, the better your chances of winning!*

*NO PURCHASE OR OBLIGATION TO CONTINUE BEING A SUBSCRIBER NECESSARY TO ENTER. SEE REVERSE SIDE OF ANY ENTRY COUPON FOR ALTERNATIVE MEANS OF ENTRY.

VLV KAL

FLYAWAY VACATION
SWEEPSTAKES
OFFICIAL ENTRY COUPON

This entry must be received by: JULY 30, 1995
This month's winner will be notified by: AUGUST 15, 1995
Trip must be taken between: SEPTEMBER 30, 1995-SEPTEMBER 30, 1996

YES, I want to win a vacation for two in Las Vegas. I understand the prize includes round-trip airfare, first-class hotel and $500.00 spending money. Please let me know if I'm the winner!

Name_____

Address _____ Apt. _____

City   State/Prov.   Zip/Postal Code

Account #_____

Return entry with invoice in reply envelope.

© 1995 HARLEQUIN ENTERPRISES LTD.   CLV KAL

FLYAWAY VACATION
SWEEPSTAKES
OFFICIAL ENTRY COUPON

This entry must be received by: JULY 30, 1995
This month's winner will be notified by: AUGUST 15, 1995
Trip must be taken between: SEPTEMBER 30, 1995-SEPTEMBER 30, 1996

YES, I want to win a vacation for two in Las Vegas. I understand the prize includes round-trip airfare, first-class hotel and $500.00 spending money. Please let me know if I'm the winner!

Name_____

Address _____ Apt. _____

City   State/Prov.   Zip/Postal Code

Account #_____

Return entry with invoice in reply envelope.

© 1995 HARLEQUIN ENTERPRISES LTD.   CLV KAL

OFFICIAL RULES

FLYAWAY VACATION SWEEPSTAKES 3449

NO PURCHASE OR OBLIGATION NECESSARY

Three Harlequin Reader Service 1995 shipments will contain respectively, coupons for entry into three different prize drawings, one for a trip for two to San Francisco, another for a trip for two to Las Vegas and the third for a trip for two to Orlando, Florida. To enter any drawing using an Entry Coupon, simply complete and mail according to directions.

There is no obligation to continue using the Reader Service to enter and be eligible for any prize drawing. You may also enter any drawing by hand printing the words "Flyaway Vacation," your name and address on a 3"x5" card and the destination of the prize you wish that entry to be considered for (i.e., San Francisco trip, Las Vegas trip or Orlando trip). Send your 3"x5" entries via first-class mail (limit: one entry per envelope) to: Flyaway Vacation Sweepstakes 3449, c/o Prize Destination you wish that entry to be considered for, P.O. Box 1315, Buffalo, NY 14269-1315, USA or P.O. Box 610, Fort Erie, Ontario L2A 5X3, Canada.

To be eligible for the San Francisco trip, entries must be received by 5/30/95; for the Las Vegas trip, 7/30/95; and for the Orlando trip, 9/30/95.

Winners will be determined in random drawings conducted under the supervision of D.L. Blair, Inc., an independent judging organization whose decisions are final, from among all eligible entries received for that drawing. San Francisco trip prize includes round-trip airfare for two, 4-day/3-night weekend accommodations at a first-class hotel, and $500 in cash (trip must be taken between 7/30/95—7/30/96, approximate prize value—$3,500); Las Vegas trip includes round-trip airfare for two, 4-day/3-night weekend accommodations at a first-class hotel, and $500 in cash (trip must be taken between 9/30/95—9/30/96, approximate prize value—$3,500); Orlando trip includes round-trip airfare for two, 4-day/3-night weekend accommodations at a first-class hotel, and $500 in cash (trip must be taken between 11/30/95—11/30/96, approximate prize value—$3,500). All travelers must sign and return a Release of Liability prior to travel. Hotel accommodations and flights are subject to accommodation and schedule availability. Sweepstakes open to residents of the U.S. (except Puerto Rico) and Canada, 18 years of age or older. Employees and immediate family members of Harlequin Enterprises, Ltd., D.L. Blair, Inc., their affiliates, subsidiaries and all other agencies, entities and persons connected with the use, marketing or conduct of this sweepstakes are not eligible. Odds of winning a prize are dependent upon the number of eligible entries received for that drawing. Prize drawing and winner notification for each drawing will occur no later than 15 days after deadline for entry eligibility for that drawing. Limit: one prize to an individual, family or organization. All applicable laws and regulations apply. Sweepstakes offer void wherever prohibited by law. Any litigation within the province of Quebec respecting the conduct and awarding of the prizes in this sweepstakes must be submitted to the Regies des loteries et Courses du Quebec. In order to win a prize, residents of Canada will be required to correctly answer a time-limited arithmetical skill-testing question. Value of prizes are in U.S. currency.

Winners will be obligated to sign and return an Affidavit of Eligibility within 30 days of notification. In the event of noncompliance within this time period, prize may not be awarded. If any prize or prize notification is returned as undeliverable, that prize will not be awarded. By acceptance of a prize, winner consents to use of his/her name, photograph or other likeness for purposes of advertising, trade and promotion on behalf of Harlequin Enterprises, Ltd., without further compensation, unless prohibited by law.

For the names of prizewinners (available after 12/31/95), send a self-addressed, stamped envelope to: Flyaway Vacation Sweepstakes 3449 Winners, P.O. Box 4200, Blair, NE 68009.

RVC KAL